Underneath

Ian D. Hall

Beaten Track
www.beatentrackpublishing.com

Underneath

First published 2022 by Beaten Track Publishing
Copyright © 2022 Ian D. Hall

Paperback ISBN: 978 1 78645 538 3
eBook ISBN: 978 1 78645 539 0

Beaten Track Publishing,
Burscough, Lancashire.
www.beatentrackpublishing.com

Underneath

Before

The remains of the body had lain undiscovered for some time when Sarah Calster crept through the house in the hope of finding something worth stealing and disturbed the settled layers of dust on the windowpane.

The owner hadn't been seen for months, but as he'd been virtual recluse for the best part of a decade, nobody thought it was strange; nobody really cared. The word was he'd gone back to South Africa to receive an award and take up his previous teaching post, so his house was left to become its own mausoleum. The back garden was so overgrown it merged seamlessly into the forest, itself clotted with tightly bound trees that the sunlight struggled to penetrate to the ground below.

The grass verge at the front of the house had been religiously cut by a well-meaning neighbour who had known the owner since childhood, when they had both been evacuated to the area during the war and had suffered the same fate when a German bomb fell on the British Small Arms Factory in Birmingham one November night, one losing a father, the other both parents. Sometime after, the one whose father had perished came home one night, having seen the wreckage of a German aircraft at the edge of the woods, to find their mother, in a fit of anguish and depression at the senseless waste of life, had hanged herself from a wooden beam in the kitchen.

The teenage burglar sniffed the air. The atmosphere was thick with musty dampness with an undercurrent of something pungent; the flashlight flared on the scaled bodies of a couple of silverfish that scurried across the floor and under the stove. Suppressing the urge to vomit, Sarah consoled herself that at least they weren't cockroaches or she'd have screamed loud enough to attract the attention of someone in the village. Cockroaches were never found in this part of the New Forest, but in the same way that spiders were supposed to suddenly spin themselves into existence if you were scared of them, she wondered if her fear could think the vermin into being. She dismissed the notion with a shudder. It was that or climb straight out that window, scramble over the wall and race back to her friends waiting by the crossroads sign. She could tell them the rumours of hidden wealth were just that—village gossip spread by those who wanted to see the owner spooked.

Sarah barely knew the man; she didn't know anyone who did, certainly not in her age group. Her mother had told her he'd once travelled to Africa as part of his scientific studies and published several journal pieces on his experiences, but when he turned forty, he cut himself off from society, his visits to the local pub dwindling to once a month, then one in three, then not being seen at all except by a few close friends, one of whom was his well-intentioned neighbour. The last time anyone recalled seeing him was the day Jimmy Carter was sworn in as America's bright young hope.

Sarah's father had chimed in wheezily at that point, pushing his glasses up his nose as he tilted his head to look at his wife. "I saw him after that, perhaps July, maybe August—yes, August. It was the day after Elvis died. He was out at the front of his house arguing with Mr. Bennett who used to run the post office. I was cycling past on that old five-speed thing I had before it got run over by that van on the road to Bramwell. Well, anyway, it was pretty heated, the argument that is, and Bennett told him he would have to pay something towards the petrol costs if he wanted him to bring groceries to his house as well as his letters."

Sarah's father had turned his attention away from his wife and daughter and started mumbling to himself, fully aware of the despairing look his wife had shot him, the one that told him he was being tedious and hogging the conversation.

Sarah smiled wistfully at the memory. She missed her father greatly, and as she silently moved through the rambling house, she thought, had he still been alive, she might not have fallen into bad company and even worse habits.

She stopped at the doorway of one room and looked inside, the flashlight providing a partial explanation for the smell she encountered when she climbed through the broken window. The room was spacious, and in another time it would have probably been a grand dining room. She imagined a family all seated in formal attire around a table, the father at the head carving generous portions of lamb and beef as his wife looked on with love in her eyes, proud that their children had all turned out polite, happy and respectful. Shaking off the illusion, Sarah cast the flashlight over the upright glass tanks that lined the walls from floor to ceiling. In the middle of the room was another glass tank, a fifteen-foot-tall monument that held enough soil to grow potatoes to feed that imagined proud Victorian family.

Sarah stepped closer to one of the smaller glass tanks. She suspected they were aquariums like the one at Carl's place. His mother spent a fortune on the upkeep of her beloved exotic pets, but unlike her aquarium, these tanks contained no water, no fish, no plastic coral or castles. There just seemed to be a kind of sawdust on the bottom, yellowing and mouldy.

1

Sarah tapped the glass gently. Nothing moved.

Stepping back, she counted how many tanks there were: not including the giant one in the middle of the room, she counted two hundred and forty; surely they couldn't have all been empty. She walked around the room, peering into those at eye level, but she saw no movement, no signs of life. Attached to the ceiling, she noticed a set of solid metal runners that ran the length of the room with a spur across to the centre, and as she swept the light around, she spotted some metal steps, hidden behind the open door.

Gripping the steps, she tried to shift them, to pull them around so she could look into some of the higher-up tanks, but they were stiff and too heavy, so she gave it up as a bad job and returned to investigating what she could see. Drawn back to the central tank, she shone the flashlight up along its length to the ceiling. It was one vast, uninterrupted piece, no joints, just a flawless, square pipe that, as far as she could tell, went up through the ceiling and down through the wooden floor. The entire contraption was filled with soil, and when she looked closely, she saw a network of small tunnels. Again, she tapped the glass; again, nothing stirred within.

Returning to the smaller cases along the wall, Sarah noticed a circular indentation in the left-hand side of the front-facing glass. She poked her finger in it, and the glass slid across easily, presumably so the tanks could be cleaned. With the front now open, she scooped up a handful of sawdust, scraping through it in case it concealed anything of value. As she did, a mound fell to the floor, and she jumped back in surprise when she saw what looked like the ravaged remains of a tarantula. Luckily, she wasn't as scared of spiders as she was of cockroaches, although she'd never been this close to one of these fearsome creatures.

She kicked it lightly, and it shifted across the floor with the motion, but that was all. Any life that had resided in those half-eaten remains was long gone.

By now, the room had lost its charm, and Sarah decided to get on with the job at hand and continue her search for anything valuable that she could sell, so she and Carl could buy pot for the weekend and the party at Bramwell. She closed the door and carried on through the rest of the house. If she had stayed, she would have noticed what remained of the spider's carcass move seemingly of its own volition as what was eating it from the inside came out to investigate the motion it had sensed.

As Sarah ascended the stairs, the smell became more pungent, and it was more than the mustiness of a house that hadn't been aired for a while. Reaching the closed door to what she presumed was a bedroom, she turned the handle and pushed the door open, discovering why the man of the house hadn't been seen for months, for there he was, surrounded by cobwebs and decay.

Sarah placed her hand over her mouth, stifling her scream, and admonished herself for falling into the trap she mocked others for. The dead were no threat. However, the man's body, like that of the tarantula, looked as if it had been partly eaten, loose, rotting skin overlaying sinew and ragged flesh and in places bare bone. While his fingerprints had been lost to time, the base of his left thumb still bore some muscle, while the right thumb was riddled with holes as if it had woodworm. Sarah was not a girl to shy away from looking where fifteen-year-old girls shouldn't be looking, and besides, the man had clearly died in his sleep, naked and alone, so she couldn't help but notice that his privates also seemed to have been eaten away. Indeed, there was nothing to suggest he had ever been male.

It was when she looked at his head that Sarah decided she had seen enough. Where the nose and mouth should have been, there was a wide hole, his lower jaw hung as if he'd died from laughing, and his ears were little more than flaps of skin. The eyes, those observers of life, were gone.

Sarah no longer cared who saw her or how loud her escape was. She bolted down the stairs, back through the kitchen and over the crumbling back wall without breaking a sweat. She ran up the hill towards the crossroads and didn't stop even when she saw Carl and his mate, who looked at her oddly as she sprinted past, all the way to the Sander's Arms.

"Call the police!" she instructed the bemused bartender, too out of breath to explain that the old man who for so many years had played on the pub's crib team, famously scoring a maximum 29 hand to lift the country trophy, was dead.

Chapter One

I THINK YOU MAY have been right when you said turn left a couple of miles back," Robert Romsleigh admitted, pulling into a layby and meeting the gaze of his teenage daughter in the rear-view mirror. She scowled at him over the folded map, which she held the same way she would a menu from the family's favourite restaurant—a decently run curry house in Moss Side.

The restaurant had closed now, and the three would miss their weekly Saturday ritual, which had begun as a means for Robert to pull both his children away from their mother and the fear she had instilled in them through years of harsh treatment, drama and suspicion. The day the divorce came through, Robert begged for his children's forgiveness and promised they would eventually be okay, perhaps better than okay.

His son seemed to have made the transition more easily than his sister, perhaps because he was younger, more resilient, less troubled. Bela had taken time and patience, and who could blame her for not always being on the same page as her father? He'd moved her away from Manchester, away from her friends and a few close calls with adolescent first crushes. It was the only way he could protect her at the time, but that was before the police had become involved when, on Bela's thirteenth birthday, her mother stalked and then verbally abused her at a restaurant in the Arndale Centre where she was having a birthday meal with friends. According to witnesses, her mother had called her awful names, and when Bela refused to acknowledge her, she slapped her daughter around the face and shook her before trying to pour lighter fluid over her. Only the quick actions of the waiter stopped the attack from ending in tragedy.

Casting all thoughts of the near-miss from his mind, Robert restarted the car, preparing to do a U-turn. The New Forest roads were oddly quiet, certainly compared to the ones he was used to driving around his former hometown. These days, he only went there to watch football with his children or when he was forced to travel to Styal Prison to endure the latest ravings of the woman he had once loved but who now sickened him.

The last time had followed a request from her solicitor, who felt his client deserved to know the reasons Robert had uprooted the children from their schools and friends. Despite the lawyer's threatening undertones, Robert had thought he might take some destructive thrill from seeing the hurt in his ex-wife's eyes, believing it could never be as awful as the damage she had wreaked on him, Bela and Stuart. He was wrong. Hearing her cries of desperation when he informed her that her children didn't want to see her anymore—even if they had wanted to, the judge had decreed the abuse too severe—broke Robert's heart. Indeed, had it not been for his mother capturing the abuse via hidden camera, Robert may well have backed down. It was hard to believe that the woman he had loved had beaten their children, scarred their arms and legs with cigarette burns and their minds with visions of the men whose company she kept while Robert worked night and day to keep the family afloat.

That was before Kaleen's tears turned to a guttural, maniacal laughter and she gouged his face with her nails, one coming dangerously close to tearing out his eye. He didn't care how long she stayed in jail; his only concern was ensuring his children were never put in harm's way again, and leaving Manchester had seemed the best option, although it came with its own set of problems, not least Bela's rumblings of discontent.

"What are you doing, Dad?"

"Going back to that turning."

"No. Keep going. There's another way into the village. I didn't see it before, but if you take the next left—"

"The village?"

"Well…" Bela fidgeted. "I just thought it might be better to…get an idea what's in store with the locals before we meet Auntie Stella."

Robert nodded and smiled at her in the mirror, relieved when she smiled back. For once, there was no pain there, her red curls framing her open expression rather than shielding it from a world that had wronged her.

"Right then," he said.

"No, left."

Such innocence in that joke. It may have been forced, it was hard to tell with Bela, but it sounded natural enough to Robert's ears, and for that he was grateful. He signalled and pulled out of the layby, following her directions.

"Can you wake up your brother?"

Bela sighed but must have done as he asked, as he heard a yawn and caught the motion of a stretched arm and then noise of a kerfuffle—just the ordinary fighting back of a younger sibling rudely torn from the pleasantries of a dream.

Stifling a laugh, Robert glanced over his shoulder. "Are you all right, Little Nemo?"

"Dad, watch out!"

Instinctively, Robert slammed on the brakes, and it was as well he did, as he stopped just short of careering into a gang of motorbikes that took the corner at speed, almost all of their riders clad in leather and denim, their steel horses screaming as they whooshed past the car. A few flipped the finger at them, and one shouted something obscene and largely indecipherable, although Robert caught the gist.

"Great. Just what we need—the local chapter of Junior Hell's Angels making our lives a misery. I'm sorry, kids. Are you both all right?"

Bela waved away his concern, unclipped her seat belt and dropped out of sight, emerging a moment later with the dishevelled map in her hand. The car ticked over, giving Robert a chance to re-establish his composure and make sure his son was all right while Bella studied the map, her nose crinkling as she did so.

"What's up, Bela?"

"This road. It shouldn't be here. The map says it's a bridleway."

"It is an old map," Robert reasoned.

"It was printed last year, Dad. There's no way they built a massive road like this in that time."

Knowing she would obsess over the incongruence for weeks and that nothing he said would change that, he let it go and moved off once more, this time keeping his eyes firmly on the road ahead and turning left when Bela instructed him to do so.

As they passed the mile marker for Bramwell, he noticed a crudely written sign, a board hanging from the crossroads point which declared that Emmets were not welcome. He glanced at his backseat passengers, relieved to see they were looking out the side window at the first houses and signs of village life. They hadn't noticed the red-painted warning.

"Look, there's the pub. I bet they have real ale—not that plastic muck they serve at the ground."

Keeping to a low speed, he drove on through the village, the occasional stare from the locals they passed making a lie of Robert's promise of acceptance and a fresh start.

"They're not looking at you, Bela. They can't see you, Stuart. They're just trying to figure out who the stranger is in the foreign car."

Bela nodded in agreement and kept her eyes on the rows of cottages, the little shops. He'd warned her there would be stares and whispers, but none of these people knew her history. She could reinvent herself, be a mystery that lit up their uneventful lives.

He had told her that with truth in his heart; he had seen her cringe when people she had known for years reacted in distress and alarm when they saw her face. And, thanks to her mother, Bela knew he had bribed other children and their parents to play with her. In time, some had become real friends, but others had continued to openly taunt her.

"Take a next left, Dad, or we'll end up back on the road to Bramwell."

"Yes, Sir, Captain Bela, Sir. Permission to beep the car horn when I see my sister, Captain Bela, Sir."

Bela and Stuart laughed, belying all they'd endured while their father wasn't there to protect them, but he was now. That was all that mattered.

"There she is, look. Waving."

Robert beeped the horn like he was urging Ian Brightwell to bare down on goal and set up the mighty Quinn to score, all the while knowing that, like his team that season, it offered more than it could deliver. He stopped outside the house—their new home, made possible by a sizeable donation from his sister and the passing of their mother—and got out of the car. As he hugged his sister, he felt the sorrow of the past drift out of sight for a while. All was going to be well in Downmere.

Chapter Two

N<small>O MORE THAN</small> two miles away from this touching scene of a family starting their lives anew away from the prying eyes of journalists and true-crime voyeurs, Harry Collins sighed as he looked upon his troop of lads struggling to erect their canvas tents and prepare the ground for their weeklong orienteering course.

"Takes me back," one of his assistants called cheerfully from where she was securing the last of the guy ropes for her tent. The woman had turned up at the Scout hut a year ago and enthusiastically volunteered her services. Harry had worried about her roughing it up with a group of lads more used to the comforts of home, but it was clearly not her first time under the stars.

"Woodstock in sixty-nine," she continued. "Twenty years of age, arrived last minute—didn't find out about it till I was almost ready to come home from a year of travelling. Great times. Did you do anything wild like that, Harr...I mean, Scoutmaster?"

Harry shook his head. He'd been born at the start of that decade and very much doubted that his staunchly conservative, unfalteringly Methodist parents had even heard of Woodstock. He grinned to himself as he imagined how his parents would react if he told them his newest assistant lived with a woman she'd met at a Simon and Garfunkel gig in 1968. If his mother could hear Millicent now, waxing lyrical about free love as if it were a suitable substitute for piety and prayer, she'd have turned deep scarlet and started talking about the fine weather they'd had of late.

Catching Harry's grin, Millicent beamed back at him and continued talking about her travels, telling of how she once tripped on LSD as the crowd around her swayed to the music wafting across the fields near Bethel, and how, after Woodstock, she had come home to resume her studies, finally graduating from the Open University in the mid-1970s and taking up a position at a local comprehensive school where she doubled as the matron's deputy.

Millicent paused her monologue to help the two boys closest to her, whose tent was sagging like a line of wet washing. When she'd joined their troop, she'd told him she'd been raised in the Jewish faith but had no truck with organised religion, instead preferring to engage in activism, although she was not what Harry would consider a 'typical' feminist. Here was a woman in command of her own life, and no man was going to tell her otherwise, yet she was happy and vibrant and full of soul.

One of their young charges howled with laughter at some quiet joke that had passed around the camp but stopped when he caught the glare of his Scoutmaster. Harry's tightly pursed lips stood firm against the tide of youthful anarchy, and the boy returned meekly to following the example shown him over the course of the last few weeks in how to raise a tent.

This was Harry's first camp in charge, and he needed tough people around him to make it a success. Millicent fitted the bill perfectly. The lads were scared of her, but they also respected her. She had a wealth of experience in dealing with children, having guided many youngsters from a troubled path and on to university, or at least away from the clutches of the police and the prospect of prison, and she knew the ins and outs of camping and the joy of heading back to nature.

Harry's other assistant had been part of the scouting system as long as he had, both having joined up as boys, Harry out of deference to his parents, who held Baden Powell in an almost zealous esteem and saw involvement in the movement as a Christian virtue, and his friend Fife because it meant for one evening a week and some Saturdays he could avoid being in the same room as his mother, still bound by the grief of losing her only daughter to measles. Fife, whose real name was Philip Piccolo, had been the former leader of the group but had needed to step back from responsibilities when his mother had attempted suicide the previous summer. Only the quick actions of a kind bystander stopped her from taking the final step off the platform.

Harry took the large trestle table out of the minivan and set it up, making sure the pegs were in place for the maps to be held down when he went over the routes and rules for the next few days.

Fife and two of their troop, Jacob Betley and Kevin Sillatoe, appeared from the edge of the forest, their outstretched arms laden with wood for the campfire. Harry told the boys to stack the wood neatly away from the area designated for the fire and then helped his friend by relieving him of part of his load.

"Come back for this lot, lads. Mr. Piccolo needs a cup of tea before he starts to chop any of it down."

They grinned at each other, comrades in arms, and went off to collect the rest of the wood while Harry filled the kettle and got the stove going. It didn't take long for the water to boil, and he made tea for the three of them. Millicent drank hers on the move—she was making good headway with the six tents—while Harry took the opportunity to have a sit-down with his oldest friend.

"You ready for this, mate?" Fife asked. "It's your first big test as a Scout Leader, after all."

Harry thought for a moment, staring into the metal cup of dark liquid. "I think so, although, big boots to fill, Fife. I wish you'd reconsider stepping down. Somehow it doesn't feel right that you're answerable to me. However, I am grateful that you decided to come along to give us a hand. Couldn't have been easy to put your mum in respite care for the week."

Fife turned red, caught out in a lie. "Well, actually, mate, it's a bit longer than a week. I've had to put her in a facility—that one on the edge of town. I could no longer cope on my own, and my aunt refuses to leave Italy to help me look after her. She said I could take her to Rome, but Mum won't travel—refuses to leave the area where her daughter and my dad are buried. It's for the best."

This was news to Harry, and sad as it was for Fife's mum, he was secretly overjoyed that his friend could re-join the outside world.

"Does that mean you'll be coming back to the troop again? If so, I will gladly step down. The parents would undoubtedly love to have you back in command."

"No, I'm not coming back. This week, this trip, is my last one. I'm going away for a while, Harry. The plan is, I'll assess you—that, you already knew—and then, on Saturday week, the house goes up for sale. The money will pay for Mum's care so I can finally go to New York and connect with my cousins over there. I'd have told you sooner, but I was scared what you might say."

Harry was surprised his jaw hadn't hit the ground. He'd never expected Fife to leave England. In 1972, he'd pledged loyalty to the Queen, knowing that his father, had he been alive, would have disowned him for his treachery, given the family had suffered interment on the Isle of Man just for being Italian.

"I don't know what to say. Are you sure about this?"

"As sure as I can be. Since last summer, since Mum walked up to the station and decided she was going to end her suffering, I've been plagued by guilt, I don't want to think about it anymore. I want a family of my own. Mum always stopped that, kept reminding me of my duty to her, to the memory of my sister, and it's suffocating. The facility—you remember it, it had that huge fire years ago? I remember the rumours, but that's all they were. No one believes that damned journalist, regardless.

"I met with the facility manager, and here I am. A week in the New Forest with a friend and a group of lads to pass on my navigational skills to, then I'll be getting on that plane and meeting up with family, eating lasagne and meatballs and drinking vintage wine for a while."

Harry didn't speak; he simply held out his hand, but Fife didn't shake it. Instead, he gave his friend a warm embrace— the kind that said goodbye. Harry caught Millicent watching them, a smile on her face, and suspected Fife might have sought her advice on how to broach the subject with him.

"Well then, we'd better make the most of the week ahead. Did you see any sign of rabbits? I've been reliably informed they are in abundance here."

Fife turned slightly pale. "Betley, Sillatoe and I came across a couple about a mile into the forest, but you couldn't have eaten them."

"Why? Don't say you saw signs of myxomatosis!"

Fife swallowed down hard and looked like he might vomit. "They were dead," he said, "but it wasn't myxomatosis as far as I could tell. They were covered in a mass of ants. I guess they'd been lying there for a couple of days, perhaps shot by some kids from Downmere, killed for entertainment, not food. Whatever, they were in a bad state of decomposition, and the ants were having their fill, crawling over them, making what remained of the fur ripple."

Harry placed a hand on his friend's shoulder and told him to put the scene out of his mind. There would be other chances to show the boys how to live off the land, he was sure.

Chapter Three

ALAN TARKY HAD watched the cars come and go through the small village all his life. Occasionally, the occupants would get out and take a stroll, perhaps to the public house for a 'quaint' country meal, their children screaming and tearing around the beer garden as they consumed their own body weight in soft drinks while their father relaxed and spoiled himself with a second pint and his wife, second wife or even girlfriend with more than bedtime aspirations watched on approvingly. He'd done his best for his family, after all; he deserved the reward.

That same family man would later crash his car somewhere in the New Forest and see his family hurt or worse for the sake of a moment's peace and quiet away from responsibility. Tarky had no sympathy. While everyone was entitled to heal at the end of a long workday, it didn't give them the right to relinquish control.

Tarky used to take great pleasure in laying down the law to such people. He would hunt them down in the beer garden and publicly shame them, wagging his index finger underneath their noses and bringing down heaven's wrath upon their souls until they rounded up their offspring and their wives and put distance between them and the village of Downmere. Not even the continued threat of being banned from the pub himself was enough to stop his sermons. He knew the village and its secrets; he knew the owners of the Sander's Arms. Each evening, after he locked the doors of the church, he would partake of a small glass of sherry and reflect upon how such matters had seen him become the village's moral compass, absolving the confessions of the day and the sins of the night. For there were many sins in this village, and Tarky prided himself in his work both as the Shepherd's administer and advocate of the Lord's vengeance.

And vengeance, in whatever form, he would undertake.

It was his insistence—more honest folk around him called it interference—that saw Sarah Calster placed into a youth custody centre after she admitted to breaking and entering into the old professor's home. Tarky had campaigned to have her arrested and tried for murder, but the powers-that-be proved—to the public, not to Tarky—that she was innocent. The professor who had locked himself away with his research had met a tragic but natural end.

Tarky had not trusted the police after that, not that he'd trusted them much before, but at that point, he lost respect for the justice system and instead, for fewer and fewer parishioners, had become a sword for the Lord's work.

It was a surprise, then, to the old vicar when a car drove slowly through the village with no signs of stopping. The driver, who looked vaguely familiar but had the air of someone who didn't want to draw attention, tilted his head toward a young girl in the back seat and merely pointed out the Sander's Arms as they passed by. Tarky frowned, the prominent lines forged by years of deep religious thought and worry for his parishioners' eternal souls creasing his forehead as he contemplated who this new family might be, which side they were on. For in his mind, it was a war between those on the side of right and those who were unrepentantly wrong.

He made a mental note to enquire who these new people were and mentally set them aside for the time being. There were bigger problems to deal with today, a case of 'petty vandalism' as the local policeman had described it in his report, but to Tarky, it was wanton desecration of several graves. There was also the issue of the motorcycle gang that had started loitering on the fringes of the village and rode through it without due care. More concerning still, the day after next would see the return of one Miss Sarah Calster. Despite appeals to her mother—from those in the village with its long memory, and from Tarky in light of the woman's devotedness in the years since she was widowed—she steadfastly refused to stop her daughter visiting for the first time since her father's funeral.

The old firebrand vicar remembered the day well. Black clouds above the pulpit as well as in the sky led to a sermon that moved many, and not in the way he had imagined. He weathered the storm of complaint from the more vocal members of the congregation: some had tried to get him removed from the parish, citing the excess of his authority, and he fought hard, laid down all that he had done for the village. If those higher up the ecclesiastical ladder pushed for it, well, as he had pointed out behind closed doors, he knew most of their secrets.

Secrets. That was the name of the game. Know your enemy from the inside out. The devil, as all those who came out of their homes on Sundays could attest, was amongst them, and no greater worshipper of Satan could he find than Sarah Calster.

The service for James Calster was supposed to have been a sombre affair; a man of good faith deserved excellent graveside manner. Despite his request for a more liberal end to his life, Tarky proceeded with a couple of stirring hymns, a passionate plea to keep his wife in their thoughts and the sanctity of the church and the village in high regard, and to report any signs of mischief so it didn't become a scourge on the land.

All was going to plan until, halfway through the service, Sarah Calster arrived handcuffed to a prison officer and took a seat at the back of the church. Visibly shaken by her appearance and the shock of her return, Tarky wanted to cast her out as if the devil were within her but collected his thoughts wisely and stopped short of pointing the finger and crying heretic and murderer.

Gone was the hair colour that screamed defiance, the so-called punk look that had once filled him with a sense of foreboding, tapping into his deepest fears far beneath the surface, the nightmares of his way of life not just dying out but being eradicated, wiped out like a virus. His family had survived the Great War and the Spanish Flu. He had seen conflict intrude upon his religious studies, and when the free love movement had called to question his beliefs and virtues, he had stood tall and resolute at every turn. Yet he could not deny that in that moment, he had been afraid.

It was the same fear he felt now as he pushed that day out of his mind and walked down the hill to the church, the old centre of village life. She was coming back. While she had stayed away, his concern had ebbed and dwindled almost to naught. Now she was coming back for another go.

Tarky tried to think of other things as he wandered along the road, stopping occasionally to talk to the locals, the butcher, the baker and the undertaker, a clasp of hands and thanks for Mrs. Bennett who was on her way home from cleaning the church and told him the flowers had arrived for the service on Sunday. She would be back later to arrange them in the normal fashion, she said, once she had seen to her Jack's lunch.

Tarky thanked her again, this wonderful, God-fearing woman with whom he enjoyed many a conversation. His mood lightened even further when he bumped into Brigette Maloney, a conscientious and dutiful daughter to her parents and the parish, who had been the apple of everybody's eye when she was the first from the village to attend the university at Southampton. She had still come home every night, forgoing the rituals of the student experience, instead relying on her work to set an example. Her news that she and her husband of one year were expecting their first child was a blessing: new life, new possibilities; new blood to keep the village going.

Tarky took Brigette's hand and clasped it warmly, saying a small prayer for the baby's health and future happiness. He opened his eyes and smiled at the woman he had once held in his arms as he baptised her. In his church, all denominations were welcome as long as they loved the Lord.

His smile soon disappeared when he saw the figure of his nightmares. Sarah Calster, as large as life, stood not five yards away from them, dyed red hair, her clothes as garish and unsuitable as they had been when she was a teenager seeing that boy Carl, another wastrel running wild and doing as he pleased.

Sarah saw Tarky too, and their eyes locked in silent, mutual contempt as she advanced a few steps.

"Hello, Brigette."

"Hello...S-Sarah." Brigette flustered in embarrassment.

It was a fumbled exchange between two people who had grown up in the same area but were socially and mentally miles apart. Brigette made her apologies to Tarky and walked briskly off up the hill, her speed increasing with each footfall.

"You're back early," Tarky remarked. "I wasn't expecting you till after the weekend. How long are you intending to stay?"

Sarah smiled sweetly at the man, her derision and disrespect bubbling beneath the surface, but she knew how to play the game. After years in detention centres and a stay in prison for something she had not done, it would be fair to say she hated the man responsible, but a display of emotion would not send a strong enough message.

"Sorry, what?"

Tarky raised his voice slightly, his own anger threatening to explode. "I said, how long are you intending to stay in the village? A truly short visit, I hope?"

Sarah looked up the hill to the Sander's Arms. The thought of a pint in the place where she had been arrested all those years ago had cheered her on the journey home. Beyond that lay the crossroads, the signpost that pointed to destinations with more drive in them than this small-minded village and its despicable so-called man of God.

"Downmere is my home," she said. "My mother is ill, and I want to take care of her. You of all people should understand the concept of family and duty. You have banged the drum of its virtue since before I was born."

Tarky moved closer. For the first time since she was a small girl running around the graveyard and he had smacked her backside raw for being disrespectful to the dead, he was within touching distance of her. His nose caught the scent of her perfume, and it made him gag, but he refused to show it, refused to look at her face, instead keeping his focus on the church beyond her, relying on it to give him strength and comfort in these troubling times. He leaned closer still, as if he were whispering sweet nothings to her, the older man seductively bringing the younger woman to her knees.

"This was always a good village, Ms. Calster, till you and your kind decided to test us, till you got away with murdering the old man and put Carl in the ground." Tarky paused to smile and lift his hat as one of his more progressive sheep bade him a lovely afternoon. He waited for them to pass by before he spoke further. "No one wants you here. No one needs you. We can all look after your mother, so do yourself a favour. Go back to wherever you crawled out from and break their hearts, because mark my words, Sarah, I will do everything in my power to stop you breaking ours again."

Sarah stood impassive, staring past him at something she could not see, a memory, a phantasm of recall that would not reveal itself.

For a brief moment, Tarky permitted himself to study the face of the young woman. She was beautiful, he would be mad to deny it, but she was, and always would be, evil. He smiled broadly for public show and then, without a goodbye, he continued on his daily mission, forcing his thoughts to return to the other threats to his flock—the influx of motorbikes tearing through the village and the red swastikas sprayed on several graves every night, some gravestones even being uprooted and smashed as if they were made of glass rather than solid stone or marble.

The car that had slowly passed through the village forgotten, Tarky adjusted his glasses as he strode intently towards the church to survey last night's damage and look for clues as to which of his teenage charges would be paying the heavy price in retribution.

Chapter Four

SARAH CALSTER LEANED back against the whitewashed stone wall of the bar and allowed the mellowness of the small cigar and pint of Guinness to soothe her frayed nerves. She couldn't say she had not been expecting such an encounter, but she'd hoped to have had at least one glass of alcohol down her throat before it happened.

The bus had stopped going into the village a few years back, not long after she had broken into the old man's house. The company that ran it found that nobody used public transport anymore; they either had access to a car or, in the case of the few teenagers that did use the facility, preferred being picked up away from the prying eyes of nosy neighbours who reported back everything they saw to their parents, or worse, as Sarah was all too aware, to the power behind the throne of the village: the rigid moral compass in black, Alan Tarky.

Sarah had got off the bus at the stop on the outskirts and almost walked straight into a group of kids messing around and making the most of a freedom they would never find in the village. The slight aroma of weed caught Sarah's nostrils, and the faint memory of a night in bed with Carl filled her mind.

One young lad, in an intentional display of machoism designed to impress his friends, stepped in Sarah's way. He couldn't have been more than fourteen and was dressed in tight, blue jeans, new trainers and a T-shirt that had some band name on it that she didn't recognise, although the accompanying picture seemed to be of a bloodied corpse surrounded by freakish vampires.

"Excuse me, please." Sarah smiled sweetly, at which the grinning teen swept his arm and bowed mockingly, eliciting giggles from his companions. Resisting the urge to push the boy to the floor and lay into him with her feet, Sarah thanked him, glancing back over her shoulder as the teenagers noisily boarded the bus and bundled down the aisle, pushing each other, one girl groping their leader's backside, another taking an elbow to the ribs and receiving a punch in retaliation. The bus pulled away, and one of the girls poked out her tongue at Sarah. In petulant revenge, Sarah gave her the finger. The girl seemed shocked but recovered quickly enough to bang on the window, her lips issuing an obscenity unheard by Sarah, who cheerily waved as the bus pulled away, taking grim satisfaction from the girl's sullen scowl and what looked like respect on the leader's face.

The walk to the village was about a mile, which gave Sarah time to think, to get her head together. Would she be recognised? The interaction with the group had given her hope that perhaps the villagers had forgotten the girl who broke into a private house and found a dead body, who saw her boyfriend fall to his death as he clambered up to her bedroom window and who, in the final part of this trilogy of blackness, brought her lung-cancer-ravaged father's suffering to an end by placing a pillow over his face. It was this last act of mercy, agreed to by both her parents and, reluctantly, herself, that had given Tarky the ammunition to see her jailed for manslaughter, with the suspicion of her involvement in the other two deaths forever hanging over her.

***

Keeping one eye on the stranger sitting with her back to the wall, Darren Curran placed the pint glasses in the washer and pressed the green button. Each time the door opened to admit another of the local lunchtime brigade, the woman anxiously scanned the new arrivals before returning her attention to her long-lasting pint of Guinness. Whoever she was expecting, they had yet to arrive. Darren poured himself a soft drink—no alcohol until he'd called last orders—and wracked his brains, trying to remember where he had seen the woman before.

The young barman's train of thought was interrupted by the surprise appearance of the Bennetts. He smiled at them both with genuine pleasure and received in return a scowl of irritation from the more dominant of the pair.

"Darren, have you got a ploughman's or something for this great lump of lard? Not that he deserves it. I come home from the church to feed the fool, and he's thrown out all the bread. Feeding the birds, he said. A whole loaf, Darren! What do you make of that?"

Darren knew better than to think the formidable Mrs. Bennett was asking for his opinion. It was no secret that she was the driving force behind the Bennetts' personal and business dealings, having kept the post office afloat when they ran it and making enough profit to give them the retirement she thought they deserved.

"Feed him, Darren, but no beer. He can have a glass of water. Here's five pounds—he can pay me back later." She raised a stern eyebrow at her husband, who shrank an inch or two as Belinda Bennett, nee Fanshaw, placed the note on the bar, spun on her heel and walked out of the pub.

Lionel Bennett shrugged at Darren. "I told her the bread was stale, but the truth is, I just didn't want to stop in the bungalow another day. I haven't been out on my own for a month, not since the bowel operation. Bloody woman. I know she means well, but there are times I think I'd be so much happier without her."

Darren laughed. He respected Belinda Bennett. She had given him his first job when he left school, and she'd taught him the virtue of honest hard work, which was more than his mother had done for him. However, he also recognised she had a mean streak. He suspected her friendship with the vicar had a lot to do with that: his sense of absolutism must have influenced her outlook over the years. Nor did Darren blame Lionel for his moment of marital sacrilege. He could imagine how frustrating it was for the poor old fellow being under the thumb of a wannabe tyrant.

"I still have a bit of Stilton left and some bread. I can throw in a tomato or two, and that would be on me. I won't say a word if you want to spend that fiver on a couple of beers."

Lionel's eyes lit up and a grin set in as Darren collected a pint glass and set it under the pump. Having never known his grandparents, Darren looked up to the Bennetts as role models, and it gladdened his heart to do something nice for them—Lionel especially. He'd never really recovered from his set-to with the professor in what now seemed a lifetime ago. It had taken a while, but somehow the old man had pulled through enough to carry on serving the public from behind his grill, counting out stamps, weighing parcels and giving the village a reason to take heart in bad times.

Looking at him now, it was hard to believe that it was only a few years back when Lionel had singlehandedly shovelled snow from the village high street one truly awful winter's morning, carefully and heroically making sure the path was cleared so the shops could open. He'd also arranged for the older folks to have their paths cleared during the day by the youngsters. Mr. Bennett had a knack for getting everyone to contribute to village life, something Reverend Tarky could only aspire to, although he'd praised the postmaster to heaven and back in his sermons for at least a month after that blizzard.

"Here you go." Darren set the pint of beer on the bar in front of Lionel's usual seat—woe betide anyone else who tried to sit there. It was a prime spot from where all could be surveyed. "I'll get that lunch for you now," he said and walked out to the kitchen, leaving Lionel to gaze at the strange young woman who was coming to the end of both her cigar and her pint.

The kitchen was quiet at this hour of the day. Most of the regulars had been and gone, the soups and the sandwiches all demolished, the prawn cocktails served and eaten, but there was always a little left over for the staff to eat.

As he put together a plate of food, Darren's mind wandered back to the blizzard. He'd been a small boy at the time, barely able to stand in the snow without falling into it, but he'd helped as best he could. When tragedy or danger struck, it was all hands to the pump—

He froze, the Stilton in mid-air as a memory emerged of a snowball fight and a girl aged ten, maybe eleven, always in trouble, throwing snow-covered pebbles at the other children.

Absently, Darren tidied away, trying to think of the girl's name. It had been years since he'd even thought of her, the last time being when rumours spread that she'd suffocated her own father. The vicar had refrained from comment, although he did let slip that she'd confessed she wanted her father to die. That seemed to sum her up for the village. She was a reckless, damaged kid who had put her boyfriend in the grave and then, not content with that, murdered her father.

Sarah Calster. He remembered now. But why was he thinking of her?

It couldn't be her, could it?

Darren walked back into the bar, all set to tell Lionel a ghost had returned to the area, but the old man wasn't there. His drink barely had three sips taken out of it, and across the room, where the girl had been, was nothing but a thin layer of smoke lingering against the ceiling and the dregs of Guinness in the bottom of a lipstick-stained glass.

Chapter Five

ROBERT ROMSLEIGH BREATHED what his sister believed was a genuine sigh of relief and smiled as his son ran off ahead, ploughing through the door like an unstoppable train. A great weight had been removed from Robert's shoulders, one that for many years had threatened to subsume him in a pit of anger and despair. Stella had tried to help, but until it became clear that Robert was telling the truth about the domestic abuse, she had, to her shame, sided with his ex-wife, knowing her brother could be difficult. She had never known him to be violent—more stubborn, set in his ways, refusing to see beyond his point of view—however, unlike their father, he had never raised a hand, even with a man, preferring to use reason, no matter how flawed, to drive his argument home.

Stella was thankful their mother had managed to record Kaleen's abuse and prove to the court that the children needed to be with their father. It was a decision that came horribly and devastatingly too late: certainly, for Stella and Robert's mother, the emotional turmoil was too much, but perhaps the heart attack had been a blessing in disguise.

Watching her brother now, as he looked over the property he had so far only seen in photographs, the undisguised joy on his face reminded Stella of another time when he was happy, before he met Kaleen at that party at university. He approached the front door, hesitated and turned back to look at her and his daughter, silently asking for permission to enter, heartbreakingly still in that place where such a gesture had to be granted.

27

"Don't be daft, Robert. It's your home. Go in, explore. Bela and I will start emptying the car."

Robert smiled, on the verge of tears, though not of sadness. He had lost so much, no wonder he looked pale and still in shock. For Stella, the pang of regret for having not been fully at his side was hard to bear, and she vowed, as she handed the first heavy box to her niece, that she would not let him deal with such destructiveness alone again.

The home she had found for him was paid for out of the proceeds from their mother's will. She had thought about renting a place for him, but the prices in the village were absurdly high. The surrounding towns were moderately cheaper but still barely within reach. Besides, she wanted him close, and her home was only a two-mile walk away, back out on the road to Bramwell.

"Dad's found the garden at the back of the house, Auntie Stella," Bela shouted, breaking her aunt's train of thought.

"Excellent. I'm hoping he'll put his gardening skills to use and grow some vegetables for you...and for me. He always had green fingers. Did you know that your grandmother wanted him to become a market gardener like her dad? *Your* dad had other ideas, though. For him, a university education meant the world. He'd always wanted to teach history." Realising her niece was itching to get on with unpacking, Stella stopped short of further reminiscing and joked, "Fat lot of use that is when you kids think we've always had video games."

***

Bela smiled, understanding her aunt was doing her best to keep the day cheerful. She grabbed the next box from the pile: it contained Stuart's toys and collectables. "I'll take these upstairs, then make some tea," she said, already halfway up the path to the house.

Glad as she was for this fresh start, it was marred by how her dad had dealt with the situation and the scars she wore. They were hundreds of miles from her friends in Manchester, but, crucially, they were away from her mum.

This 'new' house, she had learned from conversations with her dad over the previous month, had been built in the early 1900s, and thanks to her aunt, it had been modernised and all traces of the previous owner eradicated. Inside, it smelled clean with no mould growing on the walls or ceilings. More importantly, there were no creepy men hanging around, leering at her and making suggestive noises.

She placed the box on the new table, which Auntie Stella said had been delivered the day before, and filled the kettle, enjoying the splash of cold water on the backs of her hands. Through the kitchen window, she could see her dad in the middle of the long garden. In the pictures, it had been so overgrown it was impossible to tell where the garden ended and the forest began. Now it had been neatly trimmed and decluttered by a gang of workmen, allowing dappled sunlight to spill over the grass and her dad's relaxed features.

The kettle boiled furiously, the water agitated as if it were fed by the fault lines and crevices of Yellowstone Park, and it made her pause, remembering being in the bath while all around her burst into flames, then the arms of a fireman, then darkness until she woke up in the hospital, scarred forever, but at least the nightmares had stopped.

She opened the window and called out to her dad, telling him she'd made tea and that he needed to help with the boxes, making sure that she laughed as she did so. Over the past few months, she'd realised guiltily that she took out her anger on the people closest to her. Some of it came down to being a typical sullen teenager, and perhaps she had a better reason than most to dwell in a dark place, but that was no excuse for throwing hissy fits when she didn't get her own way.

As Bela pulled the window shut, a small movement caught her eye. An ant scuttled along the window ledge and down into a crack between two tiles. The insect moved so quickly, Bela might not have noticed it but for its strange colour. A black ant would have blended in with the shadows, but this ant was a fiery red, like a drop of blood on legs.

"Great. That's the last thing we need," Bela muttered and picked up the kettle, tipping the remaining hot water down through the crack, imagining the ant's fear as it scurried along its purpose-built highway desperately searching for a corner to hide in and escape the rushing hot tide.

Feeling bad about causing the creature harm, she turned away, wishing she hadn't acted without thinking, but it was done now. She collected two of the cups of tea she'd made and carried them out to the front of the house, surprised to find her aunt was engaged in conversation with a man. At first, Bela assumed it was a friendly chat with a neighbour, but as she wandered closer along the gravel path, she spotted her aunt's uneasy expression—the kind that said *follow my lead and don't say anything.*

"Bela, I was just telling Reverend Tarky that you're moving in today." There was a hint of nervousness in Auntie Stella's voice, which seemed strange if this man was a vicar.

"And you must be Bela," he said and held out his hand to her. "It's good to meet you. We have a few people of your age in and around the village. I'm sure you'll fit in well." All the while he was talking, he was shaking her hand and staring at her face rather than looking her in the eye. Bela considered how she'd react if he asked about her disfigurement. Not that it was any of this man's business.

As he finally released her hand, her father appeared at the front door, his initial welcoming smile turning to a look of bewildered irritation.

The vicar strode to meet him and again thrust out his hand, continuing to smile when her father kept his hands firmly at his sides, although Bela noticed a subtle change in the man's demeanour.

Out of the vicar's sight but noticed by Bela and her father, Auntie Stella was frantically signalling to her brother to play nice, to go with the flow of local life.

***

"Not the handshaking kind, I see." The man's tone was friendly enough, but he didn't seem the sort to let a slight like that drop, even if he understood the reasons for it.

"Not at all, Mr...?" Robert asked.

"Reverend Alan Tarky. It has been my humble pleasure for many years now to serve the village and the outlying area." The pride in Tarky's voice was unmistakable. However, Robert ignored it.

"Well, Reverend, thanks for stopping by, but I'm sure you can appreciate my family has had a long and exhausting couple of days in moving from Manchester to the village. While I don't wish to be rude, we need to get settled in before we start integrating ourselves into what I hope will be a good life here."

"I fully understand...Robert, isn't it? A long day with much on your mind. I noticed you arrive—you slowed down as you came through the village. Very respectful. I like that in a man. I do hope I will see you at the church soon. I was on my way there, in fact, when I thought I would extend my welcome."

Robert shot his sister a quick, meaningful look. He didn't trust religion and the way it tried to control lives, to keep people down in their place by proposing they could be lifted to a higher plane.

Stella came to his rescue and gently took the vicar by the arm. "It's getting late, Reverend. Could I impose upon you to walk me back as far as the bus stop? After all, that group of teenagers could be down there—you know, the ones who hang around the Michaels' boy?"

"Of course," Tarky said genially, although his eyes flared with contained anger. He opened the gate for Stella, and as they walked down the road together, Robert heard him ask about Bela's face. Thankfully, Bela had already picked up another box and was carrying it to the house; if she'd heard the vicar's rude question, she wasn't letting it get to her.

"Take that up to Stuart's room, Bela. The sooner we do this, the sooner I can start making dinner for you both."

Bela attempted to give him a thumbs up and laughed at herself when she nearly upended the box. "See you inside, Dad."

"You will," he said. She would be okay. She'd been through so much, a vicar's words would barely touch her. Still, Robert didn't want him coming to the house again.

Chapter Six

THE FLOWERS HAD been delivered and deposited inside the knave of the church, the buds opening up at the right time for the service. The vast array of different colours and smells delighted Belinda Bennett. The experience was one she always found exhilarating, enchanting; it gave her hope in a time of growing unease. She looked around the church. Apart from the one she had visited in Vatican City while on a walking tour of Italy after the war, this was the only church she had ever been inside. She was baptised, married and had her only child baptised and laid to rest all within this sacred building and its grounds, where both her parents and several friends she had lost over the years were also buried.

Belinda, tired and feeling old, still showed her face every day, even though of late, she had taken comfort in dreaming of the wooden grave. She had tried to talk to her husband about her fear of carrying on, but he was so wrapped up in dealing with his own mortality, she didn't have the heart or the strength to go through her thoughts with him.

She had always been a dedicated believer in Christ and the Church, and in the last decade had increasingly sought solace in the walls of this building and the respectful peace of the graveyard beyond. It was the only place where she could express her pain at having lost her child. When the sunlight came through the stained glass and hit the cross with her Saviour on it, she felt the grace of his love.

33

The afternoon sun had moved on, and the cross was now in shadow, the face of Christ obscured by a darkness he must have known as he faced the temptations of the devil. She took one last look at the flowers and made a mental note to use the decorative glass vases for them—the colours would stand out better in those than in the plastic ones the other committee members used—and checked her watch. The vicar would be back soon.

Crossing herself in front of the figure of Christ, she walked solemnly out of the church and into the shaded area of the graveyard, past the final resting places of those nobody remembered anymore, whose inscriptions had faded, their date of birth lost to time, their names, meaningless.

She stopped and rested underneath a hanging willow. It was one of several trees in the graveyard, but she liked this one the most and had made sure her son was buried close by. The previous summer, she had paid for a bench to be placed directly opposite his headstone and in the shelter of the willow tree. She rarely saw anyone in the graveyard these days; nobody had time for the dead like they used to. The odd occasion when she did see someone, they were always in a hurry. The flowers, if they brought any, were dumped on top of the soil, no words, perhaps a quick nod or a glance to the heavens before they realised they had somewhere else to go, somewhere they would rather be.

Belinda couldn't blame them, but she did think it was a pity. To sit with those you have lost, she believed, kept them in your memory longer, stopped them from becoming a relic of the past, like a yellowed photograph consigned to a drawer along with outstanding credit card bills and free CDs from the Sunday papers. The dead deserved better than that. Here, they were still close at hand. A mother could almost reach out and touch the spirit, the soul of her lost child, and as she sat upon the warm wood, she patted the seat beside her. It had become such a habit that Belinda hardly noticed herself doing it, a subconscious invitation to sit with her, be it ghost or fellow griever. It was all the same in the end.

The grave, as always, was spotless, cleaned as carefully as the inside of the church, no moss allowed to settle, no blemish given chance to fester. Every Sunday after morning service, she placed a single red rose on the edge of the base of the stone; on the first of every month, a bunch of gladioli interlaced with larkspur and white carnations; and on her boy's birthday, twenty-five pink carnations.

Christmas was special, as was the anniversary of his death, but for both those dates, she stayed away from the church. Memories of him with his hair brushed back neatly, looking angelic in his albs and surplice, singing proudly to the village as they gave thanks for the season, for the beauty and the serenity that their village possessed—it was too much for her at Christmas. It meant she had to share him again with well-meaning others who dropped his name into conversations and were still sorry for her loss and the village's; there had not been anyone like him since.

Belinda lowered her eyes in shame as she allowed the word *hypocrites* to pass her thin, sometimes cruel lips. There were very few people she actively disliked, and most of them were fools, targets of their own making, not like in days gone by when the village was made up of no more than five or six families, all able to trace their bloodline and heritage back to the time when William took exception to being overlooked as king. The influx of wealth had been a boon to the village, with that Belinda could not argue, but like most things, new money wiped away the depth of the old ways. The village had retained its beauty, but across the ridge, on the other side of the crossroads, stood a small, gated estate, its expensive houses tasteless in their conformity, all glamour, no structure.

She had been invited to a party there once. Lionel had started to feel the first twinges of pain and refused to attend. At the time, Belinda was convinced her husband was swinging the social lead, that he couldn't face the village expanding beyond his small, familiar realm. Of course, her mind was changed a few weeks later when the blood appeared with his bowel movements, a spot here or there at first, a smear on the toilet bowl which he didn't notice, but that was only the beginning.

"Do you remember me telling you about the party, my lad?" Belinda asked the air between them. "I came down here the next day to tell you all about it—how gaudy the decorations were, not my cup of tea at all, silver and gold everywhere, an indoor swimming pool, no wood to be found—what good is a home without wood and brass? Silver is so tacky, gold even more so. Even the furniture was hard to look at without rooting through my handbag for a pair of sunglasses. So bright and full of itself, just like the owner really."

She laughed at the shared joke between mother and son. He would have quite liked the furniture, she thought, and would have ticked her off, with kindness, for being so old-fashioned.

"Old fashioned...we'll have none of that. Who was it you went to first with your little secret? Not so much of one, though, was it? I knew—I think even your father had noticed—but we didn't mind. Of course, we talked about you. Sometimes we tried to help you...I don't know if you knew that. It was a different time. The world suddenly became so very real to us. Our fortress had been breached, and in came this horrible disease." A tear ran down her cheek and settled on her chin, glistening in the sunlight before being swept away.

"Now what did I say? You're not to make me cry when I come to visit. We save the tears for behind closed doors. Nobody must ever see the weakness of emotion." She waved off the imagined apology. "It's all right, no offence taken," she answered, a wavering in her otherwise immaculate voice. "It's your anniversary next week. You won't mind if I don't come and see you, will you? Yes, I know you don't like me going up to that...place, but I don't have any choice, do I? You couldn't trust me enough to tell me what you were thinking—now, see you've gone and upset me again! Hush, hush. I know you didn't mean to break my heart. It was all just such a shock— Oh my, I shall be in trouble, The Reverend Tarky is coming up the drive and I haven't put out the flowers yet. You do keep me talking."

Belinda Bennett rose from the bench and acknowledged the vicar with a smile and a cheery wave, surreptitiously patting her son's gravestone as she passed it, stopping in her tracks when she felt a small rumble. It seemed to come from underneath her feet and was followed by a series of loud, disturbing thuds and the sense that the Earth was baring its teeth, preparing to devour her. She set off again as quickly as she could, though her legs were not as sprightly or in shape as they once were, and she saw from the urgency in the reverend's eyes that he too felt the physical vibration. If anyone was going to save them, it would be God and his instrument on Earth.

A small surge pushed her off her feet, the momentum almost throwing her into the vicar's grasping arms, and she felt herself being dragged away from the graveyard and onto the concrete path that surrounded the church as the earth gave one final, internal boom as if it had swallowed too quickly and was letting out a giant burp. If it hadn't been so terrifying, Belinda might have given a small chuckle. The last time she had felt this frightened was the morning she found her son's final note to her, the one which explained how it had all become too much, how sorry he was for being unable to carry on with that disease coursing through his body, not now that everybody knew, thanks to Sarah Calster and the vile rumours she was spreading.

The noise had been so loud that a few people came out of the nearby bungalows and cottages to see what had happened, including the eternal spinster Stella Romsleigh, whose expression was one of bewilderment and concern. How bad must it have been for someone who hadn't said more than two words to her since her son died to finally show her consideration? Belinda couldn't stand it and slowly turned around, ignoring the vicar's plea that she save herself from witnessing the destruction.

It was as though a small bomb had gone off. The images of far-off lands tempered by war came flashing into Belinda's mind. *An earthquake,* she tried to convince herself, but there before her was the devastating scene of a churchyard devoid of serenity and peace.

Where once had stood beautiful memorials to the dead, now was an expanse. Her mother and father, her neighbour Joyce who had been drinking heavily one night and was killed outside her own home by a boy on a bicycle, the tree, the bench and the open field, it was all gone, in its place a cratered landscape, like a moon scarred by a meteor shower, except this one had come from below.

The devastation extended to the edge of the sprawling forest, and nothing of the dead had survived intact, not even her boy, his coffin now lying twenty feet deeper, open to the elements, the skeleton, like the others who had sought eternal rest here, in pieces, shattered beyond hope.

Chapter Seven

MILLICENT MAPLES HAD set the trail out exactly as Harry had requested. For some, it was a short introduction to tracking; for others, it was a chance to develop leadership skills and become more than they had been able to be as they struggled with family issues and, in one case, severe neglect.

She was grateful for the chance to come on this expedition. At first, she hadn't been too sure if she wanted to take up Harry's offer and become a Scout leader and had at one point thought it might be a wind-up. Even once she'd found out the offer was genuine and he'd assured her that he could put her skills to good use, she'd worried how a group of teenage boys would react to having a lesbian in their lives.

Not that it should have mattered, and being a teacher helped, although there was something more intimate about staying with a group of teenagers out in the open than there was to being cooped up with them in a classroom. She had learned at Woodstock that a tent and the fresh air could bring out the worst in some males, many of whom had been young enough to be governed by those first unpredictable surges of testosterone and were relentless in their efforts to get her to sleep with them while Joan Baez sang lullabies of heartache.

Millicent respected Harry immensely, even though at times she felt his deference to his parents' beliefs was a little outdated for a man of his age. He still lived at home, no girlfriend in sight: one evening in the pub, as he downed his third pint, he'd confided that there had been two women whom he had loved and in both cases had distanced himself from them because of his mother's wish that he 'marry a good girl'.

His father was a strange old duck too but quite amiable as long as the topic was neutral—pre-war train routes throughout Britain, the state of English county cricket or the nuances of the local brewing company's latest ale. However, move the discussion on to politics and he'd have shamed half the far right for not being far right enough. He wasn't that bad, just forthright in his views on certain subjects. He was born in a different time when attitudes were handed down from Victorian society. Still, at least he didn't argue that AIDS was a warning from God to homosexuals, as his wife believed. That had been enough for Fleur, who had made it clear the second they were in the car and heading home that she never wanted to meet up with Harry's mother again.

If Harry had Millicent's respect, then Fife had her middle-aged sapphic heart. She had never known such tenderness in a man. He was passionate without being a bore, caring without asking for attention, and as loyal as they came. It had taken her a while to coax out of him his problem, how he'd had no choice but to put his mother in a home as she was too much for him to cope with. Fife was the same age as Harry, but he hadn't aged well. He was always well presented and not a bad-looking man, but his mother's suicide attempt had taken its toll.

Millicent placed the final set of instructions down on the ground: the coded message of 'return to base' would surely be decipherable to both teams. If they correctly followed the course, they would find several other clues that they would need to remember for the days ahead. Harry had made this clear to the parents as well as the boys themselves: this was an expedition, not a babysitting service. It was about discipline and self-control and acquiring new skills.

Millicent had silently cheered when Harry delivered that speech the previous Christmas. He concluded by telling them that if they didn't agree and thought he was being too hard on them, they could leave after that night and not return. He wanted commitment, every single one of them playing an active part in the troop, no half measures.

Fife had not been present that evening, and the words used in anger and cajolement were not a jibe at his time in charge of the group but at society in general. The town had been in a malaise for some time; the teenagers, who had always felt trapped by convention, had become listless, the great weight of the past hanging over their heads. Nevertheless, as the evening came to an end, Harry had slumped in a chair and wondered aloud if he had gone too far. Millicent had given him her sternest scowl and admonished him—with care. She had seen how the town had changed in the ten years since the strange occurrences at the farm.

Returning to camp, Millicent shook her head but smiled indulgently at the silhouette of Harry, enhanced by the sun, smoking a crafty cigarette. She heard a loud boom in the distance but paid it no heed, her mind still replaying what she'd said to Harry that night, and they'd both been proved right, as not only did every boy return, but other parents had phoned to see if they could enrol their boys into the troop. Three of the parents also enquired about becoming helpers.

Leadership, Harry, it works both ways. Perhaps she could put it on a T-shirt.

She greeted him with a wave as she got closer, and he in return held up a mug of freshly brewed tea.

"How did it go? Did you get all the signs down like we practised?"

Millicent grinned and accepted the mug with pleasure. "Every last one of them, boss. A couple of dead ends, the clues laid out exactly as we planned—even saw Fife at the halfway point with the water. The boys won't know what hit them."

Harry laughed. The plan had been set, and with any luck, the boys would sleep well tonight. He had a big stew in the pot for them, and then bed. No messing about.

Only young Dylan Brown wasn't taking part in the trail. The journey down here had been rough on him, and he'd vomited several times, notably all over his blankets. Luckily, Harry carried spares for such eventualities and sent the boy for a lie-down with a bowl next to him.

"Are you going to segregate Dylan from the others, boss?" Millicent asked.

"Why? Do you think it's more than travel sickness?"

"Better safe than sorry, I say."

"You might be right about that." Harry considered for a moment. "He'll have to take my tent then, and I'll bunk in with Fife. Trouble is, he snores like a jackhammer, but it's that or the Land Rover, and my back will hate me for it."

"I'd offer my tent, but—"

"No, don't you worry. As long as Dylan doesn't throw up all over my tent, we'll manage a night or two."

***

Fife checked his watch again. The second group should have reached the halfway marker around fifteen minutes ago, even considering the two misdirections Millicent had placed into the trail. He recalled who was in that group and found no reason to panic. It would have been a different matter a year ago, with Kevin Sillatoe in the pack. Indeed, as leader, Fife had come close to excluding him a few times. But the boy had turned himself around of late and was turning out to be one of the best in the troop. He was responsible and compassionate towards others, especially the new boys who had joined since Harry's rousing speech at the Christmas party.

Still keeping a lookout for the group's approach, he remembered a moment when he'd lost his cool with the lad, something he regretted now he looked back on the event with greater clarity.

The previous summer, they'd joined forces with the local Sea Scout group so the boys in his charge could learn about canoeing and sailing. The twelve lads he'd selected out of a total of twenty had enjoyed the experience, six weeks of hard work and plenty of fun, give or take the occasional mishap, such as Derek Small going backwards down a weir. The look of terror on his face resulted in the Sea Scouts taking the mickey out of him but also accepting him as one of their own, so much so that in the October, Derek had asked if he could join the other group. His reason: he wanted to join the Royal Navy when he left school. Fife had clasped him on the shoulder and smiled proudly. He'd proved what could be done with cooperation.

The only undesirable spot on the whole summer came when Kevin Sillatoe had changed out of his dank, mucky clothes in the Sea Scoutmaster's new car, leaving a trail of dirt and a wet patch on the back seat. The Sea Scoutmaster kicked up so much of a fuss that Fife had felt compelled to pay for the car to be cleaned, inside and out, and had made Sillatoe offer an almost grovelling apology. If he'd had even an inkling of the turmoil the boy was going through, he'd have taken a very different stance instead of insisting he pay half the cleaning bill.

It was only when he saw Sillatoe walking to school a few days later, sporting a raw black eye and a broken arm that he understood who was to blame for the boy's behaviour because Fife was as culpable as Kevin's father in this. He'd let his frustrations with his mother spill out and worsen the chaos in the young man's life.

It was at that moment Fife knew he had to step back, leave the organisation he had served faithfully and deal with his own monsters, to make amends to Kevin Sillatoe. He had found some comfort in talking to Millicent. She had allowed him to express his fears and confess the damage he'd done. Between them, they came up with a plan, the first step being to approach Kevin's father. The police wouldn't touch the old brute, but Fife had tried to get him to acknowledge that his son had problems and needed understanding, not constant derision. The old man had scoffed and given Fife a hard time, and it took a further intervention on Millicent's part, along with the threat of investigation by social services, to put the man on a straighter path.

Since then, Kevin Sillatoe had come on leaps and bounds. No longer running around with a bad crowd, he had buckled down at school, and while there was little chance of him ever going to university, he was less likely to go the way of his old man and end up in prison on a string of charges for GBH, assault and robbery.

Twenty-five minutes had passed since Sillatoe's group should have reached the marker. The instructions had been clear: *do not start the second stage of the trail until you have checked in with Mr. Piccolo.* Kevin wouldn't have disobeyed an order. Fife tapped his watch and cursed under his breath. The final clue pointing to the meeting spot was two hundred yards away, close enough he would have heard them, which meant they'd got lost before that. Erring on the side of caution, he decided to go find the boys.

Before (1940)

one fincome elderly cabbage of him and ever past him and over the bridge invalle meele.

Later the plant and him and and joined around.
this take trees as had lot, when it used to light to up-land after being by and circuit for. Having lost me learning the parents and not his parce does the readers surprised a their made to the bathos, and reality of Burning, it was

They finally cut down her body three hours after the boy was discovered on the front step of his house crying silently, his coat sleeve wet, full of grime and covered in dried snot bubbles. He had tried to keep anyone from entering, sticking to the mantra instilled in him by his mum that strangers were never to come into the house; he only relented when the two burly, stern-looking policemen and two slightly friendlier ambulance drivers agreed to remove their shoes. One of the policemen was on the verge of clipping the cheeky beggar around the ear for his trouble but stopped mid-swot when the next-door neighbour gave him a glare so vicious she could have stopped an enemy bomb from falling on the street purely with the power of concentration.

The boy knew she was dead; he didn't need adults to tell him what was plainly so. He had seen so much death in his short life—houses hit by nightly raids, fires indiscriminately claiming children, parents and grandparents alike. The Nazi bombs didn't care. They were, like the Command said, just doing their job. Blindly, mechanically following orders.

He had been out playing on the fields and in the woods beyond the River Rae. For the first time since his dad had been killed in the air raid that destroyed the factory where he worked, his mum had allowed him to go and play, with a promise he'd return before it got dark. The potato fields had been too difficult, too muddy to play in properly, and the men had chased him off, one throwing a hefty cabbage at him as he ran past them and over the bridge into the woods.

Parts of the plane's wreckage could still be seen dotted around the three craters it had left when it tried to lighten its payload after being hit by anti-aircraft fire. Having lost his bearings, the pilot looked for his position as the squadron continued on their route to the nation's industrial city of Birmingham. It was all in vain, the pilot taking one last bullet to the head as his plane spiralled to the Earth below. Meanwhile, on the ground, the gun operator was enjoying a few glasses of whisky after the raid, unaware that beyond his little bubble of reality, that of the boy's father was ending as the factory and its heavy machinery crashed around him.

The boy could hear the men inside talking, whispers of be careful with her, show some respect and the occasional untoward joke, all filtering through to the young boy sitting on the step, no longer sure of where he was to go. He put a cold, mitten-less hand into his pocket and pulled out a small, empty box he had found near the crash site. It had once housed matches, probably left behind by one of the witnesses who had seen the plane come hurtling down as it took another hit, this time to the tail; it was sheer luck the bombs had been released onto the woods below and not gone off inside the plane when it crashed.

Inside the spent box were several ants he had found crawling around the destroyed partial left wing that was still drawing crowds. For many, it was the first time they had seen a German war machine; for others who had lost friends or family, to be so close to an instrument of death as it roared its final breath felt like victory.

The ants scurried around the box looking for a way out, but each time they climbed the side, the boy gently pushed them back down and smiled, not out of cruelty, but out of a spark of interest and awe that they had survived when the mighty trees had been turned to ash.

From behind, the boy heard the four men making their way through the house, their footsteps stuttering between reverential quiet and procedural compliance. Not wishing to get in the way of his mother's final departure from their home, he moved aside as the older-looking policeman led the way, followed by the two ambulance men and then the final policeman, the kind one, who bent down to look the boy in the face.

"We've made her comfortable, lad. An undertaker will be along soon to deal with her properly."

The neighbour who had stood on her step throughout tutted loudly. "What's the boy supposed to do in the meantime? Play on the step in the dark till you deem her death a priority?"

The policeman, to his credit, didn't rise to the angry taunt of the frustrated pensioner.

"I don't want to tell you there's a war on, missus, but as you can imagine, with another raid last night, resources are a bit tight. What time is the boy's father due home from work? I can sit with him till then."

The neighbour softened her anger, having heard the planes in the near distance, their ire this time focused on the Black Country. "The boy's father died a few weeks ago," she said. "When the British Small Arms Factory was destroyed. He hasn't got anyone. No aunt or uncle, just his mum, bless her soul." She crossed herself.

Frowning, the policeman walked over to his colleague and began an earnest conversation, which drew the attention of the two ambulance men, who had been putting away their meagre supplies. The older policeman seemed exasperated and reminded the young constable that the boy was not their concern. There were other problems to deal with, especially this close to Christmas.

The two policemen argued for almost five minutes, during which the workers arrived home from their jobs in the factories that lined the River Rae. By the time the younger policeman returned to the doorstep alongside the neighbour and the boy, quite a crowd of onlookers had gathered.

"I'll stay with the boy till the undertaker comes, then I'll find a place for him to stay tonight." Turning his attention to the boy, he said, "You know how to make a cup of tea? Put the kettle on—I'll join you in a minute."

The boy did as he was told and walked through the house to the kitchen. Out of the corner of his eye, he saw his mum's body on the dining table, a solemn sheet covering her from her feet to the nape of her once slender, perfect neck, now bearing the marks of the rope that had killed her. His young mind could barely understand the enormity of suicide; he just hoped that she had found his dad.

While the kettle boiled, he took the matchbox out of his pocket again and counted the small ants, all alive, no doubt wondering when they were going to be set free. He almost jumped out of his skin when the heavy hand of the policeman came down upon his shoulder.

"What you got there, lad?"

The boy showed him the contents of the box, and the policeman smiled.

48

"I think you should let them go, son. They won't like being cooped up like that. It's cruel. You wouldn't like it, would you?"

The boy shook his head, and under the guidance of the policeman, he went outside into the yard and released his newfound friends from their cardboard prison.

Returning to the kitchen, he was given a cup of sweetened tea, which he drank as the policeman told him he hadn't always wanted to join the police force. It was a concession to his father, who'd wanted him to have a job with prestige in the community, yet it seemed all he ever got to do was break the news to some poor family that a loved one had died, arrest black marketeers or shout at all and sundry to put their lights out.

"Funnily enough, I wanted to be an entomologist and study insects. I was especially intrigued by myrmecology—the social aspects of ants."

For the next hour, the policeman shared some of what he had learned from his observations of ant society, his lecture only broken by the arrival of the undertaker.

The policeman told the boy to go to his bedroom and find some pyjamas, clothes and toys, promising that until he could find a safer place in the country, he could stay with him and his sister.

The man kept his promise, and it was with great sadness a month later that the boy left the small, terraced house the policeman shared with his sister, to be evacuated to Downmere, a remote village where the policeman's aunt lived. The man's kindness and generosity had left an indelible mark on the boy, so much so that when he heard the policeman had been shot dead by a thief looting a jeweller's premises, the boy honoured him by dedicating his life to carrying on the man's research.

Long after the world had descended into peace, the woman who had kept him safe and given him a home also passed on, having seen her only niece follow her brother into the beyond. With no other living relatives, the woman left her large house to the boy, now a man, and he began to build a true place of study.

Chapter Eight

SAMANTHA MCCARTHY'S LIFE had not gone to plan. The fresh start had been ideal for about a year, but the head injury and memory of being attacked while getting out of her car continued to plague her, to whisper in the back of her mind that she had only survived by sheer luck.

After her daughter went to live with her father in Hong Kong, Samantha moved to London and rented a house from a friend who also secured her a job at one of the big nationals of the day. With all bar a few connections severed, she moved into the house off Brick Lane in the East End and never went back home, instead fading out of people's thoughts and memories forever.

That was not true, of course. Some still thought of her from time to time, remembering all she had done for the town, but as each day passed, as every season changed, the less her name was spoken, the less her face retained its power over the people of Perchester.

For the first few months out of hospital, she had grasped everything she could in order to feel alive, throwing herself into her work, making headlines and being the type of journalist she had always wanted to be, exposing the corrupt, revealing the secrets of the wealthy and the political classes, uncovering the truth.

Her psychotherapist had intimated that she was doing it out of guilt when what she needed to do was confront her own past. She had left a man who cared for her to deal with the aftermath of the destruction of her hometown. Even the act of sending her daughter away was a punishment, a distancing of all she had held dear at one time. Samantha only saw the therapist a few times after that and finally hit rock bottom in the early hours of a balmy summer morning as she sat in the Blind Beggar, drinking whisky and arguing with a tourist about the Kray Twins and pretending the previous evening hadn't been a shit show. Starting the day drunk, she'd got progressively worse as the hours went by, the pinnacle being when she wet herself as she was introduced to the star of the theatre premiere she was reviewing, the urine running down her leg onto the plush carpet of the green room.

Her boss Andrew Fillus had made excuses, of course. *She is such a huge fan of yours, I believe she has had a crush on you for ages*, laughing it off in public but shoving her roughly into the back of a black cab as soon as he could without raising too many eyebrows. His words echoed in her mind all the way through London's busy, illuminated streets.

It was after she had to be restrained in the pub the following morning that Andrew's words finally hammered home. If she was not willing to undergo counselling, if she continued to put the paper's name and reputation to the test, then despite their years of friendship, he would, regrettably, have to let her go. He could no longer carry her. *Take a few months out, go see your daughter, write a book.* He told if she came back sober in three months, she would still have a job and he would welcome her back with open arms.

After the police released her with a warning and the tourist and his family accepted her apology, refusing to let some unfortunate woman's bad day hinder their holiday, she acted upon Andrew's advice. She called the paper and told them she was going to take a three-month leave of absence for personal reasons. The statement was taken without argument, the sound of silent relief resonating down the complexity of telephone wires. By the time she made it back down Brick Lane, Andrew was waiting for her outside the house with a bouquet of flowers and a warm smile of friendship for the woman he knew had almost destroyed herself trying to make peace with events that were out of her control, that she had allowed to control her.

The conversation had been difficult and tearful, but Andrew had been incredible, offering a shoulder in comfort, which she'd welcomed but soon dismissed, knowing she didn't deserve his or anyone's sympathy. He'd booked her ticket to Hong Kong and even driven her to the airport, but the best thing he'd done for her was to tell her not to come back to the office. When she returned from visiting her daughter, he said, there would be money in her account to start over, move on, learn to be herself again.

Initially, those words hurt, as if he were summarily dismissing her, but as time went by, six months being cared for by her daughter and new son-in law, a gentle man who listened to her tale without interruption or blame, she knew her boss had been right. On the day she returned, he was waiting for her at the airport and didn't hide his pleasure in greeting this new, clean and sober Samantha McCarthy, a woman in control of her life again.

Andrew Fillus had kept to his word and gone beyond. He had put together a severance package that reflected the esteem in which he held her, and it was enough to go home, should she wish to, or start again somewhere new, somewhere quiet and boring, where the world didn't care what day of the week it was or what national emergency was making headlines for the boys to gossip over as they traded stocks or which party leader would ensure their days continued in champagne and cocaine.

Thus, it was with a new sense of perspective that she had said goodbye to Andrew and her old life at Waterloo station and headed west to the village of Downmere. From hard-nosed journalist to bookshop owner, from a bottle of whisky every morning to a cup of tea before opening the door, it was a complete change of lifestyle where her only concern was how best to avoid the procession of gaggling faithful who clung to every word of

Reverend Tarky's passionate sermons...until the day the earth caved in.

Samantha had kept to herself as much as she could over the years. Her husband Bertie and the shop kept her grounded and gave her all the excuses she needed to avoid socialising. *No, sorry, can't make Thursday to discuss the parking arrangements for Easter, Bertie has an appointment in Avoncross. Oh, this Wednesday? I am so sorry, Mrs. Bennett, Bertie has his weights that day, you know for his legs...* and so it had continued. Occasionally, when the moon was right, she would play host and make merry, albeit behind gritted teeth. It threw the locals off their stride; Samantha couldn't say that didn't bring her a certain satisfaction.

Like others in the village, she'd heard the loud rumble and felt the small shockwave. She'd watched helplessly as books tumbled from the shelves like paperback lemmings, too many to catch. Her husband popped his head around the door, and she saw in his expression fear and suspicion, and she could not blame him. That Sunday, years ago, when they'd shared a quiet lunch in the Grey Fisher pub in Avoncross, she'd told him everything— the drinking, the fits of temper, the counselling—and was quick to assure him now.

"It's all right, Bertie. It wasn't me. I think it came from the bottom of the hill. You get back to the archiving and I'll pop down the road, see if there is anything amiss."

Bertie Myers never needed telling twice. He nodded in agreement and closed the door that separated his office from the bookshop. Samantha quickly picked up the fallen books, sighing bitterly at the splayed, creased pages that would see their protagonists suffer more than once.

With the books back on the shelves, she joined the other villagers congregating on the cobbled pavements and milling about in the road. Some had started walking down the hill, their natural tendency for snooping urging them onward. It wouldn't have surprised Samantha to find out they had packed flasks of tea and rounds of ham and cheese sandwiches. When nothing happened in your lives day after day, it was hardly astonishing that you grasped whatever opportunities for excitement came your way.

There was no point locking the shop: if anything were to happen, Bertie would need to be able to roll out unhindered rather than wasting precious minutes searching for a set of keys he hadn't used in five years. By now, the high street was packed, others from beyond the crossroads having joined the impromptu village gathering, and in one heaving mass, they flowed down the hill, past the parade of old shops and thatched roofs.

The crowd buzzed cyclically as rumours and conjecture surfaced and were quickly squashed. Some rattled the older residents; some gleefully attracted the younger ones. *The church has fallen down. The vicar has been impaled by the cross. Mrs. Bennett and the gardener were found in a compromising position beside the begonias.* It was all tosh and nonsense, but it didn't stop the chatter.

From the direction of Bramwell, a fire engine could be heard approaching, and the crowd became even more agitated, moving more quickly, paying no heed to the new people in their midst or the man emptying out his car at the side of the road. Nobody cared, nobody except for Samantha McCarthy, wife of Bertie Myers. She slowed to make sure the stranger was okay, jolting as people bumped into her and had the audacity to grumble at *her* lack of consideration.

She only saw him for a brief second. He'd turned his back as soon as he noticed her looking his way, but it was enough to jog a memory, to kickstart an impulse she had long denied: the curiosity of an investigative journalist. Otherwise, she might have put it down to mob mentality, of being absorbed into a community that would readily raise pitchforks to defend their village, and perhaps that was so. Whatever the cause, she knew beyond doubt that she had seen the man's face before.

Chapter Nine

SAMANTHA MCCARTHY WOULD later regret not taking more of an interest in the history of the village, the sensational stories spawned from gossip, half-truths buried in the quicksand of the past, for as she searched her memory for the reason why she recognised the new man, she neglected to notice who was missing from the crowd.

In Samantha's defence, nobody else noticed Lionel Bennett was missing either. Not even Darren Curran, the closest thing Lionel had to a friend, registered his absence from the mob marching down the hill to the church, where a distinctly dishevelled Belinda was being led away by a fireman. Indeed, the only person who noticed Lionel was not with everyone else was a woman who had left the village as a girl and was on her way to see her mother for the first time in many years.

Lionel hadn't cared about being seen. He'd wanted her to see him and knew the exact moment she did. She stopped outside the bookshop, feigned browsing in the window and then made an act of deciding which way to go. To the left led to the old forge, disused and fallen to ruin, and the Thorn Hill Hotel, at this time of year patronised by a few permanent residents and hanging on by the seat of its pants. To the right was an open road that led, eventually, to the next town.

"Go on, go back to your mummy," Lionel hissed to himself, the words catching on his false teeth, the harsh, urgent sentiment burning the back of his throat in his hatred for the girl behind his son's final days of despair.

His anger turned to puzzlement when Sarah Calster reached the crossroads wooden signpost, stopped, turned back and, looking him dead in the eyes, sat on the recently mown verge. His rage returned in full force when, still staring right at him, she patted the grass beside her.

The old man's mind raced. He should have expected something like this. She was bold and not easily frightened, except for the day she found the professor's corpse and had run screaming past the pub. It wasn't that frightened girl he saw now. Rather, he imagined a patient spider, capable of putting its prey out of its misery yet watching in cruel satisfaction as its meal ceased its thrashing frenzy and gave up all hope.

Believing he could get her to admit her wrongs, Lionel took the bait and crossed the road, toiling to keep the pain hidden as he reached the verge and looked down upon her, the wicked girl turned woman.

"Hello, Lionel. Won't you sit down? It's hurting my neck looking up at you. Besides, the sun will do us both good."

"Why did you tell people about my boy? You broke his mother's heart."

Sarah nodded in earnest agreement. "Please, Lionel, sit down with me. I won't bite."

For some reason he could not readily explain, he did as he was asked...*instructed*, and they both looked down the hill. In the distance, they could see the throng milling about outside the church, not well enough to pick them out individually but enough to get a grasp of the situation.

"I used to sit here a lot when I was a girl. I felt like I was looking down on the village the way it looked down on me. I imagined you all could be stamped out—just one foot placed with enough pressure would wipe out the entire village. No one would miss it, not really. It's a small hive filled with small minds, uninteresting people scurrying about, tearing others apart piece by piece."

Lionel was about to interrupt but quickly closed his mouth. He wanted to hear what Sarah Calster had to say for herself.

Sarah smiled, not a hint of bitterness on her face. On the contrary, her expression was one of calm reflection, a sense of unburdening.

"You're learning, Lionel. Perhaps being out of your wife's shadow allows the real you to come out. You all damned me. I had nothing to do with the professor's death. I admit I went in there to rob him. I wanted money for beer and a smoke. My dad was dying, my mum couldn't get a job. Apart from Carl and a couple of others, no one in the village would talk to me. Your wife, the saintly Belinda, crossed herself whenever she saw me, and don't tell me she didn't have a bible handy to hit me with if she got the chance. Yes, in the strictest sense, I killed my dear dad, but he was in pain. He asked us to ease his suffering. Mum couldn't do it, so I did as I was told, and I went to prison for it."

Lionel scratched his face, a small itch demanding attention, a further tickle on the back of his neck.

Sarah leaned forward and hugged her knees to her chest as if to shield herself from an imminent attack.

"I told people about your son purely out of spite. I really didn't want him to die, certainly not the way he did. To hang himself like that..." She let the words dangle in the air, malevolence in the guise of sincerity, the spider coming out of its funnel sensing that its prey was struggling. "It was horrendous."

"What did he ever do to you?"

"Nothing, except get sympathy for catching a disease when he didn't have to. I couldn't have cared less that he was gay, unlike everyone else in this stinking village, the hypocrites who consoled you and then behind your back viciously took your lives apart. All I did was put it out in the open, let you see how your so-called friends were out to destroy you. I just wanted him to admit that he was ill."

The kindness of a soft kiss with fangs slipping silently underneath the skin, an analgesic before the venom hits the nervous system. Lionel felt something sting, almost inconsequential, and quickly disregarded it.

"What did it matter to you?" Lionel demanded, although he noted that his anger was slowly subsiding. He hated confrontation at the best of times and would normally have deferred to his wife, whose anger burnt long after the oxygen had run out.

Sarah moved her arms from her knees and rose to her full height, now looking down on the old man.

"Do you ever question why the church is at the bottom of the hill?" She put a hand over her eyes. "When I was little, I was told it was to keep a closer watch on hell, that Tarky went down to the crypt at night and performed rites to make sure hell didn't crack open." She paused as a fire engine, sirens blaring, eased through the crowd and drew to a halt outside the church gates. "It seems he finally failed."

Another sting, and another. Lionel felt as if he were slowly being wrapped in silk, the threads of his life slowly enveloping him.

Sarah picked up her bag. She didn't offer to help the old man up from the grass; she didn't offer him comfort or repentance. All she had given him was a possible reason why she had announced to the world that his son, his beautiful, graceful, polite, dedicated boy, had AIDS.

"Don't follow me again, Lionel. If you see me in the village, please ignore me. I'm here to care for my mum. The girl I was, that screwed-up piece of shit, she's dead. I killed her long ago."

Leaving that revelation ringing in his ears, she gave him a wide smile, her teeth showing, her lips shining in the late afternoon sun, and she left.

Lionel couldn't have followed her if he'd wanted to. His home, the pub, the post office where he had kept the secrets of the villagers and lines of communication open, became a blur as his eyes closed and his limbs slumped numbly. His final moments alive were filled with the constant pricks of strong mandibles piercing the skin, digging down beneath the flesh of his back, neck, arms and legs. He tried to call after the departing young woman, but his tongue had swelled, barely fitting inside the human cavern.

He wouldn't be found till almost nightfall. By then, several cars would have passed by, the drivers not seeing him. Even if they had noticed him and stopped, it would have been too late. It was perhaps fitting, then, that the person who found him was the last person who had seen him alive, and when she did, she allowed herself to shed a tear for the old man.

Chapter Ten

IN THE SPACE of an hour, Harry Collins and Millicent Maples had gone from pride in their troop to mild concern about how much time had elapsed since the first group's return, to finally going out of their minds with worry when neither Fife nor the rest of the troop had shown up by eight o'clock that evening.

It had all started so well. The first group returned well inside the allotted time. A record for the troop, Jacob Betley led them into camp and was cheered by the lads under his command, who each high-fived him, basking in the pleasure of their success. Harry was overjoyed to see such unity, an excellent piece of teamwork. He clasped Betley on the shoulder and gave him his best well-done smile, but as time ticked by and there was still no sign of Sillatoe's band, Harry began to smell a rat.

As the boys ate their food around the campfire, he observed them, looking for clues that Betley's crew had done something to put Sillatoe's group off the track. Betley and Sillatoe had, at one time, been inseparable, as thick as thieves, and while Fife had issues with Sillatoe, Harry had always suspected it was Betley who was behind most of the trouble they got into.

He couldn't confront the boy, not here; it wouldn't do him or the newly invigorated group any good. Stepping away from the fire, he gave Millicent the signal to keep an eye on things and walked as far as the car park, where he attempted to radio Fife, to see where he was and if he had seen the other boys. He got no answer. It was unlike Fife to not keep in touch, to not keep to the plan. Admittedly, he had completely lost it when Sillatoe had ruined the interior of the other leader's car, but he wouldn't abandon his post without just reason.

Harry had faced many tests in his short time as leader, and something deep in his gut told him this was his biggest yet, but he didn't allow this to colour his mind. Inwardly, he might have been crippled with doubt and concern, but on the outside, he felt in control.

It was a control that gave way to sheer relief when he returned to the camp and saw in the distance young Sillatoe running at full speed towards them, the other boys behind him fighting to keep up. He could hear the boy shouting and saw Betley's face change from majestic smugness to one of freezing doubt. That was when Harry knew for sure that Betley had created a diversion for Sillatoe's team.

As Kevin drew nearer, Harry could see that he was caked almost from head to foot in mud. Harry still couldn't make out what the boy was shouting, but Millicent did, and she sprang into action, her arms out wide to stop Sillatoe in his tracks. Betley leapt to his feet and rounded the fire, putting flame between him and the sheer, guttural fury emanating from Sillatoe.

Millicent did her best to keep the boys apart, but Kevin's size and wrath were too much for her to contain, and the other boys, who had previously been cheering on their champion, backed away. Initially, Harry thought it was because they didn't want to come between the two older boys, but as the wind picked up and made the flames dance with greater fierceness, he realised it was because Kevin wasn't covered in mud at all. He was covered in manure.

"You're a fucking piece of shit, Betley." Kevin Sillatoe exploded with rage, completely missing the irony in his choice of insult.

"Why? What happened? Did you get lost, mate?"

"You know exactly what happened. You changed the directions and laid a false trail. I had to run after Kelly to stop him going down the embankment, then I went down the sodding thing myself and ended up almost drowning in pig shit."

"Suits you. Shit for a shit. It's supposed to be good for your skin, isn't it?"

One of the boys let out an innocent laugh, regretting it when Sillatoe took a swing at him and connected with his jaw.

Sillatoe went to pick up a length of wood from the fire but was stopped by Millicent, who locked her arms around the boy's waist and kept hold as the rest of his group finally, sheepishly, reached the fire circle. Millicent whispered in Sillatoe's ear, her grip seemingly getting firmer, despite now sharing some of the manure.

Harry had managed to do the same to Jacob Betley, the only difference being that he couldn't bring himself to talk to the boy, or not without risking a warning from the police about his conduct. Betley struggled in his arms, kicking out, screaming with the same aggressive rage as his former friend.

While the older boys fought their captors, the young lad, whom Sillatoe had stopped from falling down the hill, explained that they hadn't even reached the halfway point when they came across the corrupted markers. Harry was impressed by the boy's courage and maturity. Barely twelve years of age, he told the story so straight that both leaders were left in no doubt what had happened. It was a simple if malicious prank, and Edward Kelly laid no blame. However, it wasn't the trail that almost sent him down the embankment; it was the huge mass of tiny lights coming together as one.

Harry looked at the boy, and then at Millicent. She shrugged, equally bewildered.

"I saw nothing," Sillatoe said. Even in his rage, he had turned away from the confrontation to listen to the young Scout. "I saw you on the edge and thought you were going to walk right off it. That's how I ended up falling down it myself."

"You didn't fall, though," Edward said. "When you grabbed my arm and swung me away, the ground…it shifted somehow, like when you pour water on a sandcastle and it still looks solid but it isn't. As you went down, the lights seemed to split apart and then blinked out of existence. I thought at first it was Mr. Piccolo looking for us, but…"

Young Edward Kelly realised for the first time in his life that he had a captive audience. The two adults and over a dozen lads were hanging on his every word, and his mouth suddenly felt dry and tight. He looked at Kevin Sillatoe, imploring him to believe what he was saying. "I saw it move, I swear. If Kevin hadn't fallen into…well, into the shit, I think he might have rolled into the darkness."

Edward looked down at his feet, unsure of what to do next, his chest feeling heavy with anxiety, hoping that nobody laughed, or worse, called him a liar.

It was to Kevin Sillatoe's credit that he let his argument with Betley go. He sat on a log beside the fire and stared into its fiery heart, sagging as the anger drained out of him. Every boy present followed his lead. It didn't matter how old you were, there were moments when even the most implausible of tales knocked the wind right out of you.

"I believe you, Edward," Sillatoe said finally, his words echoed by others of the troop, including Jacob Betley, whom Harry had released when the story came to its conclusion.

Harry had never seen such a downturn in spirits before. Not five minutes ago, Kevin Sillatoe appeared in such a frenzy that Harry was genuinely concerned for Betley's life. Now the whole troop, including its two leaders, were open-mouthed and silent in shock. Edward didn't have the imagination to make up a story like that, the ground moving, small glowing lights suddenly blinking out of existence.

Edward Kelly raised his head and cleared his throat. His expression was a mixture of embarrassment and determination. "There was something else. A low, crunching sound. I could hear it above Kevin's shouts as he tumbled down the embankment."

"What was it like, Edward?" Millicent asked. She, like everyone gathered, seemed to be holding out on this being high jinks, a tall tale that could not be saved from midnight and a face illuminated by a torch.

This time, there was no hesitation, no faltering in the conviction in Edward's voice.

"Like chewing. You know, when you're sat down to dinner with your dad and his mate and they're both chewing with their mouths open, lips smacking together, teeth rattling. If you do it, you're for the high jump, and you want to say something, but your dad gives you that stare, so you say nothing. Well, it was like that, like a hundred open mouths chewing on a plate of solid meat."

A shiver went up Harry's spine, and he was glad to see he wasn't the only one rattled by Edward's description. Even the normally unflappable Millicent looked shaken, and the boys, from the youngest to the oldest, were pale and silent. Harry almost willed Betley to say something outrageous, a well-placed *fuck you* for making them all feel foolish, but it didn't come.

It was Sillatoe who broke the back of the unsettling quiet.

"What about Fife...I mean Mr. Piccolo? He wasn't at the meeting point, and he couldn't have gone past us. We'd have seen him. Koresh stayed by the trail marker the whole time, so we had a point of reference, just in case."

Fife. A flash of shame surfaced across Harry's brow. In the melee, he had forgotten about his friend. He tried the walkie-talkie again, only static responding to his call. He had to take control of the situation.

"Right, Kevin, get yourself cleaned up as best you can. I'll run you down to the village in the morning and get you some fresh clothes. In the meantime, Jacob, you're to lend Kevin some clothes—if they smell afterwards, you know whose fault that is."

The looks on Sillatoe's and Betley's faces were priceless, and at any other time, it would have amused Harry no end. However, something inside him was gnawing away, telling him his friend was in trouble.

"Except for Jacob and Edward, the rest of you boys, eat, clean your plates, change and into your tents. No messing about tonight. I don't want to find out from Miss Maples that you've defied me. Kevin, when you're clean enough, you're to keep watch with Miss Maples, understood? Jacob, Edward, you're coming with me. Let's find Mr. Piccolo."

Betley scurried away to find some clothes for the subject of his earlier prank, while the other boys quietly went about loading their plates with food and settling down to eat.

Millicent caught Harry's arm and softly voiced her concern. "Perhaps we should think about taking the boys back tonight."

"Until we find Fife, we cannot even think of leaving. Besides, several of the parents won't be home this weekend. If we can't locate Fife tonight, then we shall appraise in the morning, but for now, please, Millicent, let's behave as normally as we can."

Jacob Betley and Edward Kelly appeared at their Scoutmaster's side, Kelly scoffing down hunks of bread and carrying a flask of tea for them all. "Just in case Mr. Piccolo needs it," he said.

"Good thinking." Harry smiled at the boy and then at his assistant, seeking her assurance that she would follow his lead.

"Is your walkie-talkie working?" she asked. Harry confirmed it was, and without a second glance, he and his two young charges set off for the trail.

Chapter Eleven

ROBERT HAD SAT on his own all evening. He hadn't seen Stuart, and Bela had picked at her dinner then fallen asleep in the front room with a duvet over her. It was unlike Stuart to not eat. Robert had heard him through the floorboards, but when he shouted for him to come down and at least have a sandwich, the boy got into a mood, and a door slammed, followed by a faint utterance of, "Sorry."

Robert let it ride. The move had been tough on them all, but kids, especially when they were pulled away from their friends, tended to act out of character. He had learned that from working at Ridgemont, a senior school that had been failing for years, the headmaster of which couldn't seem to move beyond his post-war teacher training. Many of the pupils there came from backgrounds that Robert realised retrospectively were similar to that of his own children. After all they had been through—the fire, the threats, the verbal and physical abuse, the insanity of their mother—he was confident that in time, Bela and Stuart would overcome this obstacle too.

Loading the twin cassette player with his favourite mix of songs, Robert settled in for an evening of organising his study, with the record player in prime place, as it should be. The main room was the perfect choice for setting out his new life, work and play in the same place, comfort and learning, solitude away from teaching, the chance to lock the past away. That would always be difficult. Bela and Stuart had overcome a lot, but at some point, they would have to confront what had happened to them. Stuart was already quiet in front of his sister, only acknowledging her when it suited him or when he was asked to, and even then Bela barely gave him a second glance. Robert wasn't sure how he could bridge that chasm between them.

On the kitchen table was a freshly sealed pack of cards and a new cribbage board just waiting for Bela to give her old dad a game, but as he listened to her snoring, the scars, those terrible disfigurements on one side of her face and neck always making sleep sound as if she was mimicking a Gatling gun, he accepted he would either have to wait to enjoy a few rounds of his favourite game with his daughter or undo the plastic wrapper and deal himself a few hands of solitaire. It was that or start unboxing his books, and he didn't want to play with history tonight, not the stories of kings and regicide.

No sooner had he made a cup of tea, unwrapped the cards and settled in for an evening of solitude than it was brought to an end by a gentle knock on the door.

Chapter Twelve

THE REVEREND TARKY could not help feeling overwhelmed as he looked down at the pit in front of him, cordoned off by streams of police tape and lit by a series of lights that the fire brigade and a local army crew had put together with great urgency and skill. Tarky had stayed nearby all evening, ignoring the advice of both the army and the local inspector who was on site to offer support to the local community.

Mrs. Bennett had been escorted home by the manager of the Sander's Arms and a kindly spoken policewoman. Belinda's grief was understandable, as it was for the rest of the folks in the village, all of whom had at least one person they loved in the church's safekeeping.

They had, initially, all come down the hill to gawp at the devastation that had happened under their noses, in their village. He even saw a few faces who hadn't been to church for a while, absentees from prayer and salvation. He made a mental note to call upon those wayward sheep over the next few days and hammer home how much he needed them to come together now in the name of God and their community.

Eventually, they had been dispersed by the police and returned to their homes, all but a few teenagers who had come back on the bus and were unaware of what had occurred. They thought they were being discreet, hands covering their mouths, the semi-muted words interspersed with giggles and snorts of derision. They insulted him and desecrated God's house, all the while hiding behind banter—*only kidding, Tarky.* He hated this generation; they had no respect. He would rather deal with a group of well-meaning, devout churchgoers searching for signs of impending doom than sit down and talk to this group of local teenagers.

A cruel image presented itself to his mind's eye. The pit offered a perfect solution for keeping the spiritual soul of the village intact. Round them up, tie their hands together, bind their feet and push them over the edge. Let their screams reach the heavens; let their pleading, their begging for mercy act as possible salvation before the Lord, or as entrance to the realm of darkness.

It was only the sound of an ambulance hurtling past that pulled the vicar out of his tempting dream. Seeking comfort from the cross on the roof of the church, he hunted for forgiveness in his soul. He had felt such temptation before in his life, and on occasion given way to it, once even embracing the pleasure that came from the illicit, the unthinkable. Was it for that reason he had been more than a guiding presence in Belinda Bennett's life since her son's untimely death a mere year after he'd returned from New York and told her he was a homosexual?

Tarky had kept his feelings such a secret that even Reynard hadn't known until he turned eighteen, when after one evening's rehearsal, Tarky invited the young man to stay behind and discuss his forthcoming trip to Boston and New York with the county choir. Tarky had recommended him several years before, praising his qualities as a singer and leader with a great range and religious background. *To hear this boy sing is to understand that gifts come from God, but it is hard work and dedication that gives him his grace.* He never regretted those forceful words of admiration, but when the time came for the boy to sing before the bishop, Tarky felt something other than pride for the way Reynard conducted himself.

It wasn't the first time Tarky had had such a relationship, but on the previous occasion, he had been a much younger, forgiving man, still finding his feet in the ways of his calling. He had been attending a garden party hosted by an aspiring young couple who introduced him to a fellow man of the cloth but of a different strand. That initial meeting had been fraught, both men convinced they were right in their belief and refusing to give quarter or mercy to the other as they discussed, over cucumber sandwiches and a small glass of sherry apiece, the finer points of God's word. It was a game of religious chess, a pawn sacrificed so that the knight could advance and thrust the spear into the king's side, the rook defending a particularly passionate issue, the queen taking counsel from her bishop in waiting.

The encounter had proved an embarrassment, a social faux pas for which both men had apologised. Yet as time went on, they found common ground and a mutual growing respect that one night turned into the sin they had both avoided for so long.

It was that same common ground that Tarky found with the boy who had sung in church every Sunday as his mother looked on with glowing pride, and later had wowed the congregation in the significant, imposing space of Avoncross Cathedral. The young Reynard Bennett's voice could give life to the heavens and cause the devil to acknowledge that there are finer ways to tempt a man.

It was the temptation, the flirtation in both their minds that for a brief while they gave into. Six weeks. That was all Tarky had with the boy who had become a man. Six weeks of letters, secrets, furtive glances across the knave as the two men sang in exultation of their God, and then Reynard went away, and Tarky was once more on his own, just a few letters and memories of stolen moments with the man he loved.

Tarky turned away from the church and its gaping hole. Somewhere down in that pit were the final remains of the boy he'd helped nurse in his last days, who'd confessed to meeting anonymous men over the course of several months in New York City, in bars, in cinemas, in hotels. It was there he had picked up the disease. He had planned on never coming back, to never be a burden on his parents, but a sympathetic phone call from Tarky changed his mind. *You were born here, you should be buried here, underneath home skies* were Tarky's final words down the telephone, words that would come back to haunt him when his love's body was found hanging from the tree, bright sunshine catching the leaves in a rare display of serenity that poets would have enthused over.

The old man stumbled and fell awkwardly to his knees, the solid concrete on which he had been standing connecting sharply with his trousers and the skin beneath. He steadied himself, catching his breath, breathing in and out until he felt the pain subside. Pushing back carefully, he looked down on the ground as if studying the scene through a large, open-ended microscope and saw a small bump in the concrete, a crack which had risen up as if it were giving birth to a volcano. In that fissure, he witnessed two of the Lord's most industrious of creatures. That these workers were alive, that the collapse of the ground and the gravestones and all that was contained between had not killed them, was a blessing.

The Lord works indeed for all, he thought, pondering on how best to incorporate it into a hearty sermon on Sunday. Then he remembered the words of the men who had taken command of the scene just a few short hours ago. His church would remain closed for the foreseeable future, while the ground was thoroughly inspected for further damage, more erosion.

Tarky had not understood what that meant, but he did impress upon them his parishioners' need for spiritual uplifting at such a time.

A thought struck him as hard as if he had fallen again and this time landed on his head. All his correspondence was in the church, locked away in his chambers—church business, personal letters, both those received and copies of those he had sent, symbols of his love, despatches of his certainty of Sarah Calster's guilt. He could never bring himself to destroy them, and now they were guarded by two soldiers.

The back door, Tarky thought on the move, relieved to see no one was standing sentry there. It was hidden by the greenhouse he had erected and a covering of bushes. He had been the only one to use it in the last twenty years, long enough for it to have been forgotten. He would have to be careful of the ground, though; the edge of the pit was within a few feet of the greenhouse.

Tarky almost made it past the pit when, from behind, he heard someone shout his name. The holler had come from one of the soldiers, who was no older than Reynard had been when he'd first admitted his feelings.

"Can I help you... I'm sorry, I don't know your name." Tarky gave the soldier his most enigmatic smile.

"It's Tibbitt, sir, Lance Corporal Tibbitt. There's a man asking for you at the church gate. Says his name is Darren. Wants to know if you've seen Mr. Bennett, sir."

Tarky was confused for a moment. Belinda had been one of the last to leave. Her suffering had seen her almost clawing at the chasm that had opened up around her, wailing as only a mother can when all she can see is a void where her child once lay. But that was hours ago. Why on earth would he have seen Mr. Bennett?

Tarky thanked the soldier and followed him around the church, the lights shining a path for him, which he was careful to stay upon, to where Darren was indeed waiting and also in a bit of a state.

"Reverend Tarky. I'm so sorry to disturb you. I know this is a difficult time, but we can't find Lionel…Mr. Bennett." Darren's hands fidgeted, wringing the cap they held as if he were a turn-of-the-century farmhand addressing the local squire.

Tarky reached out and stilled Darren's hands before he reverted to that frightened teen who had wet himself and broken down. Even now, almost two decades later, on a bad day, there were still people who would remind him and call him a pervert. Not Belinda or Lionel, though. They had taken the lad under their wing and turned him into one of the village's most dependable citizens. It was that version of Darren that Tarky wanted to see in the man before him, not this shaking vision on the verge of pulling his cap apart.

Tarky thanked the soldier who had escorted him to Darren's side and then walked with him, away from the church, asking plainly when Lionel was last seen and if anyone had searched for him. It was in that concern the father confessor of the village stepped in to take command. He would have to look in on Belinda first, of course. The poor woman must be out of her mind.

As the two men made their way to the bottom of the hill and started the long climb upwards, Tarky saw the bookshop owner wheel her disabled husband inside the new addition to the village hall and remembered he still had important papers to collect from there. For now, like his letters in the church, they would have to wait.

Chapter Thirteen

"YOU THREE, YOU there. I say, stop!"
From the ledge of the embankment, Harry Collins peered into the darkness. Even with his and both boys' torches shining down the slope, they couldn't see the bottom, but it had to be a good fifteen feet or more. It probably didn't feel like it to Kevin Sillatoe, but he'd been lucky; the huge pile of muck had cushioned his fall, saving him from breaking an arm or a leg or even his neck.

"I said stop! Don't you understand a simple instruction?"

The voice was clearer now, closer, more defined. It was also filled with anger and a sense of danger that sent Harry's hackles up, especially with two young lads in his care. He decided to adopt a friendly approach and raised his hands in the hope the other person would understand.

"What are you doing near my land? I keep my horses down there. If you keep shining a blessed torch at them, it's liable to scare the poor buggers."

"My name's Harry—Harold Collins—and I'm a Scoutmaster. My troop are camped just over there, by the old road to Southampton. We mean no harm. We're looking for one of our leaders. He hasn't been seen for a while, and he's not answering his walkie-talkie." Harry smiled, unable to gauge the other person's face because they were in the shadows of the trees. He did, however, recognise the sound of a shotgun being snapped into action and immediately stepped between the boys and the assailant in the shadows.

Harry had only once before had a gun pointed in his direction. A former female acquaintance offered to teach him how to fish and use a rifle, then proceeded to put the same rifle to his temple and said she'd pull the trigger if he didn't come to his senses about their relationship. Terrified and not knowing what else to do, he had run, and the one shot she pulled off went flying over his head. The following summer, he had attended her funeral and found out she'd had a drug problem, which perhaps explained why she'd sent him a card the previous Christmas asking why he'd been avoiding her since their fishing and hunting trip. Harry replied, pointing out that threatening someone with a rifle was not the best way to display affection and told her never to contact him again.

She had sent him a two-word reply in an envelope dowsed in sickly perfume with pencil-drawn flowers along the edge. *Fuck You!* It was probably the best he could have hoped for.

"Keep your hands where I can see them. I'm coming over." The voice had become lighter, less threatening, and Harry realised it had been put on for show.

From behind one of the trees, a tall woman, easily six feet in height, stepped into view. Harry lowered his torch so as not to dazzle her, and the two boys followed suit.

"You're trespassing," she said.

Harry fumbled with his torch but managed to turn it off. His nerves weren't helped by Betley muttering that the woman must have killed Fife.

"We mean no harm. I...we are looking for Scout Leader Piccolo. As I said, he is lost. We didn't see any signs indicating this is private property. If I give you my walkie-talkie, you can call my other leader. Her name is Millicent Maples, and she'll verify who I am. If that doesn't satisfy, please call the local police, a man named..." For a moment, he forgot the name of the policeman he'd liaised with when he'd organised this trip—not surprising in the circumstances. Another click of the gun sent Kelly scurrying behind Betley. "Ellis Mere, Constable Ellis Mere." Harry shouted the name and shut his eyes, expecting the bang of the gun firing at any second. It took a moment to register that he hadn't been shot and, in fact, the woman had disarmed her rifle. Even so, he felt light-headed and quickly sat on the grass before he passed out and toppled down the embankment himself.

"Mere, you say? I know him. I don't like him, but I know him. I'll take it on trust that you are who you say you are." She thrust out a hand to pull him up. "My name's Phillipa. Phillipa Dawns. I own the stud farm on the road to Cadnam. I graze my own and some of my clients' horses here. Sorry about the gun. I was driving through and heard a loud rumble, sounded like a building collapsing. Figured I'd best check the horses weren't too spooked. As for this old thing..." She snapped the gun back together and took aim at a tree to their left. The gun issued a dull click. "It doesn't work. My dad had it decommissioned in 1987, didn't want anyone to steal it and cause serious injury. It only takes one deranged fool, after all."

Harry wondered if the boys had soiled themselves, as he felt he may have done. It would serve Betley right for his actions earlier in the evening.

"One of my boys fell down the embankment, landed in what I now gather was horse dung," Harry explained. From behind, he heard Betley snort. He ignored the boy and continued. "Edward here thought he heard noises before his friend fell down, like people eating."

"I said chewing," Edward Kelly corrected. "You know when people eat with their mouths open and you can hear their teeth grinding?"

Phillipa Dawns addressed the boys. "Your other leader, what did you say their name was?"

"Fife," Betley answered.

"Philip Piccolo," Harry said. "He had a walkie-talkie on him, but he's not answering it. We searched by the station, the halfway mark, and it wasn't there, so we followed the boys' trail to here."

Phillipa nodded her understanding. "Well, we can see if he's fallen down the embankment, although if he didn't land in the horses' daily constitutional, he'd have had a tough landing. The field may be lush, but it stands on an old quarry. My Jeep's just off the side road—we can drive round and take a look. That is, unless you want to take the shortcut?"

The boys made the decision for Harry; they raced ahead, leaving the Scoutmaster no choice but to follow.

The air around them seemed to blacken as they rolled down the steep hill towards the gated fence which led to the field. The silence was disconcerting. It wasn't the first time Harry had camped in the New Forest—alone or with the Scouts—but he couldn't recall it ever being this quiet, almost as if the land was bound and gagged.

They reached the metal fence, and Harry was staggered by its size and its length.

"I can't afford to take chances," Phillipa explained. "I want to build a new stable block down here too. The one I currently use has been past its best since my dad died, but I can't afford to move permanently yet, and this is the best I can manage. The fence runs the entire perimeter, over ten-foot-high chain-link, electrified and monitored."

"Are your horses generally this quiet at night?" Harry asked, although what he was actually thinking was if Fife had fallen into the field and injured himself, he'd have been stuck until someone came to feed the horses the next day. "I don't know a lot about them, but surely you'd hear them whinnying or something?"

Phillipa didn't answer. They had reached the gate, and she brought the Jeep to a grinding halt, dirt and gravel spinning off to the sides. Edward Kelly, who had beaten Jacob Betley to the front seat, grunted loudly as the seat belt abruptly halted his forward trajectory. Phillipa either didn't notice or didn't care; she jumped out of the vehicle and ran over to a control panel, pressing a series of numbers and stepping back as the machinery whirred into life and the imposing gate slid open.

Harry was uncomfortable with the sheer scale of the place. It had the feel of a prison camp about it, the top of the fence only missing three German words to make it as sinister as his gut was telling him it was.

Phillipa stepped inside the compound and opened a small metal cabinet. A second later, the immediate area flooded with light. Phillipa returned to the Jeep and gunned it through the gate, ran back to key in the code a second time, then back to the Jeep. The gate clanged shut behind them as they set off, following a tarmacked road along the inside of the fence. As they followed the perimeter, several horses poked their heads out of stable doors. Even Harry could tell they were agitated by something.

It took a while, but at last, they reached the bottom of the embankment, the Jeep's powerful headlights illuminating the pile of muck Sillatoe had fallen into. This time, Edward Kelly was ready and braced for the sudden stop. Phillipa urged the two lads to walk with her to inspect the pile of manure, but even from a distance, it was clear there was nobody else there. Harry's walkie-talkie sprang to life, and he excused himself and walked away from the small rescue party.

"Millicent, this is Harry."

"Have you found Fife?"

"Not yet. We're in a field—the one Sillatoe fell into earlier. The landowner is helping us search. Is all okay at your end?"

Harry couldn't decide if the delay in her response was due to a poor signal or stalling for time, but it only added to the stress he was under.

"All okay with the boys," she finally answered. "We have a policeman on the site, though. It's the constable you were in touch with. Another person went missing today, a local. He wants to know if we've seen anything odd, what with the collapse of the graveyard at the church."

Harry stopped pacing, unsure if he'd heard her correctly. "Sorry, Millicent, repeat that last bit."

Millicent did so, and Harry felt the sheer lunacy of it descend upon him, a heavy weight of foreboding rocking his sense of place and reason.

"How bad was the collapse?"

"The constable said over seven hundred graves sank about a dozen feet into the ground. Apparently, they have the army over there guarding the church. It was a miracle nobody was injured. He insists we're safe where we are, but to be honest Harry, I'm not happy about it."

Millicent wasn't given to losing control, and Harry was about to reassure her that they'd be back soon to hammer out a solution, when Betley shouted him.

"I have to go, Millicent." Harry signed off and went in search of the others. They'd moved on from where the manure hugged the incline, and it took a moment to locate them. He could see Phillipa on her knees, and she seemed to be crying, almost wailing in despair. Betley was waving something in the air, and as Harry got closer, he saw it was Fife's walkie-talkie. Wordlessly, Betley pointed to the field a bit further on, and Harry took a few more steps before he stumbled to a stop. Cast in the damp glow from the stable lights were the dead bodies of some twenty horses, many with chunks taken from their flesh, a few appearing as if they had died of fright, unable to escape whatever had spooked them. Even from this distance, several looked as if they had been eaten alive, their carcasses ripped open, more bone than flesh, only the tattered remains of their heads giving any indication that they had once been majestic and noble animals.

Betley shouted again. "Look, sir—past the horses."

Illuminated in the background were the silhouettes of three large mounds, each at least six feet in height. Harry switched on his torch and swept the beam over the three hillocks. There, draped over the one furthest from them, was a body dressed as Fife had been when he'd left the camp earlier that day. Without a second thought, Harry ran towards his friend, barely hearing Phillipa's anguished cries for him to stop.

He was almost at the mounds before he did stop and could only watch in horror as the body moved up the slope like a limp flag carried upon the arms of a Mexican wave. Reaching the peak, it stilled for a moment, then started to sink, and in one awful second, Fife had been pulled underneath.

Chapter Fourteen

I N THE ENSUING darkness and the melee of uncertainty
and gossip that had seen the population of the village make
their way up the hill and back to the comfort of their own
homes or the pub, nobody had noticed that one of their own was
missing. Not until it was far too late.

Sarah Calster looked down on the dead body of Lionel
Bennett and surprised herself by shedding a tear for the old
man with whom she had spent time earlier in the day. It was
only by sheer accident that she had come across his body first:
had her mother been in better health, Sarah wouldn't have left
the house, but her mother had started down the same track her
father had a decade before. Along with Sarah, she had nursed
the man through what turned out to be a long, drawn-out fight,
in the last minutes of which her mind had deserted her and she'd
begged her daughter to grant her father's last request and end his
suffering. Now, despite the consequences and the price Sarah
would have to pay, she was asking for the same for herself.

***

Alice Calster was overjoyed to see her daughter again. In
the instant between the gentle knock on the aged door and
welcoming Sarah home with a hug and a kiss on the forehead,
the images of seeing her run riot around the graves at the church,
the heavy, forceful raps by a succession of police officers who'd
brought her home from yet another party where she'd been

found smoking cannabis, the suspicions of underage sex, the frantic concern when she didn't come home at all for a couple of days, the anonymous letters and phone calls, including one accusing her of sleeping with a married man and breaking a priceless vase in the process—all of it was overshadowed by the way she cared, the moments in which, unseen by all except Alice and her late husband, their little girl was the most special person they could have ever hoped to love.

Sarah had heard it all before and remembered on a few occasions her father waking her up in the middle of the night just to talk to her, to tell her that they loved her and were worried sick but would always stick by her.

These thoughts continued in the minds of both women as they sat across the faded yellow kitchen table from each other, the kettle continually on the boil, an endless game of refilling the pot keeping them away from the words they desperately wanted to say to each other. It was only the ringing of the telephone that stopped the questions of when Sarah expected the rest of her possessions to come, whether she was okay for money, if there was anybody special in her life. She eased herself out of the old wooden chair, but her mother intervened, telling her to stay put.

Alice went into the front room and answered the phone, her initial cheerful greeting soon dampened by a series of exclamations of *oh my dear, how awful,* and *well, he can't have gone far.* The words were punctuated by surprise. No, Alice hadn't heard the loud disturbance earlier, hadn't felt the rumble under the ground. It wouldn't have mattered if she had—she wouldn't have got that far down the slip road before she'd have needed to stop and rest. She left the rest of the village to gossip and investigate these days.

"You know Lionel, who used to run the post office?" Alice asked, returning to the kitchen. "Belinda Bennett's husband?"

"I know who Mr. Bennett is, Mum."

"He's gone missing!"

Sarah stared at her mother. "I only saw him this evening. We sat on the crossroads pike, chatting. When did he go missing?"

"Darren—that was him on the phone—he's with Belinda now. He says she was at the church earlier, when the graveyard caved in—did you know about that?"

"Yeah. It happened just before I saw Mr. Bennett."

"Right, well, you didn't mention it."

"I thought you'd know, Mum."

"I didn't. But anyway, Belinda didn't notice Lionel wasn't in the house when she got back, probably wouldn't have noticed at all if Darren hadn't turned up, so Lord knows when the poor old fool went missing. Darren's beside himself with worry. I think the lad feels guilty for getting caught up in the excitement. I told him to find the reverend. Fancy forgetting that someone you love exists."

***

It was those words that echoed around Sarah's mind as she stood over the dead body of a man who had believed he had one final fight in him, who had picked an argument and found that the wind had left his sails long before he was able to mount a verbal attack.

"It's a joke, isn't it, Lionel? You wanted a confession from me, some sort of apology, but all you got was a kiss good night from Death. No Saint Belinda, no Tarky. Not even the boy who looked up to you as a father thought about you until it was too late. You may as well have gone to that tree in the forest so the ghost of your own lad could have ignored you too."

Had anyone heard her verbally spit on the man as his spirit fled his body, it would have served as further proof, if that were needed, that she was more at home with devils and demons than with angels and kindness. But there was no malice in her speech, or none aimed at Lionel. It was just an observation. A final sermon from the pulpit of Sarah.

"Nobody stopped for you. Nobody paid any attention as you lay there. At least several cars must have gone past, and a fire engine. Someone must have seen you slumped over. Lionel, dear Lionel, if I was the last person on Earth to have shown you even an ounce of interest, what does that say about this goddamned village?"

With the final prayer uttered, Sarah told the dead man she forgave him and vowed to stay with him until someone else came, knowing that with her history, she would be blamed for his demise, but surely there was no way she would be held in suspicion for long, not with all those strange marks on his bloated face and hands. Even through the material of his shirt she could see them, tiny bite marks, like something had burrowed into him and tried to feast upon him but found him unappetising.

"Too sick, huh, Lionel?"

A tear itched her cheek, but she didn't bother to wipe it away; she let it fall naturally. From behind her, she heard commotion, a display of fret and fear masquerading as concern for a man they hadn't bothered about earlier. She spun around to meet the voices head-on, a little put out that there were no flaming torches, no angry horde of villagers demanding that the witch be burned for murder by seduction, fucking her victim until his heart gave out, pledging his soul to Satan as he came.

It was always going to be Reverend Tarky who found her with the dead man's body. In a way, she felt sorry for him. It couldn't have been easy to stare into the abyss, to see the foundation of his faith crumble before him and have the devil in his kingdom once more. That would be enough to scare any good man, although, as Sarah knew all too well, Tarky was not a good man.

"What in heaven's name have you done?" Tarky roared like thunder.

"Before you start on me, Reverend, you might want to take a closer look. Mr. Bennett's covered in bite marks—maybe he went into anaphylactic shock? Whatever, I've been with my mother all evening, and *you* need to practise what you preach because you're the one to blame this time, Tarky. You and Belinda and this whole bloody village. You left him up here to die."

With those words, Sarah breezed past the reverend, feeling lighter than she had in years.

"Where do you think you are going, Ms. Calster? You have some explaining to do!"

"I'm going home. My mother's all alone, and as you know, she's not well. You know where to find me."

"I'll have the law on you. Mark my words, I will see you burn in hell!"

Sarah stopped and turned back to Tarky, whose eyes were bloodshot with rage, spittle swinging from his chin. She smiled and shrugged. "Let them come."

Chapter Fifteen

ROBERT ROMSLEIGH LOOKED up at the waxing moon, a bright beacon of hope reflecting light from the remote, uncaring Sun. This was the best time to think, bathed in the silver strands of the Earth's dance partner. Robert had long fancied that those in ancient history who declared the Sun cooperative and subservient had not misunderstood how the heavens worked but had done it on purpose to give credence to humanity's importance, the Sun keeping its tentative distance as it asked for the Earth's hand, then scurrying back to the gods in the corner. *I did it, she said yes. Now what do I do?*

Robert disliked the daytimes. There were too many people around wanting conversation, too many students who stored their intellect in the smallest, unyielding box and then were mystified when he failed them. Dealing with them had driven him to the point of so much distraction that he couldn't see what was happening at home. The nighttime was different, clearheaded, a chance to reflect upon the day and understand the darkness around him.

He wasn't going to open the door but changed his mind when Bela stirred. Another knock came, more aggressive this time.

Before him was a tall, middle-aged woman, thin and waspish-looking with an undisguised greyness around the eyes, a telltale sign of a former drinker who wore her battle wounds with a certain measure of pride. It was a look Robert had almost ended up wearing himself, and he was so fixated on the woman's features that, to his shame, he didn't notice the man in the wheelchair in front of her. Under the circumstances, it seemed only decent to invite them in.

"My name is Samantha McCarthy, and this is my husband Bertie Myers. We own the bookshop up the hill." The woman thrust her hand forward with such vigour it caught Robert unawares. Recovering quickly, he shook her hand.

Bertie was less forthright than his wife, but still shook Robert's hand with a strength that belied his apparent condition.

"Spinal problem," Bertie explained. "Rather large and inconvenient operation many moons ago. There was always a risk that the procedure would leave me in even greater pain. Doesn't stop a handshake though, does it, Mr. Romsleigh?"

Robert smiled politely at the pair, only moderately surprised that they knew his name before he'd given it. Stella had warned him how fast news travelled on the Downmere grapevine. Nevertheless, he wasn't giving an inch until he knew what they wanted. So the evening continued in courteous enquiry, the bookshop owners showing a respectful knowledge of Robert's two books on the plague and its effect on religion during the Middle Ages and one contributed paper, for which they gave him far too much credit that left him feeling slightly off-kilter.

Robert's eyes narrowed when the woman skirted the real reason they had dropped by. He knew what was coming; he was used to the questions, the suspicion that he was somehow responsible for the fire that had scarred his daughter. He had undeniable proof that he was innocent of the charges, that his ex-wife strung out on all manner of substances had set the house ablaze.

As it happened, Robert was surprised for the second time that evening.

"I used to be a journalist, a long time ago," Ms. McCarthy began. "I was a quite different woman then. Did you ever hear or read of a situation in Oxfordshire, strange goings-on around the time of the American bombing of Tripoli?"

Robert shook his head and noticed she seemed put out by his ignorance.

"You can look it up in the Avoncross or Southampton library when you get the chance. Anyway, I lost my way after that. Full disclosure, I began drinking an awful lot, and it was hampering my objectivity. I became careless, a liability. I went to Hong Kong for a while to stay with my daughter, and when I came back to England, I found I needed to step away from it all. If I had gone back to that…unhealthy atmosphere, I would have been dead within a year."

Robert blinked and realised his eyes were dry from having not done so for some time. He was enthralled by the woman's speech. It took a brave soul to admit where their life had gone wrong; he hoped she didn't expect him to respond in kind.

Ms. McCarthy placed her palm on her husband's face, resting it gently against his cheek as one would a skittish dog that had been beaten.

"That's when I found Bertie. I was lost, you see, on my own. I had burned almost every bridge in my effort to escape what I'd been through. It was only meeting Bertie that saved me from walking into the sea on the south coast and letting every care drift away." Her gaze dropped to the floor, and her husband took over, elaborating on the 'strange goings-on' in Oxfordshire that his wife had mentioned. As the tale came to a close, Robert sensed the time was approaching when they would ask him to reveal his secrets, and he decided to pre-empt it.

"I'm sorry, really deeply sorry. It sounds horrendous, what you've been through. I don't actually know of the events you described, but I'm pleased you're able to talk of them freely. That must be a great relief, to you both. However, I fail to see what it has to do with me."

Mr. Myers caught his wife's eye, urging her to be direct with their host.

"We, well…I would like to commission your story. I know who you are. Even if I no longer practise my old calling, I like to read the papers when the shop is quiet and Bertie is busy keeping the books straight or is involved in his own research. It's cathartic to dip into the biographies of others, and you, Robert, were not given the chance to tell your side properly. I want to tell that story for you. I want you to get the peace I never received at the hands of the media and the situation which led me here."

What the couple expected, Robert wasn't really sure, but a tirade of anger was probably not the response they were hoping for. He had no control over it. Their polite yet unsolicited request disturbed something deep inside that he had contained for so long, like taking a poker to a dormant fire that erupted in fury. He stopped short of wheeling the man out against his will but made it clear they both had to leave and were no longer welcome in his home.

By the time he made it back to his garden, the moon had descended below the treeline, leaving the pinpricks of stars less reason to be jealous, and he realised how awful he had been to the couple. He was angry, not with them but with everything that had brought them to his door, all the things he had not grieved for—his marriage, the childhood his daughter and son should have had.

Not caring who heard him, he yelled at the cowardly moon, demanding it reveal itself and remove the grin from its meteor-bombarded, pock-marked face.

"Come down and fight me, you silver-sheened bastard."

A noise from behind stopped him mid-flow. Had he forgotten to lock the front door when he threw the couple out? He turned around slowly, expecting to see a neighbour complaining about the lateness of the hour, or his sister, arms folded, giving him that stern frown she had borrowed from their mother. Instead, his boy stood there, barefooted and bewildered.

"Hey, my Little Nemo. I thought you were asleep. Did your stupid old dad wake you up? I am sorry. Forgive me?"

The boy ran to him, arms outstretched, and Robert scooped him up, holding him in a tight yet tender embrace as Stuart giggled over catching his dad talking to the moon. Robert couldn't help but laugh too.

"Daddy's done a silly thing. But in the morning, I will make it right, go and apologise to them, take some flowers, buy a few books."

***

From the kitchen, Bela watched her father. She had heard his outburst before he'd bundled the bookshop owners out without ceremony or indeed respect. That was bad enough. Then he'd picked a fight with the moon, and for one awful moment, she feared he had actually hit rock bottom. Somehow her brother had always managed to pull him away from the self-destruct button, and it was a knack Bela wished she had because right now, it seemed Stuart was the only one keeping their father sane.

Chapter Sixteen

Time and distance are illusions thought up by cynical gods to make us believe there isn't a connection to all that we do. For every person who feels a cold breeze in midtown Manhattan and wraps their coat a little tighter around them, the smell of aromatic ground beans luring them to take shelter in the coffee house near Central Park and wonder whatever happened to the bar at the end of 77th Street West, there is some poor soul who has seen his house ripped apart by a tornado further inland. The connection between the two is made by a television report that inspires empathy in the one enjoying a latte in a small but popular coffee house about the other, who has no food, no clothing and nowhere to sleep tonight.

Barnaby Wilkins was the epitome of that person sitting in the coffee house, whiling away his time with little regard for the world around him. He found that his reality made more sense the further away he was from any storm that was brewing. Only once had he invited people from the village to his home; only once had he made the mistake of trying to impress the residents and old families with his charm and insight.

His house—amongst a dozen that were built, despite serious opposition led by Reverend Tarky and that old busybody of a retired postmistress—was a mere mile away but far removed from the old ways of the village. Thus, he was as surprised as anyone when she turned up at his house for the grand unveiling of his new wife-to-be. What was her name again? Did it even matter in the end? It was his house that was the real star, and Belinda Bennett had looked down her nose at everything she was shown, the unique objects, the art, the enclosed swimming pool, the gold, the silver, and the bronze. It all meant nothing to her.

A small sip of whisky to get the blood flowing, breathe in the air, watch the weight, big day tomorrow, a meeting with shareholders which would net him a few bob in the bank, a beautiful wife upstairs in their bed, silk negligée and black stockings, just the way he liked her. All Barnaby Wilkins needed now was for his dog to stop yapping in the darkness and hurry up and finish his business.

Distance. Yes, there was distance between him and the village, a yawning gorge of ideals and attitudes. He had tried to help, had offered the church a sizeable donation if they moved into a new, more modern and appealing building up the hill, but when the village found out it meant destroying the Calsters' home, the church committee had refused to countenance any such thought. He had even offered to build them a new care home at the end of the lane on the site of the old hotel, tried to buy the land on which it stood, fading away, its time of glory shelved as more people took their holidays in far-flung locations. The people of Downmere were having none of it.

"Get a bloody move on, Dante," Barnaby hissed into the darkness, only just making out the dog's outline in the light from the patio doors. The dog barked as if acknowledging the command but continued chasing imaginary creatures off its property.

Distance. It means nothing if the offer of a bridge between ideals is refused. The others in the newly built close had found ways to connect with the old, immersing themselves in the slower pace of life, but not Barnaby. For him, the village was just a name that looked good on a letterhead, the golden inspiration to which all in his position should aspire, according to his first wife, who'd insisted they moved here when their mutual friend Michael showed them the plans for the plot of land he had purchased through rather dubious means.

Barnaby sighed as the memory filtered through the pick-me-up whisky he had prepared in an attempt to get in the mood for the night ahead, but his mind filled with the image of that smarmy, lecherous, tax-dodging cheat Michael and his ex-wife in mid-grope on the marital bed, and he knew that his third wife, like his second, would be disappointed and in the morning would surely ring her friends to tell them all about his lack of success in the sack.

The dog gave a small yelp of pain, quickly followed by a deep snarl.

"Dante? What's up, pal?"

Without turning around, he stepped stealthily backwards and felt for the torch he kept on the telephone table. Keeping his eyes firmly locked on the now dim silhouette of his dog, he fumbled for his golf bag and knocked it over, sending his clubs clattering across the tiled floor. He heard movement upstairs.

"Is everything all right, babe? Is Dante inside?"

As if to answer her question, Dante growled, following up with another small yelp.

"Everything's fine, love, but just to be on the safe side, call Constable Mere and tell him we might have an intruder in the garden. No, forget that, call the security firm. Why do I pay all that money if I don't use them?"

His wife, beautiful, exotic and of welcome low intelligence, stood at the top of the stairs, wide-eyed.

"It could be that Calster woman!"

It took Barnaby a few vital seconds to understand she wasn't joking.

"Not likely! That old hag couldn't even walk across the road, let alone climb over the fence and get into the garden."

"Not Alice, you idiot! Her daughter. I took a phone call when you were driving back from London, Sarah Calster is back in the village."

Barnaby Wilkins felt the blood rush straight to his face, begin to boil and then explode.

"Why the hell didn't you tell me earlier? I would have phoned the security firm myself and had someone pass by every ten minutes. Hell, I would have had someone go over to that disgrace of a house and have her quietly removed from the area."

"For the same reason I didn't tell you about the graveyard falling in. I've had other things to do."

Barnaby grumbled under his breath, trying to keep a lid on his temper. He didn't like feeling this close to burning, as he described it, that malicious flashfire that rampaged through his mind. He had lost control a lot as a youngster, lashing out at any slight, starting fights with the other hooligans at home matches and at away games too, if he could be bothered leaving South London. Only once since his teenage years had he been so angry that he had inflicted on someone—two people—physical pain. As he bent to pick up the number three iron, he hoped it was Sarah Calster out there in the dark, tormenting his dog, returning to haunt him once more. He would take great delight in smashing his lucky club over her head and letting her bleed to death on the lawn. She would be in good company.

Screw it, he thought as he returned to the patio doors and switched on the main outside light. If the men next door complained about it shining directly into their bedroom window, he would take the club to them as well.

He never understood why they complained. He had no problem with them, well, their twenty-year age difference was a bit off-putting, but his uncle Kirk was a homosexual. Kirk had known the Krays and was a good man to be in a fight with. That's all that mattered in the East End. How well you fought.

"Call the security firm, ask to speak to Davison. Then call that bloody useless copper. Tell him I'll have someone's guts hanging off the end of this club if he doesn't get here soon."

He heard his wife hesitate on the landing before running back to the safety of their bedroom but was only satisfied when he heard the door lock click. Even if it was because he was scaring her, he felt better knowing she was out the way and wouldn't see the harm he could inflict.

One time, he had punched a rival fan to the floor. While others might have left it at that, Barnaby got a rush from it and started kicking the man in the ribs before, finally, grabbing a pint glass and smashing it into the geezer's face. He'd only wanted to know the way to the stadium.

"Never came back, though, did he? He wouldn't dare come to our ground again," Barnaby muttered to himself as he walked out into the garden, golf club in one hand, heavy torch in the other. "You want to take on something a bit bigger than a dog, you coward?" he asked the darkness and then laughed, feeling a measure of his sanity slip away, just as it had when he saw his wife being ridden by a man he had called a friend.

The dog yelped again, but this time, rather than fighting back, he legged it past Barnaby, back inside the house.

"It's all right, Dante. Daddy's got it covered," Barnaby said and took a swing with the club to show he meant business.

No sound to be heard. What had the stupid dog been barking at? He switched on the torch, the tired beam creating shadows where he had expected a face in the darkness, someone who would soon be joining his ex-wife and lover on the list of the missing.

Something tickled his stubbled chin, and he scratched at it, flicking off what might have been a gnat. He felt a sting on his foot, then another, and trampled down on the grass. Pests…so many irritating creatures in the world.

A series of further stings brought him to his knees as his feet went numb. He dropped the club and yelled. Out of the corner of his eye, he could see his wife peering through a small gap in the curtains.

The man in New York picked up the paper, the smile fading from his face as he read that the farm that supplied his friends with their weekend recreation had been destroyed by a tornado.

At that same moment, Robert Romsleigh saw his son Stuart running towards him with his arms outstretched.

At that same moment, Sarah Calster was giving a sermon to the dead man at the crossroads while four people looked upon the macabre sight of desecrated horses in a field a few miles away.

So it was that Barnaby Wilkins found at last that he had something in common with the village and its tiresome crowd.

The ants crawled over his body, swarming, injecting their venom, their toxic bites covering his skin. He opened his mouth, thereby discovering he no longer had the ability to scream, and the ants poured in, invading his body, eating him alive.

The last thought he had, before his heart gave out and his brain became nourishment for the creatures in the darkness, was of his first wife and her lover, the hole he had dug the night he found them and the note he'd written swearing blind that they had run off together.

Chapter Seventeen

HARRY COLLINS AND his two companions returned to the camp exhausted and covered in dirt, none of them truly comprehending the magnitude of the horror they had witnessed that evening.

They had stayed with Phillipa Dawns until help had arrived, including the person she'd least wanted to see, Constable Mere. While he questioned her, the stable hands, who had been at a party hosted by the owner of one of the surviving horses, led the remaining animals into separate transportation vehicles to be taken back to the stables on the Cadnam Road. Harry was impressed with their dedication to the animals and to their boss. From terrified and upset phone call to completing the job, the stable hands worked quietly, diligently, and were off site within the hour. Not one of them noticed the three monoliths or asked questions about what had happened.

After they had gone, the constable returned with Phillipa, having viewed the evidence. He was pale and silent, as shocked as they had been when they first stumbled upon the massacre.

It was that word, *massacre*, that kept resurfacing throughout the long night's conversation between Millicent and Harry as they drank tea and kept the fire going. Neither could sleep, and in any case, Harry figured whatever had made those structures had also decimated the horses and might be kept back by the fire. It was, perhaps, a fool's mercy to believe that were true, but he gladly clung to it for a while.

He couldn't have been prouder of how well the boys held themselves together, especially Edward, who'd processed the scene with a pragmatic calmness that Harry envied. Indeed, it was Edward who had discovered how the dead horses had got into the field. A section of the stable block wall had been tampered with, by whose hands it was impossible to say, but, Edward speculated, it would have spooked the horses enough that they would have pushed through to escape. By the time Phillipa discovered them, they were long dead, and the anthills, if that was what they were, would stay dormant overnight. "After all," Edward had observed with an ice-cold honesty that chilled Harry and Jacob Betley to the core, "they've been well fed. They won't need anything else for a while yet."

Again, Harry reiterated to Millicent how grateful he was that Phillipa had not been nearby when Edward uttered those words, although he also suspected Phillipa might not have been as innocent as she made out. The constable had acted strangely around her, following her every move as she gave orders to her stable hands with the same no-nonsense authority Harry had experienced firsthand, looking down the double barrels of the woman's shotgun.

"Maybe it's not her who's the problem," Millicent speculated. "Maybe he's the sort of bloke who, once he's in uniform, thinks it gives him a right to do whatever he likes. I wasn't impressed with him when he came to the camp. He made it very clear he would have preferred to talk to you."

"You make a good point," Harry said. "But it felt more than that, like he was waiting for her to slip up, as if he's long suspected her of some wrongdoing that he can't prove."

Millicent didn't comment and instead stared deep into her freshly brewed mug of tea, the tannin-stained enamel marking her years of camping experience. Harry was thankful it was he rather than Millicent who had gone to look for Fife. Tough as she was, witnessing the man's animated corpse being sucked whole into the ground was an experience he would not wish on friend or foe.

In Harry's absence, Millicent had settled everyone into their tents, and the camp was calm and still in the night, but come morning, they would need to tell the boys something. Millicent was resolute, and Harry agreed: the best thing to do was to take them back home after breakfast.

"It will take two journeys," he said, "as we have the equipment to take care of as well. My car will only take four people, five at a push, yours the same. We can get more of the boys in Fife's Land Rover and some of the equipment. We also have the problem of some of the parents not being home—the Sillatoes in particular, and Mr. and Mrs. Kelly are visiting a cousin in Yorkshire. I can't leave Kevin and Edward in the hands of strangers."

Millicent stared steadfastly back. She didn't need to say the words. It was up to Harry. His troop, his decision.

"All right," he said, "here's what we'll do. First thing, we'll ring all the boys' parents, see what's what. Then you take as many as you can in the Land Rover, and the rest of us will stay and break down the camp. I'll ask Daniel Demarco's father to come back with you—he has a Land Rover, so he can drive Fife's perfectly well. That way, we can get the rest of the boys and the vehicles home. If you leave by eight, you can be back here by midday."

"Yes, Scoutmaster," Millicent said solemnly and went to her tent, returning a moment later with a pen and notepad on which she made a list of the boys she would take first. As she wrote, Harry placed another log on the fire and looked out into the darkness. Soon it would be light and the boys would wake up, all except two ignorant of the night's horrors and the loss of their beloved former Scoutmaster.

***

Through the small hours, Harry and Millicent packed up as much of the equipment as they could and called the boys' parents as soon as it was late enough to do so. While some had moaned about their free time being cut short, most had seen the early morning regional news, which featured a report on the sinkhole or whatever it was in the village near the campsite. The vicar had been interviewed, looking shocked and devastated outside his church.

"I'm not going back unless Sillatoe's with us!" Betley yelled, his outburst catching Harry by surprise, given the two boys' encounter the previous evening, but in the hours since the discovery of the dead horses—or what remained of them in that graveyard of a field—Jacob Betley's demeanour had changed.

"We've gone over this, Jacob," Millicent answered with patience and kindness, despite his tantrum. "We can't get hold of Kevin's parents, whereas your dad is at home and will meet us at the Scout hut in two hours. Now come on, shake a leg." She pointed at the Land Rover and stared at him expectantly. Betley scowled and grunted but did as he was told, climbing into the back with the others.

Almost as if they were daring that policeman to pull them over, they managed to squeeze in all but Kelly and Sillatoe, and with some crunching of gears, Millicent manoeuvred the beast of a vehicle onto the dirt track, ready to go.

Harry turned away, defeated. His first experience in charge of camp had been a total failure, but with two horrific events happening close by and his friend presumably dead, the best he could do was protect Millicent and the boys from further danger.

Millicent shouted from the Land Rover, "Edward's grandfather just called. Fleur saw him earlier outside the newsagent's and told him what was occurring. I think I can just about fit Edward in as well."

It was, in the circumstances, oddly good news to hear. With half the equipment packed in Harry's car and the rest in Millicent's, which they could retrieve later, they would all be home, safe and sound, in a couple of hours.

Home. He had not yet told his own mother and father of his early return. He didn't much enjoy talking to his father on the telephone at the best of times. Face-to-face, he could argue a point with conviction; over the telephone, he wanted to hang up, knowing he would never be able to justify himself if he stuttered or faltered over his words.

His parents could wait. All that mattered was that the boys had understood. Once they'd learned of Fife's disappearance, they had looked after each other and gone along with the early evacuation with only one dissenting voice, and even then Jacob Betley had done it out of concern for his former friend turned arch-nemesis who had to remain at the camp.

With Edward Kelly safely, albeit tightly, packed into the Land Rover with the rest of the boys, Millicent tooted the horn and Harry waved them off. Kevin Sillatoe stuck up two fingers at them, though he was smiling as he did so.

"Come on then, young Kevin," Harry said, turning away from the departing Scouts, "let's get this lot packed up, shall we?"

***

At the crossroads to the village which had seen its name plastered all over the morning news headlines, Millicent slowed down, not by choice. She couldn't get home quickly enough. However, a policeman was blocking the way and signalled for her to turn off the engine.

"Sorry to interrupt your journey, madam. Could you step out of the vehicle for a moment, please?"

Millicent immediately complied, issuing a warning to the boys to stay put, including Edward, tucked in the front passenger footwell.

"Were you in the area last evening, madam?"

"Depends what you mean by 'area', Officer. We were camping in the forest."

The policeman opened his notebook and turned it towards her, displaying a small photograph. "Have you seen this man at all?"

Millicent studied the image. The man seemed a rough sort, part of the criminal set, she thought unkindly, but he was a stranger to her. "No. Like I say, we were up in the forest."

"Camping, did you say?"

"Yes. I'm a Scout leader."

"Can I ask what business brought you to the village this morning?"

"Just passing through on our way home to Oxfordshire."

"I see." The policeman nodded and put away the photograph, not seeming to care or even notice the Land Rover was overloaded. *Bigger things on his mind*, Millicent thought.

Climbing back behind the wheel, she started the engine and waited for the policeman to move aside before she signalled left and took the turn, glad they were on their way once more. She hadn't noticed that while she and the policeman were exchanging information, one boy had slipped out of the back door, hidden behind a bush and then, when the coast was clear, set off back towards the camp.

Chapter Eighteen

N<small>O NEED TO</small> apologise at all, Robert, if I may call you that. My husband and I fully understand the pressure you've been under, and we shouldn't have badgered you. After all, you've only just moved in."

Samantha McCarthy swiftly tore open a box of what turned out to be twenty copies of a new detective book from an author Robert had never heard of.

"Hold these, will you? I'd normally ask 'the help', but he has a date this morning with his physiotherapist." She pulled several books from the box and handed them to Robert. Before she weighed him down with more words he had no interest in, he brought the conversation back to the point.

"That is exceedingly kind of you, Ms. McCarthy—"

"Please, call me Samantha."

"Samantha... I behaved badly, and while you may put it down to pressure, tiredness or whatever other excuse, the truth is I find it hard to trust people these days. I had to leave Manchester because friends turned against me, even though they knew I'd done everything I could to protect Bela."

"And Stuart. I know you did your best for him too."

Robert blinked in surprise. "Yes, and Stuart," he agreed meekly as if it would have been the very next thing he'd said when, once again, he'd forgotten about his son. How could he do such a thing? Once was bad enough. Twice was unfathomable and unforgivable.

The morning had started off as most mornings do, with the usual bargaining for the various jobs that must be accomplished for a family home to function. With those done, Robert had told the children he was heading into the village and suggested they accompany him so they could introduce themselves, get to know the layout and the types of shops.

Over breakfast, Robert lamented to his daughter that it would more than likely prove impossible to get hold of a match programme, and as he'd walked up the hill towards the bookshop, he noted that Bela would have to go into Avoncross or even further afield to Southampton for CDs. She did love her music. There was some rather dubious pop in her collection, but she also had her own copies of his classic vinyl albums on CD. He couldn't help but smile when he thought back to her singing along to his progressive rock favourites when she was barely more than a babe in arms.

He'd thought music might be the way to win her around this morning, but she'd pulled a face and said she'd go on her on at some point. He had a horrible feeling she'd overheard the previous evening's conversation with the pair from the bookshop and already knew what was coming.

"Sorry," Robert said, realising Samantha had spoken again and he hadn't heard a word of it. "I was miles away. Thinking about the children."

Samantha laughed, no hint of malice in her amusement. "I was talking about this fool." She tapped the author's name on the top copy of the stack, now twenty-tall, in Robert's aching arms. "He's coming here Monday evening to give a talk about his fictional detective. As if the world needs yet another literary treatise on the art of criminality. Still, I've been paid handsomely for the inconvenience. The Reverend Tarky is a big fan, it seems, so he has arranged this small...what did he call it? A soiree, that was it. I can't remember the last time I saw him so happy as when he told me he'd been conversing with the author. You've met him, I believe. Tarky that is, not the author."

Robert nodded. "Yes. He took the time to come and personally welcome us to the village," he said, trying to put a positive spin on the vicar's unsettling visit. There was something about the man that rankled with Robert, and he wasn't sure what it was.

"It's all right, Robert, I won't think any less of you for not liking Tarky. I have my doubts about the man too, and besides, your Stella does love to talk." Samantha grinned. She was teasing him.

"Everybody knows everybody, right?" Robert said mock-ruefully.

"Right on."

Samantha folded the now empty box and set it to one side, beckoning for Robert to follow her to a display cabinet at the front of the shop, from which she removed an entire section of books and then, too slowly for Robert's liking, refilled the shelf with the books he'd carried for her. The whole process was completed in silence, and Robert suddenly felt compelled to fill it.

"You spoke to my sister?"

"Last night, after we returned from speaking with you," Samantha admitted easily. "Don't worry. What was said between us will remain between us. I may have been a journalist, a good one even, but I don't really like the local telegraph. I want facts, not gossip. However..." Samantha let the word dangle between them as she stepped back to admire the bookcase. "Your sister is very forthcoming when it comes to information—I could have done with someone like her when I lived in Brick Lane. I might have avoided falling foul of a few people. Won't be a second." She dashed off, and Robert heard the tinkle of the bell on the shop door. Samantha appeared outside the recently cleaned window, squinting and occasionally frowning at her new display, but in general, she seemed happy with her work. She was almost back at the door when a young woman jogged across the street and intercepted her, proceeding to talk at length and in a very animated fashion.

Robert didn't enjoy overhearing other people's conversations. Invariably, he found they were laced with social poison that was often potent enough to infect eavesdroppers. Making a mental note to ring his sister later and ask her not to talk about his life to others in the village, especially not the vicar, Robert moved away from the front of the shop, intentionally keeping his back to the two women, and browsed the history section. It was disappointingly full of books picking over the bones and skin of twentieth-century conflicts, which had never appealed to him, although he did spot in their midst a former colleague's latest publication, a work that had taken him almost a decade to research and provided an account of his great-uncle's time in and out of institutions following the horrors he had witnessed at Belsen.

Robert slid the book carefully from its place on the shelf and looked at the cover. Yes, sacrifice was indeed a patient monster waiting to devour one's time. As a lecturer in history, he knew that all too well and decided he would purchase his colleague's book and then write to him at the university and congratulate him.

Moving over to the counter, Robert checked his watch and frowned. Samantha had been outside for at least five minutes, and while he was in no rush, he had no desire the waste the rest of his morning waiting to pay for a book he was buying purely out of a sense of duty to his former colleague. Chancing a look through the window, he was surprised to see there was now a small group outside, involved in what looked to be a heated discussion, which Robert couldn't hear, but he thought he saw the word 'murder' on Samantha's lips. The older gentleman standing to her left repeated the word, at which the older woman beside him pointed up the hill and then down toward the church. The young woman who had arrived first looked tearful and shocked and said something about horses, but that was as much as Robert could discern.

The whole scene was peculiar, misshapen. He'd witnessed many a gathering like it before, with everyone vying to have their opinion heard, but this was different, a chaos of people speaking over one another with no order to their disbelief, frustration and, in the case of the young woman, heart-breaking sorrow.

Samantha McCarthy caught Robert's puzzled gaze through the window. She gave the young woman a tender hug, which seemed to appease the others, who dispersed in various directions, Samantha returned to her bookshop.

"Sorry about that." She smiled breezily as she passed Robert and stepped behind the counter. He opted for tactical curiosity.

"That looked very dramatic for first thing on a Saturday morning."

She paid him no attention, didn't even look at him as sat at her desk, leaned back and sighed.

Robert recognised her pain, having come close to it himself in the past. She was imagining the relief that could be found in a bottle, muttering some unheard mantra as she talked herself out of it. He tried to be patient, but that word, that mouthed, unheard word, kept repeating itself in his mind. *Murder.*

Finally, she spoke, though what she said made little sense to Robert. "Barnaby Wilkins is...I guess *was*...a man who lived in one of the expensive houses beyond the crossroads. He was found last night, desecrated, defiled, eaten alive. There are several officers on site now. The villagers are understandably concerned."

"And the horses?"

Samantha frowned. "Commendable lip-reading skills, Mr. Romsleigh. A couple of miles out, the local stud farm run by one of the more interesting locals if gossip is to be believed. Her stables out in the forest were broken into yesterday. Several of her horses were massacred."

Robert didn't know what to say. Like most people faced with extraordinary news, he could only utter the pathetic and predictable, "You're kidding."

If Samantha's expression hadn't given him his answer, her next words certain clarified her position.

"I may be many things, Robert, but I have never really been known for my sense of humour. Ask my old friend Kinsey. He'll tell you I don't make jokes about such matters."

Chapter Nineteen

BELA HAD WATCHED her dad walk down the path, stop at the car momentarily, search his pockets for his keys, then, thinking better of it, set off on foot past their closest neighbour's home on the opposite side before disappearing from view.

He'd been distracted this morning, and she doubted it was *all* to do with the scene he'd caused last night when that couple turned up and started talking about the past. Bela had long suspected her dad had other issues, deep problems her mother had brought out into the open rather than caused. Even so, she found it hard to squash her resentment that he had not rescued her earlier. More than that, he didn't respect her feelings. Like, for instance, moving them away from Manchester. She understood why he'd had to, but that didn't mean she was happy about it, and that was just the latest in a long line of decisions that had been made on her behalf without anyone ever asking what she thought, what she wanted to do.

There were times, lonely nights when they'd had to live in temporary accommodation, that she'd felt she could no longer cope with the problems in her life that had been created by her parents. What type of mother tries to set fire to her child on her birthday? And then, having failed, goes on a cocaine-fuelled rage and sets the house alight, disfiguring that child forever? As the hours had ticked by in that unfamiliar flat, surrounded by what few possessions had survived, her father sobbing in another room, that was when Bela realised there were only two options open to her: fight or flight.

At two in the morning, she'd decided on flight, getting dressed quietly in the dark and filling her rucksack with a few clothes, a couple of books and some tapes she'd put together. As she'd tiptoed past the dark living room where her dad slept on a worn-out sofa with the stuffing hanging out of its left arm, the pain of her fast, heavy heartbeat had made her want to throw up, but she'd ploughed on, determined to leave, not because she'd hated him, but because she could not deal with his emotions as well as her own.

She'd told herself as she opened the door that it was the best solution, a break for them both, but the flicker of the stairwell light had caught her eye, and she'd paused mid-step, and in the silence between a tick and a tock, she'd changed her mind. She'd shut the door and put her rucksack down in the corner of the room before climbing on top of the manky bed and closing her eyes.

She'd had no idea what made her stop and could only put it down to some unseen force out there in the universe that, in time, would reveal its hand, show her why staying was the right thing to do. That time came two days later when she and her dad were walking down Oxford Road and bumped into one of his old university friends who had called at the flat the evening before.

Through the despairingly thin walls, Bela had heard her dad's friend tell him that he'd been looking for him and had contacted a mutual friend in the police, who'd told him where they were staying. *"I know life hasn't been easy, mate, but if I can take your mind off it for a while tomorrow...I have two spare tickets for the match. Meet us at the Sherwood at midday."* She hadn't heard her father's reply, but after he'd said good night to his friend, she'd heard something she'd thought she'd never hear again, her dad whistling a happy tune. She hadn't heard it much since, she reflected, but maybe that would change now they were away from Manchester.

Bela sat on the wall outside her new home for a while, taking in the sun, deciding what she was going to do with her day. She'd told her dad she'd go exploring on her own at some point. Why not now? There was nothing stopping her.

Blow it, let's explore.

Setting off down the hill, she saw a bus in the distance. She didn't have any money on her but decided to follow the route it took to the next bus stop with a view to travelling farther afield in future.

Even with her hood covering part of her face, she felt conspicuous, exposed in the limelight of the day, the phantom at an opera in which she had no starring role, like she had that day on Oxford Road, the difference being her dad's friend had pressed a five-pound note into her hand and told her to go and get herself a hot dog or something, as he needed to talk to her dad for a while. She'd bought a bag of heavily salted chips and found a spot from which to watch the scene unfolding—the players arriving, people asking for autographs for their kids...

"*No, just your name will do, thanks, pal. Have a good game.*"

She'd lost track of time, listening to the gentle buzz of a gathering crowd in the distance, an occasional tribal song, a disagreement here and there, mostly friendly, one pushing past the boundary of football rivalry and brought to a halt by a mounted policeman and two other officers. Bela breathed it all in, the smell of hotdogs and onions, burgers, sweat, the pent-up frustration and the very real fear of relegation all driving the tempo of the day from underneath.

"Where did you go? Is everything all right?" Her dad appeared in front of her, his face full of concern but with an undercurrent of excitement.

"I'm fine. I saw the players arrive. Rosler looked in a dead good mood. Not sure about the others."

Her dad nodded, hardly listening. He looked fit to burst, his news almost dripping off his tongue, glistening in the sunlight.

"What've you been up to?" she asked.

"I saw Doctor D'Harrar. He wanted to meet with me somewhere off campus."

Bela felt a small swell of excitement of her own. A meeting with his former boss? That must surely mean he was being reinstated at the university! Alas, her hopes were soon dashed.

"Doctor D'Harrar feels it would be unwise for me to return at this stage. There is still too much negative press, and some of the lecturers in the department feel it might be detrimental to future funding and would impact on students in my classes."

Bela shrugged, failing to see why he was brimming with joy rather than grabbing her hand and stiffly striding from the ground, back to that hell hole of a flat it seemed they would be stuck with forever.

"They're asking me to leave, Bela," he said. "Do you understand what that means? They aren't sacking me. They're paying me off. I've been offered enough for us to leave that awful flat and live for a couple of years with a few less worries. We could move down here by the ground—imagine that! Football on tap. Then, when it all dies down and the fingers stop pointing, I can apply for a job somewhere close by. It's not ideal, but it's better than what we've had since...well, since that night and all the hospital visits."

Bela had understood then and bravely smiled. Her dad was delaying his grief, moving sideways instead of onwards, because no matter where they lived, the memory would always be there, of taking Stuart from the fireman's arms while their mother stood laughing at the inferno that had been their home and Bela was whisked away on a stretcher.

Three days after her dad's meeting with his ex-boss, he received a message that turned out to be from Auntie Stella, although he hadn't told Bela at the time. He'd gone out to make a phone call, coming back nearly an hour later, explaining that every phone box he had found had been vandalised. In the end, he'd gone to the local police station and asked to use their phone. It was a strange request, but they'd granted it, and he'd made the call that changed their family's life. Whether it was for the better, Bela was still undecided.

She'd reached the bus shelter opposite the church and stopped to read the timetables. The bus to Avoncross ran six times a day: if she wanted to go to Southampton, she would have to change further along the route and make sure the times tallied. Even then, it would take hours. Still, another year and she might be able to convince her dad to get her a moped. For now, she'd make do with walking and stay local.

As she turned away from the bus shelter, she wondered if her thoughts were making her see things because there was a floodlight—switched off, it was daytime, after all—standing above the church roof. With nothing better to do, Bela went to investigate.

At the church gate, two men in uniform looked at her sternly, their guns twitching, but after everything she'd been through, she wasn't scared in the slightest and smiled sweetly then pulled down her hood, feeling the power of invisibility once more as the two men turned away and let her pass. Had they asked, she'd have told them: *my grandmother died a few weeks ago from a massive heart attack*. It was the truth, and while Auntie Stella had stopped short of accusing her brother of worrying their mother to her death, first by marrying that woman, then by disappearing, it was plain for all to see.

"Be careful what you wish for," Bela muttered to herself, glancing up at the foreboding church blotting out the sun.

She'd wanted her dad to move on, but not like this. A small village in the middle of nowhere, a house bought from the proceeds of the sale of his dead mother's house, another decision made on Bela's behalf in which she'd had no say, and here she was, miles from home, her friends, her old life.

Her slide into teenage melancholy was halted in its tracks when a hand touched her shoulder, and she gasped, the sudden rush of air through her scarred throat turning it into what most would mistake for a scream.

Before (1963)

South Africa had been a turning point for the man. His research in the field of myrmecology had seen him earn awards and letters after his name, a doctorate before he was thirty, papers published, top universities clamouring for him, but it was South Africa that made him feel as though he had earned the faith of the policeman and his family who had taken him in during the war and given him hope when all was lost.

An award, a special dinner with his name in lights above the stage and on the programme, he felt as though he could not have achieved more. During the evening, the speeches, the presentation, the socialising, the inevitable questions and introductions, the invitations to lunch, to dinner parties or to have sex with any of the young, aspiring undergraduates in attendance, his mind kept wandering to what might have been. What would have happened if the war had not robbed him of his parents? Would he have ended up in a factory, working eight till six every day, not that there was anything wrong with that, but he had long ago accepted that to have an aspiration meant leaving what was expected behind.

Another drink was thrust into his hand by a pretty girl— a waitress or a student, he couldn't tell—who smiled at him, and he returned the gesture.

He had returned to Birmingham, briefly, after the war. His old house had survived; others had not been so fortunate.

All around the area where he had played as a child were the scars of the fascist aggressor. He stood outside his former home for a while, remembering the outside toilet, his dad singing quietly to show someone was in there, the tremendous draught that blew under the door and how in the winter, one had to hold onto the urge to urinate and chip away the ice on top of the water.

The policeman had seen to it that the house was sold for a good price and, once all the paperwork had been dealt with, ensured that the woman who had taken him in was suitably recompensed, then put the rest into an account in his name.

The war had taken everything from the boy, but it had given the man an opportunity he had not wasted.

There was never any doubt that he would end up in this position; not the awards and the pats on the back from strangers, but one driven by the need to understand the complexities of his obsession. From the moment he had seen the ants on the damaged Luftwaffe plane wing, he had been entranced, to the point where little else outside the study of insects mattered.

The army had been a useful distraction for a while: three years in Asia had provided him with an abundance of time to study closely the different variants of the ant, their diets, their forms of society, the way they lived in harmony and quite often how they destroyed each other. By not taking part in the off-duty activities of others around him, he found he could do so much more—more drawing, more research—and derive more pleasure from being close to some of the more dangerous of the creatures. He maintained those contacts in Asia after his return to Britain, and occasionally, some species would find their way across international borders, usually dissected, their cells on glass plates. Once or twice a year, a live specimen was brought into the country via a network of couriers who never asked questions and in return received a healthy sum of money.

He didn't remember drinking the contents of the previous glass that had been thrust into his hand nor signalling for another, yet as he wandered around the imposing hall of the university, he began to consider that for the first time since his twenty-first birthday, he was on the verge of being too drunk to hold a conversation.

A young couple approached him, a strikingly handsome man of Caribbean origin, whose handshake was tight and firm, and an equally beautiful woman, who held out her hand demurely for him to kiss. He obliged both, a few eyes turning in their direction as he did so, some in fierce disapproval, others smiling as if it were a welcome pleasure to see an Englishman embrace all in such times.

Once a week, he had travelled from his home in the New Forest, where he had lived alone since the woman who had taken him in had passed, and made his way to London for three days of lecturing. The rest of the time he spent happily in the village, writing, reading, studying night and day, intermittently venturing beyond his walls to walk in the forest or sometimes, when the need for human contact was pressing, to visit the local pub and play cribbage with a friend who had also lost his parents during the war and found shelter in Downmere. The only difference between them was that one had a mother for three weeks longer than the other. Both of their fathers had been buried under thousands of tons of rubble and machinery when their place of work was bombed.

One of the senior professors at the university tried, unsuccessfully, to interject into the discussion that the man and his two new friends were having. The professor wanted him to meet the sponsor who had paid for and arranged to bring him to the country—no easy feat at a time of heightened political emotions and fear for the majority of the people.

Despite being near the knuckle when it came to alcoholic wear, he still had enough politeness in him to inform the professor that he would be sure to thank his sponsor as soon as he was able, but for a short while he needed to sit down: the evening's pleasantries on top of the long journey had become a little too much for him.

"Please, give me fifteen minutes to gather my thoughts and I will seek you out, my friend."

The professor took him at his word, and the man turned back to the two young students who had caught his attention with a single intriguing proposition. He looked at them with a gleam in his eyes. It was such a marvellous opportunity, and he would certainly extend his stay beyond the allotted week if it meant he was able to see for himself the one specimen that had eluded him.

The conversation between the three of them wound on for almost half an hour before he saw the professor beckoning him over to a small gathering of people, and while he had no desire to embrace the circuit, he understood that he had to pay back in some way the courtesy extended to him, the honorary position he had been afforded during the course of the evening.

Through the false smiles, the noxious plumes of smoke from cigars and long, foul-smelling cigarettes, he joined in with their small talk, listening without caring about the fields of study in which each person endeavoured and in most cases fell dreadfully short. Every so often, he caught a glimpse of the two students whose proposal had roused in him a novel and insatiable interest.

He had made plans to meet them the following day, early, before he would be missed.

The party wound down just after one in the morning, tuxedos and evening dresses seeming to be the only things holding the attendees upright. Everyone was exhausted and drunk, while he was stone-cold sober and alert. Finally, that one creature he had never seen outside of plate photographs was within his grasp.

***

The following morning, the man waited patiently outside his hotel for the two students to arrive, his suitcase and bags on the pavement beside him. South Africa was undoubtedly beautiful, but as he watched people going about their business, he felt underneath a real sense of dread, of anger rising. Like some, he had dismissed it, not out of arrogance or racist intent, but because he felt there was nothing he could do to rectify the position.

A car pulled up alongside him, spitting up dust that caught him in the eyes. He displayed no ill feeling toward the woman driving. On the contrary, he was happy to be embarking on the adventure of a lifetime. The young man jumped out the other side of the car and put the man's suitcase and bags in the boot.

"So, are you ready to meet marabunta, the army ant?" he asked.

The man almost punched the air in glee.

Chapter Twenty

THE PRESS INTRUSION had been relatively light the evening before, a couple of cameras and a few journalists milling around asking questions of those locals willing to have their face put in front of the nation. The footage showed people wringing their hands and homed in, soft focus, on an old man's face as he recounted memories of his wife of forty years who had been buried in the church where she had been christened. Now her rest had been disturbed, and he'd been told he may never be able to rebury her, as the cave-on had unearthed a huge mess. As if on cue, a tear formed and gently ran down his cheek, catching in the grey stubble of the overwrought war hero, and—*cut*. The media had their poster child.

Somehow, the news had got out that Barnaby Wilkins had been butchered in his back garden, and that several horses owned and trained by the Dawns group, as well as one owned by a member of the Saudi Arabian royal family, had been slaughtered in a random attack during the night. There was, to Belinda Bennett's relief, no mention of her husband: the press had either dismissed his death as the natural demise of a sick, old man or neglected him for a better story. Either way, Belinda thanked God for his intervention and crossed herself as she thought of her sweet, kind husband being terrorised into his grave by that awful girl.

Constable Mere had not gone into detail about Lionel's death. The early morning village grapevine had talked of his body being covered in insect bites, which Belinda put down to tattle tales and loose tongues. She felt, deep in her soul, that Sarah Calster had played a part in his death and wished she knew why Lionel had followed the girl up the hill in the first place.

Darren had stayed with Belinda for a few hours, recounting fond interactions and memories of her husband. She refused the medication the doctor offered to help her rest. She didn't want to fall into a slumber offered in the guise of Morpheus; she didn't want to calm down and make peace with her husband's death. If she had been a more open woman capable of recognising her faults, she might have questioned how she had forgotten her husband existed for a while, why she was more concerned for her dead son and the body of the church than for someone she had promised in front of God to love and cherish. She consoled herself that Lionel was his own man and had come and gone as he pleased. It wasn't her fault he'd decided to chase after that witch. Not her fault he didn't take care of himself after his surgery.

Had anyone asked, Belinda would have denied she'd forgotten about Lionel, but the village knew. After all those years of cashing pensions, posting parcels to young relatives and dropping off bagfuls of Christmas cards every December, everyone in Downmere knew there had been four men in Belinda Bennett's life: her father, her son, the Holy Ghost, and Lionel, God rest his soul, at the bottom of the pile. She was satisfied with the constable's scant assurance that the man had not suffered. It left her conscience free to concentrate on her son, the church and poor Reverend Tarky. How would he conduct his sermon on Sunday if the army continued to refuse him and his parishioners entry?

After Darren left, Belinda settled in front of the television with a cup of tea. She would watch the news and then go down to the church herself and have words with those soldiers.

As a leading member of the community, she had a right to enter whenever she chose. They couldn't stop her.

The news team had returned to the scene outside Barnaby Wilkins' house, that dreadful, soulless building filled with gauche ornaments, hideous paintings and over-the-top décor. Belinda had always thought Mr. Wilkins unsavoury, not just for having bad taste in wives and a lack of suitable manners, but for being of poor character, and here was this journalist with a Wiltshire accent, his tie telling of his excellent university education, armed to the teeth with information that had not been common knowledge until now.

Belinda's impassive viewing was soon replaced by shock, indignation and then superiority as it was revealed that Wilkins had killed his ex-wife and her lover, their bodies having been discovered beneath the back lawn.

"This small village," the reporter gleefully informed the watching public, *"already devastated by the events of an afternoon in which its beloved spiritual centre befell a natural problem of erosion and its graveyard plummeted many feet into the earth, now finds it has been harbouring a murderer."*

Belinda turned off the television and without warning began to cry as the enormity of the last twenty-four hours tore through her, regret followed by waves of anger, sorrow, images of her son and what the disease would have done to him, her husband, cloudy but there, pointing a finger of damnation at her. How much he must have despised her for dismissing his concerns about his operation and forcing him to take on the post office after he had left the army, to stay in a village full of people like her while she left him alone night after night so she could go and sit with their son and tend to the reverend's every wish, hang onto his every word as though it were God's authority, rubber-stamped, and for what? His appreciation?

The pointing finger became a fist that hammered on the sideboard, silent yet ratting her ornamental plates, brittle mementos of royal weddings, which toppled and crashed to the floor.

In fury, Belinda charged at her husband and tried to push him away, but her old hands went straight through him, and she hit the wall. She stumbled backwards in surprise, his spectre now looming over her, her ire no match for his as he soundlessly accused her of infidelity, not of the sexual kind, but worse, through her devotion to a man with whom he could not compete, all in the name of serving the Lord.

In death, Lionel was all he had not been in life, relentless, terrifying, and in her effort to flee, Belinda lost her balance, made a grab for the curtain and fell to the floor with a heavy thump. Pain shot up her spine and sent her mind into a whirl of confusion. She kicked out, her bare foot catching nothing but air as the ghostly apparition dissolved and reformed at the place where contact would have been made.

"You always looked away." He knelt in front of her, his once-handsome features twisted into a grotesque grin of sharp, unforgiving teeth. "From the day our son came into the world, I was never good enough for you—not even second best. I was relegated, placed last in thought and deed as long as our boy, the church and that paedophilic Tarky got their measure of adoration and love."

The full head of grey hair that she had long loved stroking as he slept became a mass of small, writhing creatures, and in her horror, Belinda reared, her back against the wall. If there had been a way to claw through the brickwork and escape, she would have done so. She screamed and banged her fists against the floor, the walls, praying that someone would hear her.

It's not real. He's not here. She repeated the thought over and over as she crawled towards the door, the answer to her prayers coming in the form of shouts from outside. The door burst open, and two men and a woman appeared. Belinda collapsed at their feet, crying, "Thank God, *Thank God*."

In her relief, she hadn't noticed the image of her dead husband fade; nor was she aware of the small welts coming up on her wrists, minute injections of poison turning the skin yellow underneath the sleeves of her dressing gown, but as she closed her eyes, she could not fail to see a few of those small, writhing creatures disappear under the sideboard.

Chapter Twenty-One

CAPTAIN TRELARYN LEANED forward in his chair and examined the detailed map with a growing sense of unease. In his long and sometimes less than impressive service, he had often been privy to information that required him to employ his particular brand of barbaric persuasion. From making an alleged high-ranking IRA member talk after his unmasking by a local Oxfordshire journalist to liberating Kuwait from Iraqi hands and going to Poland's aid as the end of the Cold War drew its first, tentative breath, Trelaryn's superiors had turned a blind eye to his underhand methods, caring only that he got the job done.

As he surveyed the map that took in the area surrounding the church, he pressed the intercom button.

"Yes, Sir?" came the quick reply.

"Ms. Shernan, would you get Major Durham on the telephone, please? And could you locate Corporal Wess and have him report to me once I've spoken to the major?"

Trelaryn didn't wait for an answer, too engrossed in establishing the locations of the tunnels that had been dug out under the New Forest after World War Two. The height of the Cold War had seen further excavations, always in secret under the guise of vermin control. Nobody took any notice, and as such, the New Forest, like other places of outstanding beauty, was connected to the outside world so that the military and VIPs could quickly access the surrounding countryside in case of invasion or nuclear exchange.

Trelaryn had not been privy to this information when he first arrived on site. It was only when the major heard about the graveyard's collapse that he'd demanded Trelaryn's presence and briefed him on Operation Bramshaw.

Trelaryn had painstakingly studied the file marked Top Secret during the night, and while his body ached with the kind of exhaustion he felt after a twenty-mile training yomp through the Black Mountains, his mind was alert, tightly coiled, ready to act. The problem was he didn't exactly know how he was supposed to proceed. The map showed no tunnel directly underneath the church. There was one roughly a hundred yards from the outermost edge of the graveyard, running directly under a field. An attached note indicated that the diocese had tried to purchase the land in 1989 due to the graveyard reaching capacity. The request had been declined, as the field was MOD land, but the Church was told the owner had refused to sell because the land was particularly fertile.

The tunnel ran for almost thirty miles, with four main entrances and exits and two subsidiary exits that had been mothballed not long after completion. They had been designed so that in the event of civil disorder or a nuclear attack, the army could get from Southampton to Avoncross and, if needs be, take shelter in the purpose-built bunkers. The system had been maintained and inspected over the years, but since the turn of the decade, coinciding with the fall of the Berlin Wall and the Soviet Union's need for new friends and allies, it had slowly been allowed to fall into disuse.

There were reports of cracks having appeared even before the system became untenable and no longer cost-effective, in one case a fissure large enough for a man to walk through, and some evidence of wildlife using the tunnels for shelter. What was more disturbing, but was likely a barrack-room tall tale, was one account of sheep and deer carcasses being found a few miles inside the New Forest section of the tunnel. The only witnesses were the two soldiers who had been tasked with opening up one of the bunkers to take inventory of the equipment being stored there.

Wilma Shernan rang through to say she had the major on the line.

"Thank you, Ms. Shernan. Any news on the corporal?"

"Yes, Sir, he's on his way. Sergeant Dixon is accompanying him."

Trelaryn was puzzled as to why the two NCOs were coming in together. Dixon was known for his almost unyielding adherence to the rules while Wess frequently skirted the line between comical comeback and insubordination. He returned his attention to the major only when Ms. Shernan, one of a handful of civilians on the base, knocked on his door with an impatient air. Trelaryn immediately picked up the receiver.

"Good morning, Sir. Thank you for ringing me back so quickly. I hope I didn't wake you."

The major put his captain's mind at rest on that score. "I've been up all night reading a copy of the file, as I suspect you have. That…cave-in is not down solely to the army. The tunnel was reinforced, and there has been no major work carried out in the vicinity since before the war. I am, frankly, at a loss as to why it happened and over such a large area."

"With your permission, Sir, I'd like to investigate, take a couple of men and check out the area. Perhaps if we can get the relevant minister to issue a press release saying that the army is conducting a structural survey but there is nothing to be alarmed about—years of heavy rain, soil erosion, displacement of the natural ground—that sort of thing."

The clock on the wall marked the lengthening silence, and Trelaryn was about to repeat the question when the major cleared his throat.

"There have been...developments overnight, Derek. A man was eaten alive on his property not far from the village centre. His wife saw the whole thing and is under sedation at a private hospital in Southampton. So far, we've managed to cover it up as a murder inquiry. There's also a situation brewing a couple of miles from the village, where several horses have been attacked during the night and something...unnatural has appeared on the property."

Trelaryn's stomach felt as if it had been stabbed by an unseen assailant. He had led soldiers from the front, gone into buildings where he couldn't see what lay before him or what peril awaited to end his life. He was a seasoned professional, willing to do the jobs others would not, yet something about this whole situation bothered him.

"Whatever you need to do, Captain, you have my authority. I suggest you take control of this quickly. A small team, no more than six men. No need to cause alarm in the populace. Just do your job and report back to me. Understood?"

"Yes, Sir. Understood."

"Good. Take down this name. He's the policeman who was at the scene of the horse attack."

As the major spoke, Trelaryn could not help but notice there was an edge to his normal cut-glass Edinburgh accent, a hint of...fear? Surely not. More like apprehension, as if the army's chickens were not just coming home to roost but to kick the farmer out of his bed.

Trelaryn fastidiously noted down all the information and thanked the major for his confidence in him. The major didn't reply. The order given, all that remained was the sound of a replaced receiver and the long tone, quickly replaced by the familiar gruff voice of one Sergeant Dixon.

Trelaryn was all for following orders. It was ingrained into him, through hours of parade ground bashing, the quick-change drill, all driving home the oath of allegiance he'd made when he signed on the dotted line. However, that voice had pushed many a new recruit to the edge. Trelaryn recalled one lad in particular, barely seventeen, with an undiagnosed health condition that had seen him go from conscientious top of his class to sluggish failure in the space of six months. Dixon had been convinced the lad had slacked off as soon as he'd been assigned a permanent company and maintained that conviction after his recruit collapsed on the parade square and was later discharged without penalty.

Judging by the loudly barked orders being issued on the other side of the door, the years had not eased Dixon's temper. Preparing for yet another complaint about his defiant corporal, Trelaryn opened the door and was greeted by the sight of Wess seemingly about to suffer the same fate as that lad on the parade ground.

"At ease, Corporal."

Fury sparked in Dixon's eyes, but Trelaryn ignored it.

"Sergeant, would you be so kind as to sign out a Pinzgauer, flashlights, rope and the usual kit. Round up Barnes, Smallwood, Bean and three others of your choosing, and make sure they are waiting by the vehicle in ten minutes."

Dixon looked on the verge of mutiny. There was nothing that infuriated a man like him more than having his orders overruled by someone further up the chain. Nevertheless, he saluted his captain and marched out of the adjoining office. Underneath her breath, Wilma Shernan called him a couple of choice names, then, remembering who else was in the room, turned a deep scarlet. Trelaryn pretended not to have heard and asked Wess to join him in the office. No formalities or standing on ceremony: there would be time later to enquire what transgression Wess had allegedly committed this time.

"Tell me about the tunnels underneath the New Forest, Corporal. What happened to you and Cauls when you were ordered to make an inventory of Bunker Three A?"

It was hard to tell if the sweat on Wess's brow was from enduring the sergeant's bullying or from being asked to recall something he would no doubt prefer to forget. He stood with his hands behind his back, not quite at ease, attempting to get his breathing back under control.

Trelaryn waited patiently for the man to gather his wits before he pressed him again. By the time they joined the others outside, he was wishing he hadn't taken the major's phone call the previous evening.

Chapter Twenty-Two

AINSLEY CORBETT PICKED at the fraying leather of his watch strap and waited for the signal from the camera operator that she was ready to start rolling for the evening news. He was nervous but exhilarated at being the face of the headline of the day, assuming nothing of greater importance came up. His big break had been spoiled before, and it still ate away at him. This time, he'd make sure his was the face people remembered when they thought of the events in this village.

For all his excitement, he couldn't escape the feeling that he was being spun a line. The two policemen in charge had been efficient, almost clinical, giving him all the details before he even asked any questions, his natural suspicions already alerted by the fact that Barnaby Wilkins' wife had not been seen since the early hours. The police claimed she was in a hospital under close supervision and observation, which may have been true, but the situation felt as if it had been stage-managed for national consumption.

The picking at his watch helped Ainsley think, although he wasn't consciously aware of it. Closing his eyes, he went through what he had learned since his report earlier in the day. He had the name of the victim, Barnaby Wilkins, and some brief details about the discovery of two almost completely decomposed bodies near where Wilkins was found. Although they didn't come right out and say it, the police had intimated that Wilkins had been attacked during the night, more than likely by someone bearing a grudge; they didn't speculate on who.

Ainsley opened his eyes and smiled at the camera operator. She, in turn, screwed her nose up and shook her head.

That's it, love. Keep leading me on. You know I'll take you with me if you're kind to me.

***

From behind the camera, Christine Balker sighed. She had complained with great fierceness when she found out she'd been paired with Corbett and had threatened to resign. Her boss promised her this was the last time she would have to suffer Corbett's advances, as he was being dismissed after the holidays for sexual harassment. The temptation to stay and watch the man burn was too great, so Christine relented.

"Ready in two minutes for a take for the afternoon news, Ainsley," she informed him.

***

Ainsley rehearsed his opening line again: sensationalism and hard-hitting drama were what the viewers demanded now, to feel like they were dictating the agenda. He practised his serious, professional face for the camera, making sure the viewers saw a man to be trusted, an impartial observer to the events surrounding the death of one of Britain's foremost football hooligans turned businessman.

Chinmayi in the records office had been a star, finding a still from a match when teenage Barnaby Wilkins had headbutted a policeman at the ground or, as Wilkins liked to call it, 'on his manor'. At the time, the black-and-white image had caused a sensation, with newspaper editors rubbing their hands in proverbial glee as overnight sales soared and they celebrated this insight into modern British life. It wasn't until Wilkins was interviewed at the end of the eighties for a programme about the haulage industry that someone noticed a partially hidden tattoo of the National Front emblem on his wrist and scarring from the removal of further tattoos across his knuckles, making it possible to identify him as the likely perpetrator of the assault on the police officer. However, given the number of hooligans who bore similar markings, the police and press had never quite managed to pin him down. Now, thanks to his death, Barnaby Wilkins would finally be in the spotlight, giving Joe Public a chance for vengeance while Ainsley would portray himself as the advocate of justice.

"Thirty seconds," Christine warned him.

He adjusted his jacket. He'd heard whispers, of course, that there was a plan to remove him from the station.

And I bet you're at the forefront, Chrissie. Oh, I will take you with me, all right, to the moon and back and then leave you in a crater so deep you'll never climb your way out.

***

The take went perfectly, with just the right amount of sadness in his voice. He was a lecherous hack, but he had a knack in front of the camera. *Pity you won't get to exercise it for much longer,* Christine thought, zooming in on Corbett's right eyebrow, slightly raised as he talked of the two other bodies hidden deep in the soil.

"'Was this gang related?' I know you're asking at home, or is it something more insidious from beyond the grave, the settling of an old score from Wilkins' days as one of football's most notorious hooligans..."

Cut to famed black-and-white still; cue both eyebrows being raised.

"...someone in this quaint village in the heart of the New Forest finally exacting their revenge. Back to you in the studio."

"Want to go again?" Christine asked, and he replied in the negative.

"No point over-egging the plate, not if you want extra chips, anyway. Let's have a look." He walked over and watched the playback. "Nope." He grinned. "It's perfect. Get that ready, and we'll send it over. Then I think we should take a drive out to the place where those horses were slaughtered. Might be something in that."

Christine's stomach turned. She'd overheard the gossip earlier in the morning, courtesy of a group of villagers hanging around outside the village bookshop. The scene was as Christine had always imagined village life to be, full of arbitrary chaos that randomly coalesced to create neatness—clean pavements, litter-free roads—the pride in Britain's best-kept village making a mockery of the banality of its existence. Today, though, that spotlessness had been blemished by murder and slaughter. Christine started to pack her camera gear together, finding herself thankful that she lived in the grime of London.

***

As Christine packed her gear into the van, Ainsley calculated how long it would take to film a piece then come back to the village and get some reaction for the evening news before driving back to the studio in Southampton. After years on the road, filling in time with pointless twee interviews with housewives complaining about the closure of a local park or the swimming baths, bitter business owners demanding the police do something about the increase in kids thieving, car park arguments and low-level criminals on the run, there had only been one other story that came close to being his meal ticket.

He'd had all the facts and witnesses willing to come forward and speak publicly about incompetence at the Department of Agriculture, but the paper he'd worked for then had gagged him.

Clearly, favours were being exchanged behind the scenes, while he was made to look incompetent. Since then, he'd strived to carve out a career in front of the camera, becoming the go-to man for filler towards the end of the half hour, all smiles, *and finally...*

Ainsley swallowed down on his crushed dreams and bitterness. He hadn't thought about it in a long time, how his first golden ticket had been snatched from under his nose. It would not happen a second time.

He was about to ask Christine if she was ready to go when he spotted the crowd of locals standing nearby, watching them and murmuring to each other. He smiled and waved at them, and a few waved back. One even remarked how good it was to see him in their village—any chance of an autograph?

But it was the one person not waving, who seemed distinctly unimpressed by his appearance, that caught his attention. She might have aged, her hair more in keeping with a grandmother who could no longer be bothered to dye it, and whose face still bore the scars of taking spirits to bed instead of lovers. Once more he swallowed down his frustration. *What the hell is Samantha McCarthy doing here?*

Chapter Twenty-Three

ELIZABETH CROKER SCRUTINISED her school project, amazed at how well it had come together and surprised she hadn't broken it in the three weeks since she came up with the idea.

Inside the Perspex tank, hundreds of ants went about their business with seemingly little knowledge or care that they were being watched by human eyes, while she was busy drawing the creatures, studying their movements, examining their social structure and capturing their organisation in detailed notes and observations.

Her mother had been appalled when she'd told her what she was doing for the final presentation of the school year. While she appreciated Elizabeth's enthusiasm for biology, she'd hoped she'd pick a much larger variety of animal, not the dirty, scurrying creatures whose presence usually resulted in a call to the local exterminators. She'd bought every wildlife video and magazine she could find, and they'd spent hours cutting out pictures and making a collage. She'd even taken her daughter on trips to the zoo and safari park, trying to harness her compassion to the plight of elephants, gorillas or other endangered species, any of which would have created a project that she and her classmates would gain pleasure from. Still, Elizabeth had insisted on this ant colony.

In a fit of adult fury, which Elizabeth had watched with terror and no understanding of what she had done wrong,

Lucille Croker had set fire to the magazines she had purchased, ranting about how she would never help her daughter with a project again.

"You think you know better than me, that some filthy ants in a Perspex prison will impress your teacher and those awful children you call your friends?"

Elizabeth had pleaded with her mother to not be angry, her knuckles smarting when her mother swatted at her as if she were an irritating mosquito. It was to no avail. Her mother threw the final video tape into the flames, sending particles of black smut into the sky and causing a couple of neighbours to complain loudly that the smoke was drifting across their gardens. Elizabeth felt nothing but embarrassment as her mother screamed over the top of the walls that separated each property, *"Mind your own business and get back to dressing in your mother's clothes, Nigel Planter, sissy boy!"*

Worse was when her mother turned that insane rage on her. Even now, the words hurt, and as she looked at the ants in their home that she had built without her mother's knowledge, she felt a rush of anger of her own. She snatched up the tank, struck by the urge to bring it down on the garage's concrete ledge and destroy this thing that had made her mother so furious she hadn't spoken a word all through the school holidays, leaving Elizabeth to fend for herself.

But as she lifted the container of soil, leaves, mulch and ants above her head and looked up through the bottom of the Perspex, she stopped. She had cared for these dynamic, interesting creatures, had watched them grow, seen a couple die, and taken a peculiar voyeurism in their ritual of male aggression. She held the tank above her head until the muscles in her arms twinged and cramped with the weight. Feeling a surge of responsibility for these small beings and shame for what she'd almost done, she gently set down the tank and covered it with a dark sheet she'd found in a box of her dad's belongings still stowed at the back of the garage.

He'd once kept his motorbike there—his pride and joy that now resided in the yard of another woman's home, not as well cared for as it had once been. Between playing stepdad to three teenagers and looking after the small child that had caught him and his new wife unawares, he no longer had time for his motorbike. Yet he still found time for Elizabeth. Unlike some of her friends who rarely saw the parent who'd walked out, she spoke to her father every other day. Standing in the gloomy garage, she wished she could have gone on holiday with him and his new family, but as he'd pointed out, it was their honeymoon, and they were only taking the baby with them because it was too young to go with the three older kids to their grandmother's in Plymouth.

Before he'd left, he'd helped Elizabeth draw up plans for the tank and put together the foot-cubed contraption with enough soil for the ants to thrive and for her to watch them. It had taken a week, and surprisingly his new wife had encouraged them to spend the time together after school. Elizabeth's mother had hated that and flew into a rage at the mention of her stepmother.

Thinking back to her mother's reaction, Elizabeth understood for the first time the beasts of jealousy and possession. She had almost grasped them once before, not long after her father had got on his motorbike and said goodbye as she cried and begged her parents to try to make it work, to stay together. Her mother had stood to the side, her face sullen, chewing at the inside of her cheek. It gave her the appearance of a badly eroded stone statue.

Elizabeth removed the sheet again so she could look at what she'd created. The sense of power over the creatures within had already left its black mark on her heart. She had studied the ants to the point of obsession, just as her mother obsessed over her.

In a way, Elizabeth was trapped in a tank too, although she had found a way to express her freedom, proved she could survive on her own. Since her mother never came out of her room these days, Elizabeth had no choice but to learn to cook, clean and make sure she kept to a routine.

The money was running short, though, and the villagers were asking questions of her mother's whereabouts, if she was sick. Elizabeth had lied, convincingly as it turned out, to the lady at the newsagent's, the man in the post office and the owners of the chip shop where she bought her evening meal each day. The only ones she hadn't fooled were the creepy vicar and the bookshop owner, who was either nosey or well-intentioned; Elizabeth wasn't sure which.

Reverend Tarky had called at the house twice enquiring after her mother's health. The first time, Elizabeth said she was in bed with a migraine, the second that she'd been picked up that morning to attend a choral practice in Avoncross. The choral practice had been on the calendar, underscored twice in black ink, her mother's system for making sure important events didn't clash. As Elizabeth stood guard in the entrance to her home, she informed the vicar that she wasn't sure what time her mum would be back but she'd get her to ring him later. He'd seemed satisfied by her lie and made no move that gave her reason to believe otherwise, but as the day passed and she heard movement in her mother's room, Elizabeth began to wonder.

The bookshop owner, Ms. McCarthy, was different. She seemed quite a forceful woman—she had to be to have kept her own name after she'd married. She was a bit of a nuisance too, asking Elizabeth every time she saw her if she'd remind her mother to pop into the shop so they could firm up the arrangements for some author's event. Elizabeth had managed to stall her so far, but the woman wasn't giving up; she had half a mind to phone Ms. McCarthy and, in her best impression of her mother, tell her she no longer wanted anything to do with the village or its soul-destroying way of life.

Elizabeth replaced the cover and whispered good night to the creatures before closing the garage door and creeping back into the house.

Tiptoeing up the stairs, she reached her mother's bedroom and knocked softly, just loud enough that her mother would hear and answer if she was in the mood. There was no response—nothing unusual in that—but as she had done each day, Elizabeth opened the door slightly to see if her mum was sleeping or sitting at her desk. Like every day for the last two weeks, she lay on her bed, turned away from the door. Elizabeth tried asking if she wanted a cup of tea and some toast, perhaps some chips from the village. Nothing, no answer.

On the bed, her mother's decaying corpse lay in stony judgement of her daughter. Elizabeth tiptoed over to the bed and sat beside her, running her hands through the dead hair, watching the ants climb over her fingers as she ruffled the half-chewed scalp. With her other hand, she pulled the cover up over her a little. *She might be angry with me, but that doesn't mean she has to get cold.* Several ants scurried away, disturbed by the movement of their domain and food supply.

"I love you, Mum. I wish you'd talk to me."

Yet another day of silence between mother and child, but Elizabeth refused to descend into a tantrum. She leaned over and kissed the dead woman, removing an ant that latched onto her lips in the exchange.

"I'll check on you tomorrow, Mum."

Tiptoeing back across the bedroom, Elizabeth's thoughts turned to dinner. She was sure she had enough money left for a sausage supper. Her dad would be back soon, and she would be able to borrow some money for a proper meal.

Chapter Twenty-Four

IT WASN'T UNTIL Millicent had turned the vehicle left into Wendlefield that she realised how well behaved the boys had been on the journey home. Almost too well behaved, now she thought about it: she'd heard hardly a peep out of them for more than ninety minutes. She had tried to engage a couple of them in conversation, but her questions were returned with dismissive monosyllabic replies, so she had given up.

If nothing else, the quiet gave her a chance to take stock of the overnight developments, to think of Fife, Harry and her position within the movement. She enjoyed being part of young lives, helping these boys become adults, smoothing out their rough edges. As she clicked off the indicator and pressed on the brake, she thought back to her conversation with Fleur about taking a more active role in the community.

She'd considered applying for a job in the care facility in Wendlefield, but Fleur had talked her out of it. The rumours of its past persisted despite a clean bill of health from various government officials and whispers of mismanagement in what had once been deemed a model facility for recovering drug addicts and others whom society wanted to keep out of sight. After that, the Scouts had become Millicent's family, and she genuinely cared for the boys, some of them perhaps just as troubled as those for whom the facility was their permanent home.

Somehow, the small village feel had been retained, even though it now stood in the shadow of a larger town a couple of miles to the northeast. It was here Millicent had arranged to make the first drop to save Mrs. Desrail the expense of a taxi when she could least afford it. She felt bad for Linus Desrail. His father worked long hours for little pay, and his mother had been confined to a wheelchair for several years. The family struggled, continually denied help from social services, which they would have received if Mr. Desrail gave up his job, but he was a proud man, and so he continued to work all the hours he could, returning from the fields late each evening and leaving again early the next morning.

For her part, Iris Desrail was an excellent mum who managed to keep a smile on her face even though the pain in her spine often left her close to calling it a day. Linus helped her prepare the family's evening meal and was responsible for all the other household chores. The least Millicent could do was ensure he spent one evening a week with boys his age. It was the closest Linus was getting to a normal childhood.

Millicent drew to a slow halt directly outside the small cottage that had been part of Wendlefield for as long as there had been homes in the area. A relieved Iris waited at the front door. Millicent instructed the boys to make way so Linus could get past, and one of the boys made a lewd comment about Linus's mum, loudly enough for her to hear.

"I know that was you, Jacob Betley. Only you could come up with something so disgusting."

A ripple of laughter filled the vehicle.

"Sorry about that, Mrs. Desrail," Millicent called through the open window, but Iris waved the apology away, unperturbed by adolescent innuendo. Even so, Millicent turned in her seat to deliver a scolding.

"Jacob, you will apologise to Mrs. Desrail right now, or so help me there will be trouble when we get back to the Scout hut!"

A stifled giggle sounded behind her, along with a loud *shush* from one of the younger lads at the back.

The combination of the stress of the night, the lack of sleep and a deep-seated worry for her friend tipped Millicent's patience over the edge. With a growl, she undid her seat belt and got out of the Land Rover, then flung the back door open with such force the hinges creaked. The boys stared at her, some with eyes lowered in shame, others wide-eyed in admiration or, in the case of Stanley Marsh, abject fear.

"I am sorry, Miss. I didn't mean it. It just popped out. Please don't tell my mum, she will go spare."

Millicent was too dumbfounded to answer. She couldn't even find the words to tell Linus to be patient as he shoved past her and flew into the house without stopping to say hello to his mother. Millicent tried to make sense of why there was a space where Jacob Betley should have been.

It seemed an absolute age between Linus leaving and when she finally managed to get out the question. Even then, she wasn't sure she wanted to hear the answer.

"Where is Jacob?"

Stanley Marsh's face crumpled, and he burst into tears.

"He jumped out when you were pulled over by the policeman near the camp, Miss. He threatened us to keep quiet, said if we squealed he'd make our lives hell. You know what he's like, Miss. You don't cross Betley unless you want your head kicked in."

Stanley was a big lad for his age—almost fifteen—but he found it hard to contain his emotions and had never been considered for a more responsible role in the Scouts because of it. His outbursts were legendary—a consequence of having a bullying older brother—but in the circumstances, he could be forgiven.

Millicent put a hand on his shoulder, attempting to comfort the lad, her anger replaced by fear for Betley's safety. No matter that he'd left without her knowledge or permission; it was a dereliction of duty, complete neglect on her part.

"Is everything all right, Millicent?" Iris Desrail had approached, unnoticed, and peered inside the back of the vehicle, eyes narrowed as she took in the empty seat.

"No, Iris. Everything is most definitely not all right." Millicent closed the back door lightly, knowing, despite Mrs. Desrail's overall pleasant nature, news of Jacob Betley's absence would be all around the waiting parents and grandparents before the Land Rover made it back to the Scout hut.

Bidding Iris farewell, Millicent climbed into the driver's seat and started the engine. Linus Desrail was watching from his bedroom window, his face gaunt and sad. No wonder he'd fled so quickly, but Millicent wouldn't hold it against him or any of the remaining lads. Jacob Betley was a law unto himself. She gave Linus a friendly salute and put the vehicle in motion.

As she drove back to the town, she handed Edward Kelly a card with a phone number on it and instructed all the boys to stay quiet while she gave Edward instructions to take her phone from her pocket, unlock it and dial the number on the card. The call was answered almost immediately, but she waited until she had turned the corner out of the Desrails' street before she pulled over and took the phone from Edward.

The line was crackly to the point of inaudible, and had it not been an emergency, she'd have hung up and tried again later. As it was, she persevered.

"Constable Mere, it's Millicent Maples from the Scout troop. Perhaps you can help me. It concerns one of the lads who was with us. His name's Jacob Betley, and I think he's lost in Downmere."

Millicent listened patiently as the constable explained the situation in the village, emphasising how busy he was, but he agreed to keep a lookout for the missing boy.

"Thank you, Constable. If I could also trouble you to get a message up to Scoutmaster Collins? Let him know I'll be back with Giuseppe Demarco as soon as I can."

The whole exchange took less than two minutes, and as she put her phone away, Millicent cursed Harry for his insistence that he didn't need modern technology to be a good Scoutmaster.

Without realising, she'd said the word *fool* under her breath and quickly clamped her lips together. The only boy who'd heard her was Edward, and he kept his thoughts to himself, no doubt wondering, as she was, whether she'd meant Harry, the policeman, Jacob Betley or herself.

Chapter Twenty-Five

NOT ONLY HAD the entrance to the tunnel been hidden from the public eye by ingenious military planning, but it had also become so overgrown with hanging ivy, not to mention cobwebs and an abandoned car, Trelaryn had overshot it by forty or so feet. It was Corporal Wess who shouted to the assembled team that he had found the large iron doors concealing the privately built subterranean road that ran the breadth of the New Forest.

Wess wrenched aside a handful of lush, green leaves, revealing a sign that stated the fine for unauthorised entry was more than a month's pay. "Sorry, Captain, I can't afford to go in," he said, dark humour covering his honest reluctance to venture into the tunnel.

Having heard the corporal's account of the last time he had been inside the underpass, Trelaryn understood his unwillingness and suspected if he had been given a choice, if it had been Dixon issuing the order, Wess would have clasped himself in handcuffs and taken the opportunity to be broken daily inside the Glass House in Colchester rather than go back in that tunnel.

"You're a good man, Wess. Let's get this done and I'll see what I can do to get Sergeant Dixon out of your hair."

He meant it as well. Dixon was a first-class soldier, but sometimes one needed to be able to see the bigger picture and be prepared to carry out a task that would haunt you for the rest of your days, however many or few those were. Dixon didn't have that spark of initiative, but Wess did. He just needed pointing in the right direction.

While Barnes and Bean unloaded the equipment from the Pinzgauer, Trelaryn ordered the other men to remove as much of the fauna as they could. It didn't take long for them to uncover the outline of the door along with further metal signs that warned of *Trespassers Will Be Shot*, *Keep Out* and *Danger Of Death*.

"Would rather pay the fine," Wess muttered, at which Barnes and Smallwood laughed, but Dixon once again took matters into his own hands, roaring at the corporal to watch his mouth.

"Come on, Sergeant," Bean implored. A conscientious and rather quiet soldier, he was not one for showing dissent, preferring to get on with the matter in hand so he could get back to his family and life outside of uniform. While his challenge had been non-aggressive, it was still a powerful moment and, Trelaryn noted, took Dixon by surprise.

"What did you say to me, Bean?"

The soldier shrugged, and Dixon squared up to him, his nose almost touching Bean's chin. Bean may have had a couple of inches on the sergeant, but that didn't give him the upper hand in any type of fight.

"Think you can take command when it suits, Bean?"

"No, Sergeant, but you've been riding Wess's arse for weeks now, and we've got a job to do. With all due respect, can we just get on with it?"

Dixon's eyes glazed, rage taking over. Bean stood his ground, relaxed, stoic, but ready to defend himself. It was at that point Trelaryn stepped in. Ill-discipline would not be tolerated, neither would outright bullying between the ranks, but Trelaryn suspected Dixon was suffering from undiagnosed post-traumatic stress. He'd seen many a good man go under, the strain finally catching up with them. One soldier in his command had taken his own life after the liberation of Kuwait, convinced he was responsible for the death of twin girls who had been sheltering in an abandoned building. Despite talking to senior command and being told quite categorically that he was not to blame, he went out of the barracks one night and put a bullet in his head.

Dixon reminded Trelaryn of that soldier. There was something in his eyes, a fear behind the wild and unabashed anger, but the damaging machoism had gone far enough.

"As you were, Dixon. We'll sort out any grievances in the proper manner later. Until then, as Bean said, we have a job to do, so get this door open. That's an order, Sergeant." Whether out of fear or respect, Dixon backed off immediately and followed his orders.

The large metal doors resisted the strength of the men. Too much time, age and no doubt the spread of rust had done its work, and in the end, they had to use a grappling rope, one end connected to the truck, the other to one of the door's outer hinges and bolts.

The doors were just over fifteen feet high, designed for FV4034 Challenger 2 tanks to roll through. The road beyond, at one time superior to the most sophisticated public highway, was twenty feet wide with rooms cut into the earth at strategic points along its route, providing access to bunkers 100 feet below. Had the Cold War ever heated up, this imposing feat of engineering would have been completely useless, as the storms of 1987 had done significant damage to the upper rim of soil.

Thanks to the brute strength of the truck's engine and the forceful determination of Barnes at the wheel, the door came away from its hinges, the shock of its release causing Barnes to reverse quickly as it came crashing down towards him. He dragged it back to the lane leading to the main road and unhooked the ropes.

Once the cloud of dust, ivy and soil had settled, Trelaryn shone his torch into the entrance, but it was the dank smell that was more revealing.

"Right, Barnes, Bean—I want you to take the Pinzgauer and go to the church in Downmere, relieve the two men guarding the equipment and keeping anyone from exploring the large hole. They are to return to camp and be off duty for twenty-four hours. They're also to pass the order on to Tibbitt and James to return here with the vehicle."

The two men saluted their captain, who caught their smirks as she marched briskly away from the entrance to the underground roadway, and Trelaryn couldn't blame them for thinking they had the easier assignment. The four remaining soldiers put on their backpacks, made sure their torches were working and their watches were synchronised.

**

Wess warily kept his distance from Dixon, staying at the back of the formation where he was able to see natural light for as long as possible. The bunker that he and Cauls had been ordered to clear was three miles into the tunnel and on the left-hand side. Droplets of water from cracks in the infrastructure mixed freely with his sweat—if it hadn't been for Trelaryn's calming presence, he might have deserted the small company and headed back outside while he still could. Cauls had not been so lucky. He was still in here, probably in Bunker Three A where he was last seen. Where Wess had sentenced him to a grisly death.

Seeking distraction, Wess thought back to the first time he'd been in an underground installation, the German military hospital near his childhood home in St. Martin. He recalled how the cold air and dread of the past had given rise in his imagination to the sounds of the dead scratching their way out, the slaves from France, Poland and Russia joining local Guernsey men sentenced to death for aiding the British, all of them crawling from their cold storage tomb.

It was the only time Wess had been inside the complex. His father, newly appointed as headmaster at the local school, had taken him along on his exploration of the surrounding area. Young Billy Wess had clung grimly to his father's hand throughout, and upon returning to the surface had collapsed, dry-retching, too frightened to move for the next half an hour.

As the four soldiers moved down the tunnel and came upon Bunker Three A, Wess imagined holding his father's hand once more and hearing his calm, patient reassurance that the dead could not rise.

"Tell that to Cauls," he whispered as the company of four looked through the small, wired window into the darkness of the room, unsure of what lay beyond.

Chapter Twenty-Six

SAMANTHA MCCARTHY, AS I live and breathe! What brings you to this delightful village? Could it be your nose caught something in the air other than the whiff of cheap whisky and the chance to screw someone over?"

Sam McCarthy smiled politely but felt the familiar gnaw of unpleasantness and the desire to reach deep into the soul of Ainsley Corbett and tear it apart, just as he had, in effect, done to her. After Robert Romsleigh had left, she'd switched on the TV in Bertie's office and had indeed caught a sniff of something malodorous. Seeing the former junior reporter from her newspaper turned anchorman reveal that a wanted criminal had been found dead in his impressive country home had given her more than a jolt of surprise. At his utterance of, *"As I stand here in this beautiful, idyllic village, dark secrets are being revealed in the heart of the New Forest,"* she'd wanted to slap him in front of the cameras. Always one for adding a bit of titillation and drama to the most horrific of tragedies, Ainsley Corbett was the epitome of a new breed of journalism that Samantha detested and had been on the verge of joining when she'd fallen down the East End rabbit hole, chasing the next Reggie Kray.

Thankfully, her spirit had rebelled, and with what happened in Perchester always at the back of her mind, she'd taken the exit when it was shown to her. No regrets, although it never could quite scratch the itch, which was why she'd flown from the shop after Robert Romsleigh left, barely remembering to lock the door,

151

past the crossroads where Lionel Bennett had met his end, and on towards the new estate.

She thought back to her old friend and colleague Kinsey, who could command confidence with a simple smile and had become the media face of the town where he had grown up, having almost given his life to saving it from an evil Samantha still could not comprehend. That was *true* worth. Kinsey was honest, sincere, nothing like the abject fool and vile excuse for a human being now standing a few feet away from her. She knew the second he'd recognised her in the crowd; the subtle frown that had disappeared in an instant was worth the journey up the hill on its own, and as she'd watched him close his segment and give instructions to his camera woman, she was tempted to come up with a way to make his life even more miserable.

"Still pissed, Samantha?" Ainsley Corbett smiled at her without a hint of friendliness, speaking loud enough to be heard by the ear-twitchers and gossipmongers congregated behind the chequered police tape.

"Only with you, Corbett. How did you get to the dizzy heights of local television news?"

"Hard work, sleeping with the enemy—you know the sort of thing. Same way you got the job on the newspaper!" Ainsley smiled again, this time baring his whiter than white teeth, a shark who'd found out how toothpaste works. "The last I heard, you'd come back to jolly old England and managed to wrangle a large pay-off from the paper. Good old Daddy Fillus, eh? You always were his favourite bit on the side."

"Something like that," Samantha replied nonchalantly.

"And there was me, out of work, shunned and ostracised by the print media in London. I worked hard, Sam, I worked damned fucking hard, and you stole my chance at the story of my career."

Her heart fluttered with no small amount of joy at hearing he still bore her ill for standing in his way. "That story was a nonstarter, Ainsley. It wouldn't have served the public interest to rake up the past. It still doesn't."

"Maybe, maybe not. However, with this story today falling into my lap, I've already been told to name my price, and you know what I'm demanding as part of my salary? Unfiltered access to what happened at that facility near your old stomping ground. Very nasty business, McCarthy. I believe there's still damage being done there."

Corbett bent down to retrieve the pick-up wire. It took all of Samantha's restraint to hold back from kneeing him in the groin.

"When are you leaving, Corbett?"

Effortlessly, the man stood erect again; his cool attitude matched his smile. *He thinks he's winning.*

"Well, it's been nice seeing you, but I have to record a piece about the horses that were found slaughtered nearby." He turned his back on her, shouted to his camera operator to start the van, then turned his hateful stare on the woman who had nearly killed his career. "By the way, do you have a card? Or are you living nearby? When this is over, I need to call you. You have information about Wendlefield that the world wants to hear."

McCarthy leaned in close to the reporter, feeling his stance weaken as she breathed seductively in his ear. "Go fuck yourself." Leaning back, she saw a glimmer of indecision flash in his eyes and grinned. *He still only thinks with his smallest muscle. Some things never change.*

Gathering his composure, he turned away and strode towards the van, calling back cheerfully, "Always good to see an old friend, Sam." He waved once more to his admirers, receiving a ripple of applause as he climbed into the van and it moved off.

The crowd began to disperse, the rumour mill rumbling along nicely. Samantha would no doubt get some interesting phone calls later. Pity she wouldn't be at home to receive them: she'd arranged to meet up with Robert at the pub this evening. Their earlier conversation had come to a meaningless, abrupt halt, but his desperation to talk to someone about the fire was almost as strong as her desire to see her name in print again.

Following the villagers back down the hill, she spotted, out the corner of her eye, Alice Calster watching from her gate on the other side of the road, hanging on for what seemed dear life. Samantha slowed her steps, weighing up whether she should stop and talk to the woman. The way Alice looked, it might be the last chance. She was not even fifty yet—an age Sam had passed several cheap bottles of Scotch and even cheaper men ago. Poor Alice had been through so much hardship. First her husband's illness, then her daughter's wild and reckless life, and now her own battle with the same cancer that took the only man she had ever loved. It was no wonder she looked double her age, a near-skeletal figure.

But as Samantha was about to cross the road, Alice turned away and slowly shuffled back towards her cottage, her tattered slippers shuffling along, her feet barely lifting a quarter of an inch off the ground; the dust obligingly kicking up and leaving a trail behind her that reminded Samantha of the lingering, smouldering smoke that revealed nothing but ashes in the last moments of cremation. With that grim thought, Samantha continued on her way, although she was only a few houses further down the hill when, from the Bennetts' side gate, another person appeared. This time, it was someone she very much wanted to talk to, although it was safe to say he didn't want to talk to her. He looked crestfallen, his shoulders slumping beneath his epaulettes.

"Constable Mere, just the man! I have something important I wish to discuss with you. It's about the reporter you allowed to access your crime scene."

She'd raised her voice and glanced at the stragglers, dawdling with ears perked ready for the next instalment of the tale to unveil itself. Sam turned back to Constable Mere and grinned.

"Get in here," he muttered and quickly ushered her inside the dead man's house, shutting the door on the disappointed eavesdroppers.

Chapter Twenty-Seven

THE CAN SAILED majestically through the air and was caught by the rough hand of the seasoned veteran at the handlebars. The scene was a happy one, in many ways resembling a jamboree: the mid-afternoon fire burned brightly, and people shared jokes as music played loudly. It was a celebration, both of being alive and that the job they had been employed to do had been carried off with such timing and daring.

"Did you see that silver stallion rear up? I thought he was going to kick my head in. Big bastard, he was."

A mocking round of applause greeted the speaker as he went on at length to describe how he had calmed the beast before putting a bullet in its head and then, more gruesomely, chopped the head off in front of the other horses, making them lose their minds with grief.

"I still say we should have done the whole lot, doubled our pay."

"They give me the creeps!"

"What, horses? Lovely creatures! Used to ride them on the downs as a lad. I could have been a jockey, you know. I had the nerve for it."

"Shame you didn't have the flat stomach, lard arse."

Laughter broke out, the still air allowing it to reach the otherwise deaf ears of Martin Willis. A pawnbroker and credit sales manager by trade, he had fallen on hard times. Despite half the city sailing close to bankruptcy, he had found a way to turn their misery into profit for himself. People just didn't have the presence of mind to turn to their uncles anymore.

He surveyed the crew before him, all present other than Dale, who had scarpered before the end of the night's work. Martin had expected him to turn up at some point with his tail between his legs, but unlike the rest, he hadn't returned to their out-of-the-way camp. He would find his share of the money severely reduced for his action, even if Dale was the one who had introduced Martin to the client.

"I thought I made it very clear. We only needed to kill half. We wouldn't have made any more money for killing them all." Willis leaned back and kissed one of the two women in their midst with a near savagery, her squeal of delight belying her false pretence of being shocked.

"I would have done it for the sheer joy," Angus McGreely said, raising his can of beer in a toast. "I never knew that such gratification could be found."

"You're a sick bugger, you know that, Angus?"

McGreely rose to his full height and playfully made as if he wanted to fight the boss, prompting more laughter from the others.

"Settle down, settle down. Look, we've done our job. We didn't draw suspicion by making off as soon as the deed was done. No cameras picked up our movements near the field, and we've shown our faces in the village so that when the time comes, that's who they'll remember. A biker gang. Just hold on tight till the client gets here, then we can go home."

"How much per horse again?"

It was the other woman in the group who asked the question, Sally Dubuque, whose angelic voice was like a siren call to would-be investors. She'd brought hundreds of thousands of pounds into the firm, yet she was as comfortable plunging a knife into the back of anyone who took her fancy as she was sweet-talking people out of their money. Indeed, it was only Martin Willis's interpretation of an occasion a couple of years ago, when she had exercised her violent predilection, that had kept Sally out of prison.

He answered her question flatly, watching for any telltale sign that she was about to turn the beer can in her hand into a weapon the same way the small knife at the end of the bar, used only minutes before to slice lemons, found its way into the back of a man who had chosen to grope the wrong woman. As per Martin's witness statement, the man had tried to drag Sally to the toilets with the intent of raping her, and she had acted in self-defence. The murder charge was dropped, the man's reputation forever ruined: even in death, he was shunned by those who had known him.

Martin backed Sally then, as he would now. She brought money and clients to the firm; she also knew several very good suppliers of cocaine. It would be stupid to dismiss her, but all the same, he was wary of her. In an unguarded moment, he might even admit he was terrified of her.

"That is a lot of blow, my friend." Sally grinned, her blood-red lips curling, her nostrils unbalanced, the overall effect more akin to pain than joy.

"Tell you what, boss," Neil said, rising from his bike seat with a resounding creak, "I will be bloody glad to not have to wear this gear again. Leather is very constricting. My wife says I constantly smell of cow—she hasn't wanted to touch me in weeks."

"I don't know how to tell you this, Neil, but your wife doesn't like touching you because she can't stand you. She's convinced you have so many sexual diseases you'll rot her from the inside out."

The camp exploded in laughter again, and Neil raised his can in acceptance of being the butt of the latest gag.

"Do we all need to stay, boss?" asked the youngest member of the company. Adesh had only been with the firm for three years, arriving straight from the University of Liverpool, where he had excelled in business studies and paid his way by supply and demand with menaces. His sadistic streak had flourished under Martin's leadership: he trusted Adesh perhaps more than any person on his team.

"Split up, you mean? Don't you want to make sure you have your reward in your hand today?"

"I trust you, boss. Besides, if I don't see you in the office in the morning, I'll download a shit ton of porn to your computer, and I don't mean the good stuff."

Martin laughed heartily and slapped his thigh. The others around the fire weren't sure how to take Adesh's words. None of them, except for Sally, had worked closely with him, and they all saw him as a mere boy, an interloper. Angus reared, ready to challenge the lad, but took his lead from Sally: the look of dread deeply etched into the already pronounced lines was enough for the usually brazen Scotsman to believe that Martin's favourite could do something like that and not lose sleep over it.

"Sure, why not?" Martin agreed easily. "You know where to store the bike, right? Leave it with Jake, change into your everyday clothes, and I'll see you bright and early at Proven and Thatch with a hundred grand. The same goes for the rest of you. If you want to stay and meet our client, it's fine by me. If you want to follow Adesh and meet me in London in the morning, all good." He looked around at his colleagues and friends. The maxim of 'never trust anyone else with your money' didn't apply to this select group, and a hundred grand was, in better times, a drop in the ocean, but he wanted them to remain loyal to the company. He'd already heard whispers that Angus was thinking of jumping ship to make another go of it with his wife in Spain.

In the end, all decided to collect their earnings the following morning. They tied their equipment to their bikes and, one by one, headed out of the camp.

"Be safe, boss," Adesh said, fastening his helmet. "Don't forget, they don't like men like you in prison." His smile disappeared behind the darkened visor, and he leaned back in his seat and turned the key. The stolen Triumph was already in the distance before Martin could wish him well.

That left just one other person: the 'mystery' woman who had joined them over the last few weeks to wreak havoc in the nearby village.

"You can remove that cheap red wig now," he said.

She leaned in to kiss his neck. "Have they gone?"

"They have. How they didn't recognise you, I don't know."

"One of them did, yesterday. Don't worry. I took care of it."

Martin narrowed his eyes and pulled back from the woman's advances. "Dale?"

"I had no choice. He threatened to blow the whistle, said it was a conflict of interest—the client getting involved with the company on such an intimate level."

"He had a point."

"I know, darling, but needs must. I asked him to stay behind and help me lock up after the job was completed. I offered him an inducement."

"Which was?"

"A further fifty per cent on top of his share."

"And he accepted?"

She ran her hand over Martin's groin. "He did."

Martin swore. The woman fluttered her eyelashes and laughed carelessly.

"Is he dead?"

"Does it matter?"

"*Is he dead?*"

"Yes, he's dead. His bike is buried deep in the forest. I left his body with the sultan's horses. I'm afraid they won't find much. I saw him being dragged into a large anthill on the field. Three other people saw it too, although they assumed it was a friend of theirs."

"So he's dead?" Martin repeated.

"He is."

"Fucking good job, I would've put a gun to his head myself if I'd known what he was going to do."

Phillipa Downs tossed the red wig on the fire and turned to her lover, kissing him gently before peeling off his fake moustache.

"Let's put the fire out. We can leave your bike in my trailer and go back to the stables. The lads won't be there until later. I have your money, plus your own fee of course. How you share the rest with your...friends is up to you." Her eyes sparkled in the firelight, the orange flame igniting passion as she grabbed hold of his lapels and pulled him into a deep kiss, her hand straying inside his jacket and then downwards, cupping his genitals through the rough denim of his jeans.

Neither Phillipa Downs nor Martin Willis noticed that in the undergrowth around them, thousands of eyes watched, disinterested in this dangerous act of lust. Soon, their hunger would be sated.

Chapter Twenty-Eight

BELA LOOKED DOWN at the boy curled protectively on the concrete floor, his face distorted in pain and confusion. He took a few deep breaths and felt across his stomach as if reading Braille. Finally, he gathered the strength to climb back to his feet and glared at Bela.

"What the hell did you do that for? I only touched you on the shoulder!"

"Because you don't scare people like that. I have no idea who you are! You could have been anyone."

Bela waited for the words to sink in, watching for understanding to seep into the boy's mind about how, even if she hadn't admitted it, his actions had scared her. She expected at least a flicker of embarrassment or some other sign that he felt remorse for creeping up on her like that.

Instead, his sly grin returned, and Bela concluded that he was what her old school friends would have called a 'bad boy', the kind no girl in her right mind should get involved with yet somehow couldn't help being drawn to.

"My name's Jacob Betley. What happened to your face? It looks like someone put a hot iron on you."

Bela was used to the inquisitive stares, the well-meant suggestions of how she could cover the burns with make-up. The urge to smack them in the face and leave them nursing a welt they couldn't mask with foundation was one she'd often fought back, so much so she chose to hide her face rather than deal with other people's neurosis.

"Next, you'll be telling me that I'd be *so pretty* if I just slapped on a bit of make-up. Well, sod off. I didn't ask for your company or your conversation." She was surprised by how brave she sounded because she didn't feel it. Either way, it seemed to knock the boy's confidence for a moment, but he quickly reverted to type, leering at her with that dangerous air of dominance some boys couldn't help displaying, especially over girls they considered weaker or playing hard to get.

Bela had seen it all before, from the boys who'd come to school the morning after a party, bragging about their conquests to anyone who'd listen when in reality they'd been too shy to even contemplate what they'd claimed to have done. She wasn't intimidated in the slightest.

"What are you doing here?" she asked, as it had dawned on her the boy was as much a stranger to the village as she was. His accent didn't sound like her aunt's or the vicar's—there was a twang to it she didn't recognise—and he also hadn't picked up on her accent not being local to the area.

"I was looking for my friend. He was with our Scoutmaster, and I went to where we were camped last night, but the Scoutmaster's car's gone, so I figured I'd walk back to the village to see if I could find them." Betley brushed back his hair like he thought it made him seem cool to the girl he'd cornered behind the church.

Bela glanced over at the soldiers. They looked bored, tired and frustrated and were taking no notice whatsoever of her or the boy. She smiled, hoping to disarm him. "Where you from, Jacob Betley?"

"Perchester, near Oxford. What's the village like? Seems a drag to me!"

"Oh, you know," Bela shrugged, keeping one eye on her surroundings, hoping that someone would pass by and she could pretend to know them. "Quiet."

"What do you do for fun?"

"How old are you, Jacob?"

"Fifteen. You?"

"The same," she lied, moving off towards the stone wall nearest the road, where she turned as if she was going to sit on it so they could talk in comfort. Jacob Betley followed, his grin broad and conceited. If she'd been another girl, she thought, she would have either screamed for help or kissed him a couple of times to keep his attention. But she had survived her mother's insanity and the near-fatal fire that had burned down the family home. She'd borne the brunt of her father's descent into depression and held him together while he healed. Compared to all of that, a fifteen-year-old boy was no challenge.

For a minute, the two strangers sat next to each other, and then, without warning, Bela pushed him over the wall to the pavement below. The drop was no more than a couple of feet, but it caught the boy unawares.

"What the fuck did you do that for? I only wanted to talk to you, fucking crazy cow."

Smiling, Bela held up her hands, showing off her long nails, manicured to points. "Come near me again and I'll do some serious damage to *your* face. You might even lose an eye."

Jacob Betley struggled to his feet, feeling the back of his head and examining his hand for any sign of blood. Satisfied only his pride was injured, he turned on the girl he had wanted to get to know.

He was his father's son, a man to whom violence meant very little. He didn't care if he was the one receiving or doling out the beating, having given and taken a broken glass in the face on more than one occasion or even given someone a quick jab with a knife for the sheer hell of it. Such was the culture in many of the public houses in Perchester. Jacob's mother, on the other hand, was a woman for whom violence had become an expression of love—a means for her husband to correct her mistakes, make her behave—and the dysfunction of their relationship underpinned their weekend drinking sprees, with her egging him on to teach whoever his latest target was a lesson.

It was in this toxic atmosphere that Jacob Betley had learned that a tough man earned the respect of the town and the love of a woman. Unlike Kevin Sillatoe, whose family had neglected him out of despair and found him too wilful to deal with except by robbing him of his spirit instead of channelling it productively, Jacob Betley was rotten to the core, a psychopath who needed stopping before it was too late.

So it was that Betley lost his temper, and while Bela hadn't been afraid before, she knew the signs, had witnessed them firsthand in her mother. Curling her fingers, she formed fists as her father had shown her, letting the pain of her nails digging into her palms boost her adrenaline, Betley lunged at her and would have knocked her flying had it not been for the hand that grabbed his belt and hurled him backwards into the country lane. He rolled a couple of times before landing on his hands and knees, snarling like a rabid dog at his attacker.

The woman who had pulled him to the ground laughed sarcastically. "She warned you, boy."

"Leave me alone, bitch. We were only talking."

"Bitch, huh? That the best you've got?" She shrugged. "I've been called so much worse, but I might rip off your balls for the fun of it. Is that what you want? To know women are not defenceless? Because we could both beat the shit out of you."

She smiled sweetly at him, and Jacob scrambled to his feet, still in two minds whether to retaliate even as he backed away from her, not noticing the army vehicle coming up behind him. Thankfully, the soldier behind the wheel had excellent reflexes and brought the vehicle to an immediate stop, leaving Betley to feel the hot draught from the engine on his face. It was only when the soldier touched his arm that Betley opened his eyes.

"What the hell? You're lucky I was slowing down or you'd be roadkill right now."

It all proved too much for Betley, made a fool of by a girl, smashed into the ground by a bitch of a woman, and now he was staring into the face of a soldier with a gun at his side and a bad case of the vapours pouring off him. He managed to squirm free and shouted out to Bela as he ran, "Nice meeting you, darling. We'll meet again sometime."

"Fuck off!" the soldier, the woman and Bela shouted simultaneously and then laughed as the lad ran back up the hill faster than he'd run since being chased the length of the town's high street after stealing several albums from Woolworths.

"Are you okay?" the woman asked Bela once Betley was out of sight.

"Yeah, thanks." Bela smiled gratefully. Despite her scars being on full display, the woman was looking her in the eyes, which was more than could be said for the soldier. With an embarrassed nod, he backtracked to his vehicle.

"If you ladies are all right..."

"We are," they both confirmed and watched as he reversed slightly and steered the noisy, heavy vehicle around them, chucking a cloud of exhaust in their direction. The woman coughed and wafted the air to clear it.

"You're new here, aren't you?" she asked Bela, who nodded. "Thought so." She held out her hand. "I'm Sarah."

"Bela." She shook the offered hand. "Nice to meet you."

"You too, but fair warning. I've not got the greatest reputation around here." She glanced loathingly at the church. "Have you met the vicar yet?"

"That old fraud Tarky?" Bela nodded. "Unfortunately."

Sarah grinned. "I think I like you, Bela. Welcome to Downmere, or hell, as I call it."

Before (1966)

He read his letter of dismissal, and therefore removal from South Africa, once more. It was all very polite, dictated in terms that would lead an ordinary person to think he was making a fuss about nothing; he should feel fortunate to have had the chance to even study in the country.

He did not feel fortunate, however. He felt sick with contained rage that Prime Minister Hendrick Verwoerd, a man who openly admired Nazi Germany, had the audacity to write to him personally and inform him that neither he nor his views on the apartheid system were welcome. He had not just been dismissed; he had been silenced, made an example of.

"I hope someone assassinates you, you fascist," he hissed under his breath. The woman in the seat next to his gave him a filthy look. Another Afrikaner of Boer descent, no doubt, a flag-waving supporter of the regime.

He smiled, hiding his contempt behind an apologetic smile, no desire to add the tension of an argument before they landed in England.

"Rehearsing for a play, a Pinter," he explained, then, just because he could, added, "You know, that wonderful Jewish playwright?"

The woman sniffed, her jaw stiffening and the distance between them growing as she shuffled uncomfortably in her seat. She looked like she'd rather endure the rest of the flight tied to the wing than spend another minute sitting next to a Jew lover. Her discomfort was of no consequence, not when he'd watched his friend's brutal torture at the hands of a gang of white youths who, spurred on by taking Gicicio's life, had whipped his wife so hard she almost bled to death and was only saved by multiple transfusions and the dedication of the nurse who stayed with her in the hospital and kept her spirits up when all she'd wanted was to join her husband in the afterlife.

As the sole witness, it was his testimony alone that brought the six men to trial, but in one of the many miscarriages of the corrupt justice system, all but one of the six walked free, claiming they had tried to break up the 'fight'. As each had left the courtroom, they'd looked him in the eye, their grins promising retribution, not from fists or a shotgun, but from high above.

He had always prided himself on being far-sighted. His time in South Africa had, he thought, enhanced the sense of balanced caution he had come to rely on, but his swift removal—informed on Wednesday, on a plane by Saturday—had caught him by surprise. He'd hope to have at least a month to get his affairs in order and arrange a secure means of transporting his specimens back to England. Instead, all he had with him were the clothes he sat in and the manuscript for his latest book, which would at least solve his immediate financial problems in the event Rachel and her family were unable to access his bank account.

The pilot's voice broke into his thoughts, informing him that they were about to descend into London, the weather was good and, adding a spark of personality to the conclusion of an otherwise uneventful journey, wishing the British passengers the best of luck for the afternoon's Cup Final at Wembley. He'd be cheering them on.

The man, who had never been interested in sport, grunted and muttered, "It's the English, you fool. The British don't care."

The woman next to him shot another glare of disdain his way, and this time, he returned it with a thunderous look, adding a small snarl for good measure. It had the desired effect, and the woman turned away, her expression of disgust reflected in the window as she counted down the minutes until she could be rid of the uncouth creature beside her.

Fastening his safety belt, he settled back in his seat and closed his eyes, reflecting on the past few years. If he were objective about it, his time studying the African variant of the ant still gave him a sense of immense satisfaction. He had ploughed into his work like never before, dedicating himself to the pursuit of knowledge. He'd secured funds from several universities that, in return, would benefit greatly from the body of work he and his two assistants produced. Only once had he needed to step back from the project when a fever laid him out for two months. He had convalesced in the small village where Gicicio's relations clung grimly to the old ways and where he had met the only woman he had ever fallen in love with.

Throughout his recovery, through the sheer agony and insanity that the fever brought out, the night terrors and horrifying hallucinations, she had remained by his side, although it was some time before he was well enough to understand that the touch of her hand was not the product of a nurse's duty but of tenderness. Alas, a queen could not be pursued by a lowly drone, a worker who must build bridges so others might follow, and it was with regret deep in his heart that he told her after their one night spent together that he was leaving and would not return, for the others would never accept him as her equal. That one night spent in another's arms, knowing that person would not be taken from him by the evil that had taken his parents, spurred him ever onward, and soon he had more than made up for lost time, finishing the project three months earlier than planned.

The plane landed safely and came to a stop, and he put aside the thoughts that hung over him like a threatening rain cloud. He rose from his seat to retrieve his manuscript from the overhead locker. The woman, whose sneer had betrayed her political nature and to whom patience meant little, pushed past forcefully, almost toppling him into the laps of a sleepy child and her mother. He took off his hat and apologised to the mother, who brushed off his regrets with an affable smile; no harm intended, no foul given. He was thankful for that. After all he had been through in the last few weeks, a stand-up fight on a plane would not go down well with any of the institutions he represented. He had known others to be reprimanded and sidelined for less.

***

In the short time he'd been away, London had changed a great deal. Young women expressed themselves in a more outwardly secure fashion, and there was a feeling of confidence and anticipation in the air, which he doubted had much to do with the upcoming football match. Standing on the concourse at Waterloo station, he noticed also that the men had the strangest haircuts. Gone were the bowler hats commonly worn before he'd left the country, taking with them the stuffy attitudes that had defined his youth. He couldn't quite put his finger on it, but everyone was marching to a different beat, perhaps that of the new queen, her pheromones pushing out the once-smoggy air of the capital so that this new colony could thrive to do her bidding.

Late stragglers rushed past, somehow avoiding him as they ran up the stairs leading to the Tube to Wembley, their rosettes and scarves declaring their allegiance, their chants battle cries from a generation that had not seen war. Perhaps he should study them, this new tribe whose passion for a game of football could so easily drag Britain into a different kind of conflict. One young boy kicked out as he raced past, cheered on by his father. "Get a move on or we'll miss the kick-off."

There goes a leader in waiting, he thought with tiredness and despair as the two merged into the crowd and disappeared with the surge that left the platform suddenly empty, clear of all but a few passengers waiting for a train that would take them away from the capital for the day. He couldn't blame them for wanting to avoid the hordes who would later party in the streets in victory or, in defeat, plot the next turf war. He had seen how ants enacted their own version of the aggressive pursuit of territory—the decapitated heads, the senseless, colony-destroying rage—and had hoped to find a way to eradicate that part of their genetic make-up, to bring if not harmony then at least an understanding of how much greater their society could be if they worked together.

With more time and resources, he foresaw a day when the garden variety ant found in the South of England worked alongside the ants of the Americas and Asia and the marabunta of South Africa, and how joyous a day that would be. Never mind the accolades; it would be a fitting end to his career, one he would dedicate to those who had fallen, died or been incarcerated in jail in South Africa. He had never met any of those men or women, but he felt for them all the same and spent a moment in silent prayer as his train arrived and he boarded, finally on his way home.

Home. He had not thought of it that way for a long time. He hoped the house had been looked after. He leaned back against the carriage seat and sighed, realising with some surprise that it was of contentment. The letter, the rushed deportation, the unspoken permanent banishment, were all in the past, and he began looking to the future. Should his equipment and specimens arrive safely by boat, he would find a way to make the ants work together across the species and build them a home, a magnificent nest and laboratory combined.

For the first time since he had been served notice to leave, he saw a new road open for him. He only wished Rachael and Gicicio could be there to see it.

Unbeknown to the man, a telegram was en route to his home, stating that all had been taken care of, and the live specimens were on their way.

Chapter Twenty-Nine

A s THE CAR turned right off Southampton Road and into the New Forest, Giuseppe Demarco reminded Millicent for the fourth time that she should think about slowing down. He understood her desperation to get back to the camp and make sure Harry Collins and Kevin Sillatoe were okay; the quicker they arrived, the sooner they could organise a search party for Jacob Betley. However, it wasn't worth the very real possibility of crashing into a vehicle or careering headlong into a wall.

Millicent had been right about the welcoming committee impatiently awaiting them at the Scout hut, most of whom were so relieved to see their children, they immediately took off, not wishing to further antagonise Mr. and Mrs. Betley and the crowd they'd rounded up. There was something of a lynch mob mentality about them, to the extent that Millicent, who had never backed down from a fight in her life, wondered if it was too late to turn tail and run back to America with Fleur, leaving the Betleys to take it up with Harry when he returned.

She hadn't backed down, though, and to her surprise, Giuseppe DeMarco had stepped in front of the human tsunami of hate, giving the single greatest speech she had ever heard. The mixture of broken English and a booming, heavy Italian accent threw Jacob's parents off-kilter. Fully prepared as they had been to verbally assault Millicent, the Betleys both flinched in the face of Giuseppe's forceful will delivered with empiric blood in his veins. Then Jacob's father muttered *dirty wop* under his breath, and Millicent braced for the inevitable fist fight.

Instead, Giuseppe smiled broadly at the man, his bushy moustache curling up at the ends, his bronzed face catching the sun and giving him the appearance of a Mediterranean god, and suddenly Millicent understood why some of the mothers spoke in hushed tones about the man. Not that such a figure appealed to her—she preferred her partners to be less hairy—but she could see how his earnest vigour would appeal to others as he shrugged his broad, athletic shoulders and addressed the crowd as a whole, his attitude remaining calm and reasonable even though his nostrils flared wildly.

It was those same flaring nostrils that greeted her as they came to the crossroads that split the village from the rest of the world. She smiled demurely and handed over her walkie-talkie, suggesting he try to alert Harry.

For the next five minutes, Giuseppe attempted to hail the Scoutmaster, swearing in Italian at the lack of response. He kept on trying right until the moment they entered the campsite and saw only one car, Millicent's, on the gravel near where the tents had stood that morning. The trestle table and cooking equipment were stacked in the back of Millicent's car. The site was as pristine as they had found it the previous day, and there was no sign of Harry or Kevin. Chillingly for Millicent, there was also no sign of Jacob Betley, and his father's final warning, issued with fist raised, echoed in her mind. *Knowing my son, you won't find him. He'll take the opportunity to leave. If that's the case, be prepared for you and me to discuss it when you come back.*

"I wouldn't blame him if he did."

"Sorry, Millicent, what did you say?"

"I was thinking out loud."

***

Harry Collins and Kevin Sillatoe had driven out to where Phillipa Downs had taken them the night before. Harry wasn't sure why, but something had niggled at him all the while they were packing up their equipment. He'd found Kevin to be a good worker away from the others, and they'd finished far sooner than Harry had estimated. He shook the boy's hand and congratulated him on a job well done—all without breathing through his nose. The poor lad still stank of horse manure.

"It'll be another hour at least before Miss Maples returns. Do you want to go to the village or…"

"Or what, Sir?"

"Well, I'd like to go and have another look at the field and the stables where Mr. Piccolo was last seen or at least ask Ms. Downs if she has further news."

Kevin thought about it for a moment or two, seemingly mulling over the options before agreeing that going to the stables was a better idea.

As they drove the short distance to Ms. Downs' property, Harry turned his mind to Millicent—how she was getting on, if she had reached Perchester yet—and accepted reluctantly that she was right. He could not afford to be out of contact like this. As soon as they were back home, he'd do something about that, with Millicent's guidance, of course. Harry didn't know the first thing about mobile telephones.

They arrived at the place where Ms. Downs had kept the horses, and Harry looked at the scene before him in disbelief. A quick glance at Kevin told him the boy was in the same state.

Outside the large metal gate, three horses stood as if they were waiting to be allowed into the theatre, their bodies rigid, only the occasional swish of a well-groomed tail betraying that they were anything other than statues. Two more horses stood a little further up the road. Harry was certain Ms. Downs had taken them all back to the main stable near Cadnam, and yet here in front of him were the same horses that had been removed the night before.

The gate opened, and several young men emerged, some bickering, all of them looking pasty. One stopped and promptly relieved himself of his breakfast. Harry looked away, affording him some privacy. Kevin, though, couldn't take his eyes off him.

"Stay here," Harry ordered.

Kevin nodded vacantly, still watching the man, who took a few breaths, straightened and then doubled over again, bowing to the gods of vomit.

What Harry was going to say or do, he hadn't quite figured out, but his gut was telling him that something was dreadfully amiss. As he called out to the men with a measure of anxiety building in him, it occurred to him that he should have waited for someone else to drive down the road and back him up or pass on a message to the authorities should the situation turn nasty.

Thus, it was with some relief that he heard a van approach slowly before it came to a stop a few feet from his car. From the van bounded a man in a tight-fitting, expensive-looking suit, and not far behind him was a younger woman, her eyebrows raised in surprise, suggesting she hadn't expected anybody to be around.

"Well, what do we have here then?" The man's tone was arrogant and commanding, like Harry and the stable hands were new recruits on a parade ground.

Harry broke ranks first, taking the initiative to both introduce and distance himself from the others.

"Hello, my name's Harry Collins. I'm a Scoutmaster from Perchester in Oxfordshire. I was here last night with the owner, looking for my colleague, who we believed might have fallen down the embankment and into the field. It was us who reported the massacre of the horses."

The man looked at him strangely, holding his gaze as he gestured to the young woman, who immediately went to the back of the van and started to pull out equipment.

"Sorry, was it something I said?" Harry enquired. As if the man's demeanour wasn't alarming enough, a couple of the stable hands mounted horses and rode off at speed. "Hey, wait!" Harry shouted after them.

"Let them go, Mr. Collins," the man advised smoothly. "I have them committed to memory. They won't evade me. However…" He turned his attention to the remaining young men. "You three are going to stay. My camera operator has you on film, so if you want to avoid prison, you'll find it in your best interests to show me exactly what is going on."

The man returned his attention to Harry and thrust out his hand. "Harry Collins from Perchester, you said? Well, isn't that a fortuitous turn of events! By any chance are you a long-term resident of the town?"

Harry didn't understand what was going on but answered, nonetheless. "Born and bred, Mr… I'm sorry, I don't know who you are. Some kind of reporter, I presume?"

"My name is Ainsley Corbett, and the fine lady behind the camera is my assistant, Christine Balker. By any chance have you heard of a former newspaper reporter and editor from your charming part of the world, a lady by the name of Samantha McCarthy?"

It took a moment for Harry to place the name, to think back a decade, but eventually, it came to him, and he smiled in recognition. "Yes, indeed. I've more than heard of her. I knew her. I was a lot younger then, mind you."

"Weren't we all, my friend? Did you know her well?"

"Not really. I used to do a paper round, mainly on the estate that was built in the sixties. I remember seeing her around a fair bit. Pleasant woman, bit grumpy at times. Why do you ask?"

"My dear chap, let's see together what these rascals are hiding from us, and then we can have a nice, long chat. Might be something in it for you—if your memory serves you well."

The journalist looked over at the stable hands and smiled disarmingly. "Come on then, let's not be shy. Show me what it is that has you three in such a tizzy and why those other two couldn't wait to get away from here."

As Harry moved to follow the men inside the gated field, Kevin shouted over to him.

"Sir, Miss Maples is on the walkie-talkie. She wants to know where we are."

"Excuse me for a moment." Harry walked back to his young companion and heard Millicent's voice crackle down the line, the dip in the road acting as a barrier. "Thank you, Kevin." He took the walkie-talkie from him. "Hello, Millicent?"

"Harry, thank God! Where are you? We've been trying to get hold of you for ages."

"You must have just missed me. I didn't expect you to be back so soon. We, that is to say, Kevin and I, are at the place I described to you last night. Something very odd is going on."

"You're not kidding," Millicent replied. "Jacob Betley is missing. The police stopped us in Downmere, and he jumped out without me noticing. He's still in the area."

Kevin swore under his breath.

Harry looked at the young lad but said nothing. He didn't need to. Both of them knew Betley was coming for Sillatoe, his former friend turned enemy.

Chapter Thirty

THE AIR WAS deathly quiet, the only sounds in Wess's ears that of his heart beating faster with creeping anxiety and the electronic beep of a console accepting the coded password that Trelaryn tapped in. At one time, he'd considered paying his way out, but he only had four years left, so he'd decided to see it through. The army paid for his counselling and until now had kept him safe. Now they were asking him to put his life on the line in these tunnels a second time.

Captain Trelaryn had ordered Smallwood to stand guard outside, to keep a sharp eye down the tunnel for any sign of intruders. He had no need to explain his decision to the men, who all knew that it was in this particular bunker Cauls' body had been found. However, only the commanding officer at the time and Wess had seen the aftermath, and from that point, the place had been decommissioned and sealed without further investigation, as if someone higher up the command chain had decided that whatever was down in the depths of the Earth was impossible to beat.

The door clicked open, the automated mechanism not yet having given up the ghost. *Shame the same can't be said for the lights*, thought Wess.

The sealed air that rushed out was nasty, an intense smell like rotten eggs or meat left to decompose in the sun. All four men vocalised their disgust and clamped their hands over their mouths to block the stench of the sick and dying. Wess had imagined the smell before, but nothing could have prepared him for the full hit of it, which brought tears to his eyes and seemed to burn into every pore, feeding the overflow of emotions he was already dealing with.

Back at the barracks, the captain had urged him to sit and tell his story once more. Wess had politely refused the offer of the chair, wanting to appear alert when in truth he was making sure he was able to leave without knocking over the chair or the captain's desk, should reliving what he had only revealed to his previous officer and the recommended therapist prove too much.

The nightmares had been bad, but he'd come through them and thought he was doing okay until one night when was on leave and two of his army buddies found him in a beer cellar, passed out and surrounded by empty Scotch bottles. That was the real trauma—how far he'd fallen while still holding himself together. He'd got through each day's work, gone on manoeuvres, had a laugh in the mess, but the laughter had been too loud, too forced, and he'd trained too hard, pushing himself beyond the level of fitness he'd had when he first signed up. That was how he'd 'held it together', by always being the first to volunteer for assignments and the last to leave the mess.

In the end, with help, he had found a way forward that wasn't a form of slow suicide. He'd set his own goals and been honest about his state of mind. However, being true to himself had come at the cost of getting on the wrong side of Sergeant Dixon, and Wess would admit, if pushed, that at times he deliberately rubbed the sergeant up the wrong way, but he wasn't alone. Most of the company couldn't abide the man, who was inflexible, coarse, bullying. Indeed, the only reason most didn't openly defy him was because he was so volatile. If Wess had sailed close to the wind by turning up on parade drunk, then Dixon was a nuclear warhead primed and ready to be dropped from a height that would leave all in its path wasted.

There hadn't been a great deal that he could tell the captain. The moments before it happened had been filled with the unassuming boredom of cleaning down equipment, testing and re-testing it. It had been a normal day until they were ordered to make their way to the lower level, the bunker itself. Even then, Wess and Cauls had expected it to be a routine, easy job: take inventory, make sure the wireless system was functional and check the call facility between the upper and lower chamber.

All had gone like clockwork. A job that would normally take two hours was completed in half that time, and it was only when they were on their way out that they realised they'd forgotten to test the call line. They spent a couple of minutes arguing over who was going to have to trudge back down to the bunker level. Wess offered Cauls four pints in exchange; Cauls tried to up the ante and promised to introduce Wess to a young woman he'd met the week before in Avoncross. It came down to a coin toss, which Wess had won, and while he listened at the door that led to the stairs, Caul's heavy footsteps accompanied by the occasional bad-tempered exclamation or sarcastic call out from an ever-faint voice, he was sure he had got one over on his pal.

They ran through the test, and for the first ten minutes, all was well, then for no explicable reason, the communication system between the two blocks failed. All Wess could hear was static, a piercing clicking that hurt his ears, and then the line went dead, all the buttons and switches becoming unresponsive. He opened the door and hollered.

"If I have got to come down these bloody stairs, Cauls, you can forget the four pints, *and* you have to introduce me to your sister as well as that girl from the Butt Of Ale."

Silence, except for the static.

"Cauls, what the fuck are you doing down there?"

Still no answer, only the sound of the static. Was it getting louder?

"Cauls? Come on, man! Talk to me!"

Running footsteps, probably sixty feet down, and the static.

Wess looked across at the machine controlling the call. The volume dial hadn't moved, yet as he stood in the doorway, the static grew noticeably louder. It was only then that he heard Cauls' scream from below and realised just how loud the static had become for it to have drowned out his friend's voice.

Latching the door open, Wess looked over the single rail that was in place to stop anyone from falling headlong into the stairwell that led to the bunker room. Seeing nothing but darkness, he took out his torch and pointed it down the concrete flight of stairs. If not for the sound of static, he would have been sure he was looking into the heart of a void. Then, in the pitch-blackness, he spotted a blemish of khaki.

"Cauls, is that you? Why can't I see you?"

He could hear him, though. Fast footsteps pelting up the stairs, heavy breaths rendering Cauls incapable of answering his colleague, then a thud and a yelp of pain.

Wess stared into the void and blinked. His eyes were playing tricks on him or else the black hole within this underground shelter was shifting, spiralling upwards. Shining the torch's beam on the walls below him, he saw a mass of black like a rippling cloak, the devil's coattails caught in a tornado, sweeping ever higher to challenge the word of man and any god foolish enough to stand in its way.

Human movement again.

"Keep the door open! I'm nearly th—" Cauls' words were cut short by another painful scream. "Help me, Wess! They're ripping me to shreds."

By the sound of his voice, Wess estimated Cauls was only one flight down, but the crescendo of noise made him hesitate, and this time, when he pointed the torch at it, the devil himself appeared before him, all teeth and legs, a writing mass of death rushing up to meet him. Something small dropped onto his head, another onto his arm and bit down. He slapped at it, squashing it against his palm, and brushed it off.

"Wess, help me, you bastard..." Cauls' voice called out in desperation before it was once more lost in the scream of static.

Wess couldn't take it any longer. It was as if the dead had risen and were scratching their way up the walls. He slammed the door and he ran, as he had from the underground military hospital, this time leaving behind not a bemused, concerned father but a friend whose last audible words to him were an accusation of cowardice.

Wess reached the sealed door that led to the underground tunnel and took a fateful look back. If he hadn't, then whatever it was that had climbed up the walls and stairs, whatever had eaten Cauls alive, would have soon found plenty of other readymade meals to devour. He saw the outline of Cauls emerge at the bunker stairs doorway, by this point more shadow than man, only one eye visible, staring at Wess in dread and fear, reminding him that Cauls was still, inside, a man.

That vision made Wess' instincts kick in, and he sealed the room off from the outside and press the decontaminate button, watching through the glass as his friend turned to muscle and tattered uniform, skin and skeleton. The mass moved, some of it caught in the vent, the rest evaporating, disappearing as quickly as it had come. Only then, as the body fell to pieces on the other side of the door, did Wess scream for his commanding officer, who had immediately evacuated the building.

Had it not been for his commanding officer placing a Section D notice on the information, Wess would have been forced to endure a military court procedure to investigate Cauls' disappearance.

One other team had ventured inside since then, and there was nothing out of place, no reason for the death of a soldier. Nobody had noticed the insignificant crack in the wall, the tiniest of holes which had been bored out. Nobody noticed because that was not what they were looking for. It had been classed as a horrific accident and the file quietly closed.

"Come on, Wess, time to walk me through what you saw here," the captain ordered with equal parts kindness and urgency. Wess stepped into the room, and instinct once again took control.

Chapter Thirty-One

A s Reverend Tarky was arranging for the Sunday church service to be held in the local village hall, Belinda Bennett was being sedated once more by the doctor, and Robert Romsleigh was wondering where his daughter could have got to, Ainsley Corbett and Christine Balker were being shown exactly what had happened to the owner of the Cadnam stud farm and a second person of unknown identity.

Witnessing the two half-eaten human beings was hard to stomach. Most of the skin had been ripped away, leaving only muscle and sinew behind, as if whatever had enacted the savagery had been disturbed and scuttled off to wait nearby until it was safe to return and finish its meal.

Phillipa Downs was at least identifiable by her face, which had remained almost untouched, a few bites at the lips and ears visible in the semi-darkness of the stable block. The identity of her associate, though, was a mystery; even the stable hands couldn't guess who it was, beyond the male anatomy, as his face had been masticated down to the bone.

"There's no ID in his coat pocket, I've already checked," the young lad who had been throwing up on the grass verge whispered hoarsely from the stable door.

"Okay. Thanks," Christine Balker acknowledged, understanding the stable hand's refusal to come any closer. She'd seen many things over the years, but nothing quite as disturbing as this. Even so, she kept her camera rolling, zooming in on the scene as dictated by Corbett's narration, the lens lingering on the face of the dead woman before pulling back to reveal the position the bodies were in, the act of love in this case a killer. What they were recording would never make it on air. The commissioning bodies would not allow such gruesome footage to be shown on British TV, but there was always a lucrative market for the snuff film.

"Fair to say they were caught by surprise," Christine observed as she set the camera back on its tripod.

"What makes you say that?" Ainsley took a pencil out of his jacket pocket, which he used to poke at the man's remains.

"Wouldn't they have put up a fight, or... I don't know, thrashed around a bit? They wouldn't still be in that position, would they? She—what did you call her? Phillipa Downs? She'd have seen whatever was devouring his face and thrown him off. It must've been over in seconds."

Ainsley Corbett prided himself on being a man of the world. He had snorted cocaine off a twenty-five-year-old's flat stomach when he was in Bolivia. He had shaken the hand of a brutal African dictator and then poured him tea. He had even stripped naked and run around the Eiffel Tower one winter's evening on the strength of a bet with a man from Afghanistan; the reward: information on how Britain was being flooded with impure heroin, part of a story that would have seen him become one of the most sought-after journalists in the world. Yet the unsettling way his camera operator had described the pair's quick death turned his stomach, and he felt it growl in protest and warning.

"You really should write necrotic erotica, Chrissie. You'd make a fortune."

Christine didn't know whether to be insulted or amused but found it easier to shrug as if she didn't care. Better that than give him any reason to think they were friends.

Ainsley's pencil hovered above the woman's ear. Christine and the two closest former employees of Phillipa Downs watched. He raised one finger to his tightly closed lips to signal for them to stay quiet. The young man who had been sick took a step backwards until he was completely outside the stables.

"Don't make a sound, any of you." Ainsley kept his eyes firmly on the dead woman's ear as he spoke. "Chrissie, pass me a camera film holder—the bigger one of the two you keep in your pocket."

Christine slid her hand into her pocket and pulled out the black plastic holder as requested, then took three careful paces over to Corbett. He took the container from her but held it within her reach.

"When I nod my head, put the lid on, snap it shut and then all of you, remove yourself from here. Don't run. Just walk back towards the gate."

"What about my camera?" Christine asked. "Am I supposed to leave it here?"

He didn't reply, for once refusing to tell the woman he considered his assistant how to do her job. Ainsley Corbett was a user, a cad, sexist to the point of embarrassment. Women either loved his bad-boy exterior or they loathed him and wanted to punish him for the way he treated them, but Christine had always known one thing about the man she had filmed and documented since he came to work for the station. He was fearless. Never once had he shown an ounce of apprehension, yet she thought she saw the pencil shake, his gloved fingers tremble as he moved the point closer to the woman's ear.

There was a movement so slight Christine thought she might have imagined it until something small and black grabbed hold of the end of the pencil. She was so focused on it that she barely caught herself in time when the sound of running outside startled her. The poor stable hand's nerves had finally shattered, and he was off like the wind.

He would be found later that night by police, slumped over a beer-stained bar in another part of the New Forest, babbling incoherently about devils that come out of ears.

Ainsley had not timed putting the creature inside the tube correctly, and now it was using its pincers to attack his glove. Despite his lack of nodded signal, Christine's instinct took over. Spying a metal bucket, she grabbed it and brought it down on Ainsley's hand, causing the creature to loosen its grip on the glove, which seemed already to be fraying. The creature fell to the floor, and as quick as she had ever moved, Christine put the upturned bucket over it. Helping Ainsley to his feet and urging the other two men to depart, she managed to get all four of them outside and away from the building. There was no sign of them being followed, nothing to add to the sheer terror she had felt when she'd caught a glimpse of the insect Ainsley had coaxed out of the dead woman's ear.

The two other men took the near traumatised Ainsley's weight and led him out onto the verge while Christine made her way slowly, steadily back to the building. A small pile of dust and dirt picked up by the wind immediately made her stop, and for a moment she was frozen to the spot, questioning her sight and her sanity. The dust settled and she moved off again. The distance between the gate and the stable was not that great, yet to Christine right then, it might as well have been a mile.

***

While Christine Balker slowly edged towards the stable, Ainsley tried to focus on the story rather than the creature that had been so close to taking a chunk out of his finger. He'd already heard the lurid tale of Phillipa Downs' deal. She'd grasped the chance to make some easy money via fraud and deception, which in itself would have made a great story for the news, although one that wasn't unheard of in the equine business. None of the hands had been told who had actually carried out the slaughter of the horses; all they knew was that the survivors had been hidden away and would later be sold at private auction. The ones that had been hacked to death, and possibly eaten by a multitude of the same creatures that had attacked Downs and her lover, had been expendable, part of a scheme to claim on the insurance.

Ainsley had made the point that surely any investigator would have known that the dead animals, no matter how badly mutilated, were not the same ones as had been placed in Phillipa Downs' care. The answer was clean and callously simple. Petrol and fire, after all, leave an incredible mess to decipher, even for the skilled animal sleuth.

***

Three times Christine had to halt her progress. She had seen only fleetingly what she had managed to capture underneath the bucket, but after witnessing firsthand what it was capable of, she had no desire to end up on its menu. Each step was taken delicately as if crossing a minefield, lest she disturb the ground and give the creatures a signal to home in on.

Finally, she reached the stable door. Even at a distance, she could hear the angry scrambling of the creature trying to escape its metal prison. Christine took one last look around for any sense of movement. The light on the camera flashed steadily. It had finished rolling and looked as though it had recorded everything since she and Corbett had wrestled the creature.

The sound underneath the bucket stopped, became a deathly silence. At least, Christine hoped it had died, but she doubted it. More likely, the creature had caught her scent and was now in a hushed frenzy, waiting out the seconds until the bucket was lifted and it could escape and eat.

That was enough for Christine Balker. She turned on her heels and ran, not caring this time about stealth. If she had to, she would run all the way to the studio offices in Southampton. She would not stop, would not falter, as long as she never had to come face-to-face with that creature again.

She needn't have worried. Aside from the one ant underneath the bucket, the swarm had moved on, and the stable was, perhaps, the safest place to be at that moment.

Chapter Thirty-Two

SARAH CALSTER AND Bela Romsleigh watched the four soldiers greet each other with high-fives and share a joke before exchanging information, which seemed to be extraordinarily brief, on what their captain had ordered was to happen next.

Bela supposed they had forgotten that she and Sarah were there—why else would they have walked away and left the church unguarded?—but as the woman who had helped her see off Betley's unwanted advances took her hand firmly and whispered, "Run," she found she had little time to be concerned about why four highly trained soldiers had neglected a basic part of their duty.

Before the soldiers had even reached their vehicle, Sarah and Bela had made it across what remained of the grass verge and to the side of the church where the concrete path held back the pit that had swallowed the graves of generations of the local dead, in some cases leaving their skulls staring out of empty eyes at the sky above.

Hidden in the church's shadow, Bela looked down into the yawning crevice that stretched all the way to the thin border of wire and uneven brick separating the church from the farm next to it. Something caught her eye as she looked in the distance, the awkward movement of a wounded animal whose gait suggested it was walking on three legs, which proved to be the case: as it came closer, the tattered joint of its missing limb oozed dark blood that dripped slowly to the ground.

"You can't go in there!" a distinctly masculine voice boomed, shattering the stillness of the graveyard and pulling Bela away from the grotesque figure that had captured her attention. Panicked, she moved to put her hands in the air and submit to a military rollicking, but Sarah held her back with an arm across her chest before she could step out of the shadows.

"He's not talking to us," Sarah whispered, nodding for Bela to take a look for herself.

Bela risked poking her head out quickly and saw that the soldier who had barked the order was addressing Tarky.

She leaned back again, pressing herself against the brickwork until she felt she was being consumed by the building and craned her neck to better hear what was being said.

"I'm sure if you ring your commanding officer, you will find there's no problem with me collecting the hymn books for tomorrow's service. I only require a little time to collect a few things—books, some personal notes—you understand?"

"Sir, my orders are to keep everyone out until the area is deemed safe. Surveyors and workmen are coming on Monday. By next week, the week after at the latest, you'll be permitted to re-enter the church."

"Are you a God-fearing man, soldier? Are you a Christian? My flock, this village, expects to be able to hear the word of the Saviour, to celebrate the love of God. You would deny them that comfort?"

"Sir, I understand what you're saying, but unless my commanding officer tells me different, you're not entering the church."

It was at that point Tarky exploded in rage, and his voice took on a strange and disturbing quality that Bela had never heard from a man in his position. There was real hatred as he lambasted the soldier, as if the man was the devil incarnate rather than just following orders.

"There is a great evil here, a presence we need to cleanse from the village before its spirit infects us all."

Sarah dug Bela in the ribs, making her jolt, but it got her attention. She whispered in Bela's ear, "That's me he's talking about. Nice to have a reputation that precedes you." She turned her face away before Bela could ask what she meant, although judging by the dimple in her cheek courtesy of her broad smile, Sarah revelled in the infamy being painted on her soul. Meanwhile, Tarky was still harping on at the soldier.

"I need to administer relief to my parish, to keep the devil herself from being accepted once more. So I'm going into my church, and no instrument of war will stop me."

Sarah poked Bela again and tilted her head to speak. "Got to love Tarky, the way he loses his temper and becomes the most frightening person alive. He spanked me once, you know, when I was a little girl. Pulled my dress up and slapped my backside I don't know how many times. I couldn't feel it when he was done, and nobody stopped him. They all said I deserved it for running around the gravestones." Sarah pointed down at the smashed granite and marble sparkling in the sunlight.

Bela couldn't believe what she was hearing. It seemed outrageous to her that a vicar, of all people, could do such a thing, but then she thought about her mother and the way she had gaslighted her and Stuart. At first, their mother had been reasonable, admittedly struggling with her mental health as her marriage broke down, but over time, they had become hostages, and the way she'd snapped, that scarily calm voice she'd used with the police officers who'd come to check they were safe... then the petrol and the fire...

Bela realised Sarah was staring at her intently, her head cocked to one side as if she was questioning where Bela had gone.

"I'm sorry," she whispered. "Things on my mind. The vicar reminded me of something…of someone I used to know."

"It's okay, but you missed the good bit. The soldier picked Tarky up and pretty much chucked him into the middle of the road." Sarah covered her mouth, stifling her giggles.

Bela peeked out but could no longer see the vicar, but she could hear him ranting at the injustice of it all and imagined his fist clenched, raised to the heavens.

"The wrath of God knows only his servant's fury."

"Eh?"

Bela considered what she had uttered without conscious thought. "The wrath of God knows only his servant's fury. It's what my mother screamed at the police just before she set the house on fire." Bela tugged back her hood so her face was fully on display. It was the first time she'd deliberately shown someone since she was released from the hospital.

Sarah gave a low whistle. "I noticed the scars before, but I'd never have guessed what you've been through. I'm so sorry. You expect your mum to love and protect you, and…that's just… I'm sorry that happened to you."

"Thanks." Bela smiled self-consciously but appreciated Sarah's kindness. It was rarely the response she received from relative strangers and absolutely not the actions of the evil presence Tarky was rallying against. In fact, in the short time they'd known each other, Bela could think of nothing about Sarah that matched Tarky's version.

"Listen," Sarah said, "I came down here for a reason. Do you want to help me? It's fine if you don't, just go now. I'll cover you."

"No, I'll stay," Bela said, at which Sarah signalled for her to keep quiet as she grabbed her hand again and walked briskly along the side of the church, ducking behind the colourfully blooming bushes and into the greenhouse.

"We must be quick. The soldiers will do a sweep of the area soon. I've been watching them since early this morning. I mean, what girl doesn't love a man in uniform, right? But it doesn't mean I want to be arrested by one." She pressed on the side of the greenhouse, and a false door gave way, opening with a deathly silence that added a measure of gothic horror to the whole experience.

Bela brushed past the exotic plants, all bearing white labels with enticing names in delicate, handwritten lettering, and followed her new friend through the secret doorway, pausing while Sarah pulled the door shut and latched it, leaving them in near-darkness.

"We can't turn on the light—it'll be seen from the outside— but I know exactly where we're going. Just hold on to my belt and tread carefully. Don't think about touching my arse either." Sarah laughed and added, "I'm kidding, by the way."

Bela laughed too, but Sarah's comment had triggered an uncomfortable memory. One of her former friends had come out as a lesbian, and the other girls had frozen her out of their group. To her shame, Bela had joined in with their name-calling, if only because for a while it meant they were leaving her alone. But she hadn't been at school the day the girls pushed Yvonne down the stairs and she'd suffered a severe concussion and broken her arm. She'd never come back to the school again. The last Bela had heard was she'd tried to take her own life, but her father found her and got her medical help and counselling.

"What are we doing in here, Sarah?" Bela asked, cutting off the memory before it spiralled into guilty self-loathing for her part in Yvonne's suffering. "The church was sealed off for a reason. I don't want to end up in a hole with the roof on top of me."

"I need something. The last time I was here, I saw it in Tarky's private chamber. Nobody else knows about it, but it'll show this village of sycophants and flatterers that he's not the man they think he is. It's my last chance to expose the two-faced creep because once my mum's died, I won't be coming back here again."

Sarah stopped walking without warning, and Bela bumped straight into her back. "Is this his chamber?"

"Yeah. I need to get the key out of my pocket. You might want to cover your eyes. The light will be brutal."

Bela closed her eyes to the point where they became slits and braced herself as she heard the sound of a key in a lock and then the click of the door opening. Reluctantly, she followed Sarah inside.

"How did you get the key?"

"Stole it from Belinda Bennett's dresser last night. I'm an excellent thief, or I was when I was your age. Had to give it up when I became a child counsellor. This is an exceptional situation, though. Now the easy part. We're looking for a diary, a journal. Once we have it, we can get out of here."

"You said the easy part?"

"Yep. We've got to get back outside and past the soldiers again."

Bela looked around the small office, at the black-and-white picture of a choir on the wall, several old books on the vicar's desk. Sarah was busy opening drawers, scattering the contents on the floor, not caring that Tarky would know there'd been a break-in when he was eventually allowed back into his church. One drawer resisted Sarah's efforts, and the whole desk shook as she attempted to wrench it open.

Bela, still unsure of why she was helping to tear apart the man's study, wandered over to a floating shelf behind the door and read the spines of the books stacked there. She'd expected them to be religious papers, but they appeared to be journals—not Tarky's, though. These belonged to a Professor Carlton L. Sandalwood. She recognised that name: her father had met him, she was sure, in reference to the anti-apartheid movement.

A snap of wood and a cry of pleasure came from the desk as Sarah got the drawer open. Apparently, she'd also found what she was looking for, as when Bela turned around, Sarah was cradling a book in her hands as if it were a newborn baby.

"Come on, let's get out of here. I have a lot to read before tomorrow."

"What's tomorrow?"

Sarah frowned, amused. "Sunday? Even without a church, Tarky still has to bless the virtuous and damn the wicked, namely me. I intend to respond in kind." Sarah tucked the vicar's diary under her arm and strode towards the door.

Bela quickly grabbed the four journals from the shelf and shoved them inside her jumper as she followed Sarah out of the room and was plunged back into darkness. The door clicked shut; the key clattered in the lock; Sarah took Bela's hand once more and guided her back along the passage towards the outside world.

High in the rafters, a bivouac of ants swayed uneasily in the draught created by the shutting of the heavy, old, wooden door.

Chapter Thirty-Three

ELIZABETH CROKER HELD her breath as Samantha McCarthy knocked on the door a third time. Elizabeth had watched the bookstore owner disappear into the house opposite with the policeman, and panic had washed over her. What if they knew her mum wouldn't leave her room, that she had stopped talking to her, refusing to eat or drink anything?

It was the crowd outside the unpleasant man's house that had first caught Elizabeth's attention, a mass gathering of locals who normally avoided each other unless there was a party or a funeral, and even then they only went on the off-chance they'd been left something by the deceased. That was the kind of crowd she only expected to see in the village—the ones who knelt piously before God on a Sunday, cheated on their wives on a Monday, embezzled from their employers on a Tuesday, stole from the community on a Wednesday, lied about it on a Thursday, told their family they loved them on a Friday, lazed around on a Saturday and started all over again on a Sunday. Such were the followers of Solomon Grundy, the two-faced puritans of Downmere.

So what on earth had brought them out to the new houses?

From her bedroom window on the second floor, she could see across the fields and right into the living room of the beastly Mr. Wilkins. Her mother had often stood behind the blinds, tweaking one of the slats so she could see without being seen and later reporting back over dinner, not caring whether her husband or daughter were taking notice. All she cared about was putting people down, and her reputation was well known. When Elizabeth was quite small, the people of Downmere had been plagued by a poison-pen-letter writer, and it had been a standing joke between Elizabeth's dad and his colleagues, then later his friends at the cricket club and later still his new wife, that he had been surprised to find out it wasn't Lucille, who knew everything about everyone. In fact, she could have given the police a timetable of everybody's movements over the past few days, had she been alive.

Elizabeth had watched with the same sense of prying scrutiny as Samantha McCarthy laid down the law to the policeman, her hands flailing wildly in defence of her point, which the policeman must have taken, as he'd nodded, pointed at his watch, and then the pair had left the house together. By then, the road outside was empty. The crowd had seen a man off the television, and that was enough. Who cared about what real people did?

Well, Elizabeth cared. She cared deeply and didn't want anyone to disturb her mother or take her away. Sure, like any kid, there'd been times when she'd seen her parents more as malicious oppressors than benevolent guides, but it had been hard enough when her dad left; she'd never forgive herself if she stood by while they took her mother as well.

***

Sam McCarthy stepped back and looked up at the three-storey house, the biggest on the estate but the least respectable these days, certainly on the outside. A dirt-brown stain had appeared on the rendering where the gutter jointed the drainpipe, and the grass at the front was bald in places, overgrown in others. The garage door had seen better days too. Then there was what was on the inside, festering in the heart of the house since the husband had walked away.

Sam couldn't blame him. She'd seen enough of the pair to understand how difficult Lucille could be. Some women couldn't help themselves. Their demands far outweighed the capability of the man they were slowly destroying. She knew because she had been just like it during her first marriage. It was only after the break-up she realised that by continuing to make other people's lives a misery, she was also making herself miserable, and she finally accepted she could be different. She found a new purpose, a reason to live. Lucille Croker had no such ambition and had simply withdrawn, not even letting her snide, malicious side come up for air these days.

It was her prolonged absence from the community that had led Sam to reach out. If Lucille was struggling with depression, she needed help, and it wouldn't be doing her daughter any good either. At one time, Lucille would never have allowed her daughter to eat fast food, yet Sam had seen Elizabeth hanging around the village chip shop several times recently. Sam wasn't inclined to build fast friendships, but as it had been with Alice Calster, she couldn't leave poor Lucille to struggle on alone. Stepping up to the door, she knocked again and listened for signs of life inside. She'd give it five more minutes, and if she didn't get a response, she'd give Tarky a phone call once she was back in the shop, see if there was any support he could offer.

Five minutes later, Sam took one last look at the house from the roadside, trying to discern if it was a movement behind the blinds on the second floor, the reflection of a tree or a trick of the eye. She checked her watch: she was out of time. Constable Mere should be arriving at the field where the horses had been slain about now, and Sam wanted to be back in the shop before he returned to the village. After all these years, she just couldn't shake the journalistic curiosity that had almost destroyed her twice before.

She'd fallen so far when she left Perchester, and she'd kept falling. Much as she wanted to believe that her world had stabilised and she was on top of things now, she knew was treading a treacherous line, one that would perhaps have been less so if she could remember what had happened when she'd investigated the strange happenings of that April week and the appearance of...what, exactly, she didn't know. She'd been told by her daughter, her boss, and her one-night lover Kinsey, but she could never quite grasp the story or rectify it in her mind how she came to be lying in a hospital bed with her head 'split open like a cantaloupe', lucky to be alive.

Lucky to be alive... She was so fixated on thinking back to what she could remember—the moment the car's engine had failed as she'd driven towards the farm—that she didn't notice two sets of very different eyes follow her as she reached the crossroads and, for reasons she didn't understand herself, turned right, away from the village and towards the old forge and the Thorn Hill Hotel. The hotel would be empty; it always was, but all of a sudden Sam was famished. She needed to eat.

***

Elizabeth Croker kept to the hedgerows, not noticing the leaves that pricked, the stems that scratched, leaving their indelible marks on her as she followed McCarthy along the lane towards the village, except McCarthy didn't take the turning to the village. Confused, Elizabeth stopped and stared in disbelief as McCarthy turned right at the crossroads and headed down the road to the hotel nobody from the village went to anymore. The last big event there was a New Year's Eve dance held in the hotel's once-fabled Georgian-inspired ballroom to welcome the 1990s—a magical evening when six-year-old Elizabeth had worn the new dress her dad had specially picked out for her, or so he'd said, later confessing over a bottle of red fizzy pop and a packet of crisps that he'd picked that night to tell her mum he no longer loved her and wanted Elizabeth to have something nice to remember. In other words, it was a ham-fisted bribe pre-empting all the damage he'd been about to inflict.

She was about to set off once more when she spotted a boy, a bit older than her, sitting on the low wall surrounding the village hall. He called out the McCarthy, asking if she had some coins to spare, but McCarthy acted as if she hadn't heard him. It was odd. He didn't look homeless, and there was something about his expression that Elizabeth couldn't interpret. She might only have been on the verge of senior school, but she'd seen enough of people's torment in her life to read it on a stranger's face.

She stayed perfectly still, unseen by the boy as he also began to follow McCarthy, keeping his distance but not so much that she wouldn't hear his footsteps behind her. McCarthy disappeared around a bend in the lane; a moment later, the boy rounded the bend too, and Elizabeth caught sight of his smile, not a grin of happiness but one that was foul-bred. She waited a few seconds then crossed over and raced to the end of the lane, paying no heed to the hedges now, as she watched the teenager stalk his prey.

***

Sam McCarthy knew nothing of what was behind her. Her thoughts were an opaque fog in which she was trying to pin down the exact moment she realised she'd been lied to about the explosion on the farm being an accident. That was why she'd warned off Ainsley Corbett. Not to destroy his career again nor even to protect state secrets. It had been the beginning of the spiral that had seen her end up in a Whitechapel pub, pouring scorn on the supporters of gangland twins and the myths and legends they had created for themselves. If he pursued the Perchester story, it would be his downfall too.

A mile ahead of her was the hotel. She didn't know it, but she was soon to have some serious questions answered.

Chapter Thirty-Four

DIXON LED THE way down the stairs, the bright electric light doing little to blot out Wess's now constant memory of the darkness that had crawled up the walls and devoured Cauls. He shivered and let out a yelp of terrified surprise when the captain's hand came down on his shoulder, light pressure intended to reassure and express solidarity.

Sergeant Dixon looked around and glowered, all set to berate Wess, but shut his mouth when Captain Trelaryn held up his hand in apology.

"As you were, Sergeant. My fault, not Wess's. I didn't think."

The sergeant muttered something neither of the other men fully caught; suffice to say, it was neither complimentary nor pleasant. Wess envisaged Dixon would have thrown him down the stairwell and claimed they'd just been mucking around if the captain hadn't been with them.

Descending to the bunker didn't take long, but all the while, Wess kept glancing up and imagining what it must have been like for Cauls, hurrying in vain to outrun whatever had hunted him down.

***

Trelaryn noticed Wess was struggling, and not for the first time reconsidered his decision to bring the soldier along. He balanced his reticence against the knowledge he would gain from the man's reactions as well as the honest, detailed account he knew Wess would later provide. Of course, Dixon's report would be in factual army speak, concise and to the point: A led to B and then equalled C; no room for error or emotion.

Trelaryn was also aware of the doubts his superiors had about Wess. The corporal's experience the last time he'd been in the tunnels had led some in the command chain to suspect he was covering up for Cauls somehow, speculating he had opened one of the labelled canisters in the bunker and died because of a joke gone awry, or that Wess was simply overwrought with emotion. Either way, with Trelaryn's backing, this time Wess would provide that one element that was always lacking from a military account: the human experience.

It was a risk, one that could easily break Wess for good, but it was one the captain was willing to take.

They reached the bottom of the stairs without incident. The door to the bunker was firmly shut, and there was no indication of it having been breached since Wess was last there. The only sign of life, of continuation, was the amount of dust that covered the stair treads, bannisters and the floor of the stairwell: even in a supposedly airtight environment, the decay of existence had found a way to penetrate a secure military installation.

Trelaryn wasn't a man for flights of fancy. His job and mind demanded exactness, truth, although he'd admit he had enjoyed reading a collection of H.G. Wells' stories one summer when he was nursing a broken leg incurred after a full, bloodied tackle on the rugby pitch in the last week of school term.

It was one of those stories that came to mind as they stood in the dust, the sense of being inferior to the world around him reminiscent of how the Martians had died, microbes and bacteria defeating the alien invasion. This much dust seemed to be a contradiction to a system designed to keep the bunker sterile in the event of war. The failsafe was intact; he had already made sure of that before saying anything yet still felt foolish for pointing it out. Wess nodded, agreeing with the captain's observation and dipped his finger into the dust, looking at it intently.

Whatever Dixon thought, he didn't share, applying himself to the matter at hand and punching in the code that would release the lock on the door so they could enter the main chamber of the bunker.

On the second attempt, the door opened with a small click. The lights had already been turned on: the switch at the top of the stairs activated the whole facility. Dixon walked straight into the room, and Wess followed behind, acting on military impulse, even if his eyes were still focused on his fingers. He put them to his nose, sniffed and quickly lowered his hand in disgust.

Trelaryn drew breath to ask what the dust smelled like, but a noise caught his attention, like a crackle of static in the air, barely noticeable to the untrained ear, but Trelaryn recognised it as the sound of distant gunfire. It had come from the stairwell, and he contemplated running back up to investigate when, with an uncharacteristically urgent edge, Dixon called his name.

He backtracked and walked into the main chamber, where he was confronted by Wess and Dixon, both pointing to the far end of the room. The sight confused the captain for a minute. All he could think was, *well, that shouldn't be there*. In the chamber's far wall was a large crack, extending from floor to ceiling—probably above and below that, judging by the way the brickwork was sagging—and it was at least seven feet wide at its broadest extreme. Soil and dirt were strewn on either side, and the crack itself was like a black hole in space with no chance of escape from the dark, forbidding, featureless chasm.

Wess walked towards the crack, examining it at close quarters for a moment before he held up his hand in front of it and then plunged it into the gap.

"It's not much, but there is some air coming through it, and something else in the background as well. The same faint trace as is coming off the dust back there." He turned on his torch and pointed it into the very heart of the crack. "Come and take a look at this, Sir."

Trelaryn went over and was amazed to see a large tunnel stretching out before him, fashioned in the same way as the one above, only this one was not made by human activity.

"It's not running parallel with the road upstairs, Sir. See how it veers off to the right slightly? How far though, I cannot tell."

Another burst of gunfire came from above, this time slightly nearer. All three of them heard it and looked at each other with what was undoubtedly the same expression of haunted concern. Gathering his wits, Trelaryn stepped back outside the main chamber and looked up. As he did so, he saw Smallwood hurtling down towards him. He was barely able to get out of the way before the man smashed into the ground, dust billowing around him. His body was broken immediately, his neck contracting like a concertina under the weight of his body, legs buckling as they caught on the rail of the first set of stairs. Trelaryn had no time to figure out whether he'd jumped or been pushed, for above him the lights were growing dim, fading out.

***

Wess followed his commanding officer out of the chamber and skidded to a halt at the sight of Smallwood's crumpled body, but the captain wasn't looking at Smallwood. He was staring up the stairwell, and as Wess followed the captain's gaze, he realised with a cold dread that the nightmare was happening again.

Captain Trelaryn stood motionless, his eyes ablaze, black tinged with reds and browns. Wess pulled at the man's arm with such force, the seams crackled, stitches snapping. Still the captain didn't move, paralysed by the growing darkness, the spreading seed of death.

"Sir, we've got to move, now. *Sir!*"

Almost dragging his captain back into the chamber and towards the crack in the wall, Wess felt a surge of adrenaline, suddenly finding a new strength.

"Should we wait for Smallwood?" Dixon asked.

"Smallwood's dead. He's out there on the floor with his skull caved in. If you want to carry him, be my guest, but we're not waiting for you." Wess's reply got a snarl out of Dixon and seemed to partly shake the captain from his trance.

"Where are we going to go, Wess?"

He didn't know, but he could hear the army coming towards them, sense the hunger driving them. Pushing the captain into the void of the crack, he urged Dixon to follow him in and was about to join them when he spotted a box marked in military stencilled type. Grenades, left as a last resort if the bunker were overrun by a merciless enemy, although Wess doubted this was the enemy the army had in mind back then. He picked up the box and took one last look at the open door. No time to shut it now; they had to take their chance in the void.

Chapter Thirty-Five

AINSLEY CORBETT AND Christine Balker were packing up their equipment when the scene outside the stables suddenly became a whole lot busier.

A police van came to a skidding halt, and three officers piled out, one from the front, two from the back. Within seconds and with the same grit-spitting finesse but a better grip on the gravel, Millicent planted the Land Rover alongside the police van.

Harry Collins and Kevin Sillatoe, who had been waiting outside the security fence while the journalist interviewed the stable lads, both grinned, impressed by the twenty yards of tyre marks embedded into the road, although Harry's smile quickly diminished when Millicent climbed out and marched towards him, clearly on a warpath.

"When we get back to Perchester, I'm buying you a bloody phone, Scoutmaster Collins!"

Harry grimaced and meekly held up his hands. "Whatever you say, Miss Maples." Mindful of the various others in attendance, not least a hack journalist who could have made a meal out of a bag of sand, he lowered his voice. "Any news on Betley?"

"Not a word." Millicent waved her arm in the direction of the police officers. "Presumably that's why that lot are here. I called them before we left Perchester."

"How did you not notice he was missing before then?" Harry hadn't meant it as an accusation, but Millicent took it as one and reared, about to lose her cool completely. Giuseppe DeMarco stepped in and calmly explained that the rest of the boys had covered for Betley, even impersonating him. Had it not been for Millicent's insistence on good manners, it would have taken longer still to realise Betley had absconded, and, Mr. DeMarco added, she had dealt admirably with the boy's parents, who could have done with a few lessons in good manners themselves.

While Giuseppe had been speaking, the police officers had moved closer, and Harry caught the eye of one. Millicent followed his gaze, homing in on the officer.

"Are you Constable Mere? I called you over two hours ago. I trust you've been busy searching for our missing Scout?"

The officer squared his shoulders and stood to his full height, while his two colleagues shuffled back a few inches.

"Miss...er, Miss Maples, is it? I will be straight with you, madam, the boy's disappearance got...slightly sidelined. Ours is a very small station, and we've been tied up with investigating a suspicious death..." He trailed off when he noticed the reporter hovering nearby.

"He means a murder," Ainsley Corbett said with none of his earlier smugness, Harry noted. Indeed, since Corbett and his camera operator had returned to their vehicle after visiting the stables, they'd seemed shell-shocked. Were it not for the arrival of the police, they'd have already been dust in the wind.

"Hold on," Harry said. "We're not sure Scoutmaster Piccolo *is* dead. He could be lying unconscious in a ditch or—"

"Who?" the constable interrupted.

"The other Scout leader who was with us. He left camp yesterday afternoon and didn't come back. He was last seen on top of that embankment over there." Harry indicated.

The constable took out his pad and pen and jotted down some notes. "What was his name again? Piccolo, did you say?"

"Yes. Philip Piccolo."

"Right. So that's two missing, two dead." Constable Mere flipped his notepad shut.

"Try four dead," Ainsley Corbett said.

"I beg your pardon?"

"In the stables. Phillipa Downs and an unknown man. Well, I say man. It's almost impossible to tell if he's human, but I'd advise you to take my word for it that the bodies are in there, along with the creature responsible—I'd say it's also what killed Barnaby Wilkins. Chrissie here trapped it under a bucket. Not sure how long it'll stay trapped, mind you."

"Mr. Corbett, may I remind you that you are a civilian. Gents, if you could…" Mere nodded to his colleagues to go and investigate the barn, and they moved off at a slow jog. "Miss Maples, Mr. Collins, as I'm sure you can appreciate, we haven't yet had the chance to look into the whereabouts of the missing boy, and that's not why we're here now. Mr. Corbett, I must ask you and your colleague to leave the site. Your superiors have been informed that a Section D notice has been put in place. Tomorrow, we will be evacuating the entire village."

The scene erupted into chaos, everybody asking questions at the same time and talking over one another, Harry included, although he noticed that Kevin Sillatoe was keeping quiet, no doubt trying to figure out where Betley had got to.

The melee continued, voices became ever more frayed and fraught, until the camera operator whistled loudly and shouted, "Oy! Don't go in there!" to the two police officers, who had reached the stable block. "Unless you want to increase the body count to six?" She turned to Mere. "I'll show you the footage I took, Constable. I'll give you a full statement—anything. But please, please do not let your men enter that building."

Mere gave it a few seconds of thought, then nodded and signalled for the other officers to come back, while the camera operator went to retrieve her camera from the van. In the ensuing minutes, Harry noticed the absolute silence.

No birdsong; no wind in the trees; everything was still and hushed, as if the forest were waiting to reveal what was on its mind.

The camera operator returned and set up her tripod so everyone could see the small screen, or everyone except the stable hands who, Harry discerned, had discovered the bodies, and Ainsley Corbett, who turned his back on the camera and spoke quietly to Kevin Sillatoe. Somehow, the rest of them managed to let the tape run to its conclusion without passing out of vomiting at the sight of the near-picked-clean bones of the man, the terror death mask on the woman's face and, finally, the creature, which was nothing like anything Harry had seen before. It was alien-like, a mutant.

"What the fuck *is* that?" Giuseppe DeMarco uttered loudly. In other circumstances, Harry would have asked the genial Italian to mind his language, but he'd been thinking exactly the same thing.

Christine Balker switched off her camera and turned to Constable Mere, locking her gaze with his. "This is being shown tonight on the six o'clock news, and you will not stop us. I suspect you have bigger fish to fry today, anyway. For one, you need to hear what those three stable hands have to say because you haven't just got a dead couple and an irate monster to deal with, and believe me when I say it is *really* pissed off. The stable owner, Philippa Downs, is a fraud. She's been scamming the owners of the horses she claimed were slaughtered. They're very much alive, as are my colleague and I, and we intend to stay that way."

Behind her, Ainsley Corbett was listening with an expression on his face that to Harry conveyed the utmost respect for his colleague.

"Well, on that note," Ainsley said, returning to Christine's side, "we'll leave you gentlemen in blue to it. Harry Collins, pleasure to meet you." He extended a trembling hand. "I'll be in touch regarding our mutual friend Samantha McCarthy. Till then, see you on the six o'clock news."

One of the police officers stepped forward to stop the journalist and camera operator from leaving, but Constable Mere intervened.

"Let them go."

Ainsley Corbett nodded his thanks and walked over to the van. As he opened the passenger door, he called back, "I second what my colleague said, Constable. Neither you nor your men should enter that stable block without some kind of full body armour. I suspect that creature is part of a larger colony, and we disturbed them in the middle of their meal. They might not be too far away."

Leaving that chilling warning ringing in everyone's ears, Ainsley climbed into the van, and it pulled away from the scene.

Those remaining looked at each other blankly for a few minutes before Constable Mere came to his senses, and he and the other two officers arrested the three stable hands on the charge of aiding and abetting in an act of fraud and cruelty to animals. None of them put up a fight or entertained the notion of escape. What they had seen had knocked the stuffing out of them, and they seemed to welcome being locked up safely in the back of the police van.

With his suspects secured, Mere directed one of his colleagues to cordon off the stables; he instructed the other to call Inspector Nicholas Bridge and inform him that the reporters had already left the scene when they arrived and to alert the army to the situation. The officer wanted to know why he was being ordered to blatantly lie to the inspector when they could have stopped the pair from driving off.

Mere shrugged. "As the woman said, we have bigger fish to fry today."

Without warning, Giuseppe DeMarco swayed, his knees buckled, and he almost fell to the ground. Only the quick actions of Harry and Millicent prevented the tall, athletic Italian from doing himself an injury. They walked him to Harry's car and sat him in the front.

"Sillatoe." Harry beckoned to the boy. "Can you stay with Mr. DeMarco, please?"

Kevin Sillatoe nodded and climbed into the driver's seat, grinning at Harry through the windscreen.

"Don't touch *anything*!"

Sillatoe saluted and promptly started fiddling with the radio. Harry shook his head and turned to complain to Millicent, finding she had left his side and was approaching the police officers.

"Excuse me, Constable." She glanced back at Harry and gave him a wink. "Before we go look for our young missing scout, can we take a drive around the area where our other leader was last seen?"

To Harry's surprise, the policeman agreed without argument, and Millicent returned to the car. When he thought they were out of earshot, he asked, "Do you think he's all right?"

Millicent kept looking ahead, keeping her voice low. "I think the film shook him up badly and he's not thinking straight."

Giuseppe DeMarco wound down the window. He seemed to have regained his colour. "What's happening?"

"We're going to take a look at the area where Fife fell. Something feels wrong about last night—I mean, aside from the fact that the stable owner was as bent as they come. Perhaps, in the cold light of day, we'll find a better answer."

"Need me to do anything?"

"Stay with Kevin and be safe." She peered past Giuseppe, giving the boy a look that said *behave yourself*. "We'll take the Land Rover, as it'll cope better with the terrain. Then we'll all head back to the campsite, pick up my car and look for Jacob."

Millicent turned away and set off towards the Land Rover. Harry waited a moment and then leaned in and spoke quietly to Giuseppe. He could feel Millicent's eyes burning holes in his back, and once he had Giuseppe's agreement, he hurried over and climbed into the passenger seat, hoping she wouldn't ask.

Constable Mere pulled back the large metal gates, and Millicent drove cautiously through the open entrance, her hand on the gearstick ready to reverse and get out of there should the need arise.

After a minute or so, she asked, "Are you going to tell me what you said to Giuseppe?"

"If it happens, you'll know," Harry replied. His answer came out curtly, but he hadn't meant it that way. He just wanted to concentrate on the job at hand, but he could tell Millicent wasn't impressed.

She wasn't the only one whose nose was out of joint: as they doubled back on themselves, Constable Mere came into view momentarily, and while he was too far away for Harry to read his facial expression, his gait suggested he was taking some flak from his colleagues for allowing civilians access to an active crime scene.

It didn't take long to reach the embankment. Millicent brought the Land Rover to a halt at its steepest point, where they believed Fife had fallen and where Kevin had tumbled into the horse manure. Bracing for the smell and anything else he might uncover, Harry got out and went as close as he could withstand.

"I don't understand it." He raised his hand so it was level with both the top of his head and the top of the heap of dung. "It's the same height as me. Last night, it towered above us."

As he spoke, a rumble came from the pile, not unlike a drain being unblocked, a gulping, sucking, wet sound that had Harry taking a few steps back and playing through a scene whereby Millicent had returned alone to tell the parents that Scoutmaster Collins had been swallowed whole by several tons of horse manure. He glanced back at her, and saw her eyes widen. When he looked at the pile again, it had decreased by a further eighteen inches.

"For God's sake, Harry. Get back in the car!"

She didn't need to tell him twice. He ran and scrambled into the passenger seat, the door not yet shut as Millicent swung the Land Rover around and headed back to the gates. Harry turned in his seat and looked out at the field, no idea what he was seeing. The earth was heaving like a body of water, and one of the three hillocks he'd seen the previous night came crashing down, breaking into small pieces as if it were made of some kind of clay. It put the fear of God into him, and he yelled at Millicent to get a move on.

"If I go any faster, I'll miss the turn at the gates." Even so, she put her foot down and took the turn without slowing, sliding around the corner and through the gates as Constable Mere ran out in front of her, waving his arms. She narrowly avoided hitting him and then swerved again, both she and Harry spotting the reason for the policeman's frantic self-endangerment. The entire stable block was collapsing, the cries of distress and pain from the animals within adding to the thunderous rumble of the bricks and tiles crushing them to death.

Millicent wasn't slowing down, so Harry stretched over her and hit the horn, catching the attention of Giuseppe DeMarco, who had already evicted Sillatoe from behind the wheel and shot off like a Formula One driver, gaining thirty yards on the Land Rover by the time they reached the road heading away from the village. Millicent threw her phone at Harry.

"Call Giuseppe and tell him to wait when he reaches the last hill before the T-junction."

"And how do I do that?"

With a sigh, Millicent pulled sharply onto the verge and slammed on the brakes, throwing Harry forward. "Remind me when I buy you that phone to teach you how to use the bloody thing." She snatched it back from him and made the call herself.

Sheepishly, Harry turned and looked out of the window, catching sight of the view in the wing mirror. One second, the police van was turning out onto the lane and heading towards the village, the next, nothing. The whole area between the Land Rover and the police van subsided, sending a shockwave through the air in all directions.

Harry wound down the window and poked his head out, watching the field they'd been in not two minutes before implode, followed by the one beyond it, and the next one. The Land Rover jolted into action again, and he quickly pulled his head in.

"Did you see that?"

"Yes," Millicent gritted out, both hands gripping the wheel as she cranked the speed up to maximum. Had it not been for Harry imploring her to slow down as they reached the top of the hill, he was quite sure she'd have kept going all the way to Southampton, never to return. Even so, she slowed gradually, putting a few hundred yards more between them and the vast chasm before she stopped. They both got out and stood on the ridge of the hill, joined a moment later by Giuseppe DeMarco and Kevin Sillatoe, all four vocalising both their relief that they had survived and their horror at the destruction.

"It's the tunnels the creatures have built," Kevin said. "There must be loads of them, millions, churning up the land."

Harry mulled over the boy's words and agreed. He couldn't think of any other reason, and with that thought came a further dreadful realisation. The tunnels may already extend beyond the fields, to the village of Downmere, and there was no time to warn anyone.

Chapter Thirty-Six

S AM MCCARTHY WAS thankful that the boy standing in front of her still had quite a bit of growing to do before he was even half the size of his father. That said, as she later told her husband and the doctor at the hospital, he knew how to pack a punch.

She remembered Betley Senior, all right. The whole family had marked her card not long after she became editor of the Perchester local paper. The boy's grandfather had done time for robbery and violence in the early 1970s, and on the day of his release, he bypassed going home to his loving wife whose temperament matched the underside of a badly mistreated frying pan, and instead made his way to the offices of the paper and put a brick through the window. He didn't even cover his tracks, and Lord knew, many in the town would have given him an alibi, not because they were his friends, but because the cost of doing anything else was too high. Better a few years banged up behind bars for misleading the police than to meet Horace Betley in one of the cold, dark alleyways that dotted the town.

The police were called, and Kinsey—much younger and fitter then—had wrestled the old man to the ground, not that Betley put up much of a fight. He was sent straight back to prison and never stepped foot in the town, his wife burying him three months into his sentence, when an undiagnosed liver condition finished him off while he sat on the toilet.

Jacob's father had never forgiven Sam McCarthy. He blamed her for his father's death, and on a few occasions, he was found in possession of spray paint near her house, having scrawled some rather disgusting anti-Chinese sentiment on the front window. Both her then husband and daughter pleaded with Sam to forget about it, let it go, but she couldn't and ran it as a headline the following week with Betley's picture below. A six-month custodial sentence made Mrs. Betley insist that her husband start mending his ways lest the same fate visit him as it had her father-in-law.

The family left Sam alone after that, but as she looked up at the teenage boy, the familiar dark-green eyes flashing with wildness, sweat glistening on his forehead, everything else around her faded into insignificance.

She had arrived at the hotel with the idea of a cream tea settled firmly in her mind, a small treat before starting the interview with Robert Romsleigh that evening. As she approached the entrance, she noticed how quiet it was. Even with hardly any guests booked in, she'd have expected some activity, a doorman to greet her, perhaps, or a concierge at the desk.

There was no one around—no guests, no staff—and in an act of whimsy, she rang the bell on the unmanned desk, admiring the silver letter opener that lay next to it as she called out, "Bell boy?" but no one came.

She wandered through the empty foyer, glancing up the stairs and into the cloakroom as she passed on her way to the dining hall, which was where she finally saw other people. Three of them, to be exact, lying on the floor, their clothes intact, but where their faces should have been...

Swallowing heavily, Sam backed off and considered the bodies from a distance, deducing two of them were husband and wife, or lovers sharing a clandestine weekend away. The third body wore a waiter's uniform, a pool of gravy and wine running together at his feet.

Sam walked on. A smell of burning was coming from the kitchen, and while she had a reasonable idea of what she'd find there, if she allowed the hotel to catch fire, it would be gutted before the fire engines made it as far as the one-way system on the Southampton Road. Hesitating at the door, she took a couple of deep breaths before entering, taking in the scene as if she were reviewing a gothic waxworks museum rather than the sight of a massacre. There was the poor unfortunate receptionist, and a man she half recognised from a feature in the local rag as the head chef, along with his sous chef and a porter, all dead, in various stages of fright, fear, and in the case of the young lass at the sink, praying on her knees, her eyelids open but the objects of sight gone, a few dangling tendrils in their place.

Sam McCarthy stifled a scream. What good would it do? There was no one around to help her, or perhaps there was. It was hard to say with the hiss of steam issuing from the stove. She turned off the gas rings and removed the hot pans, setting them on the counter before leaving the kitchen and stealthily making her way back to the foyer, staving off the memory of the last time she'd been this scared. The metal object swinging down, the woman holding it, her features blurred not through some failure of Sam's memory but because of something inside the woman, making her different.

Ghost apples. The phrase sounded in her head, in Kinsey's voice, as she reached the front desk, and she stopped, perplexed. *What the hell does it mean? Ghost apples.*

Jacob Betley sprang up from behind the desk, catching her unawares, and punched her in the face. Her nose exploded in a spray of blood, the blow knocking her onto her backside.

"What the hell—"

"I know you, lady. You thought you could run away, but you can't. You wait till I tell my dad I found Samantha McCarthy,"

The boy climbed on top of the desk, swaying from side to side, a predator ready to leap.

The gore running down Sam's face made it difficult to talk, to confirm she knew who he was. She spat a clot of blood onto what had once been a costly plush carpet and raised her hands to shield her face.

"How do you know who I am? You were barely a toddler when I left Perchester, and forgive me if I'm misjudging you, but you're hardly the type to read back copies of the national papers."

Jacob Betley loomed over her, the desk adding another four feet to his height. Sam tried to get up, but she slipped on her own blood, narrowly missing a plinth, the plaque denoting that it had once borne a bust of Cleopatra.

"There's a picture of you in our garage," Betley said. "Dad keeps it on the dartboard Mum bought him for his fortieth birthday. That's how I know who you are. I've studied your face for hours, Ms. McCarthy. You're not very pretty, are you? You probably were once, but I bet those crow's feet aren't just from sleepless nights, eh? Do you ever think of us? Of Perchester? Cos we think of you. We think you're a liar. You made up stories about Wendlefields just to sell papers, and that boy you said died?" Betley shook his head, sneering in disgust. "That didn't happen." He jumped down, landing between Sam's splayed legs, perfectly positioned to stamp on her ankles and snap them should he so desire.

"What are you doing here, Betley?" she asked, trying to remain calm.

"Scout camp." He kicked her foot. She sucked air in through her nose, refusing to show her pain. "How about you? Do you live here now? I hope so. My dad loves a day trip."

Sam thought she saw someone come through the door, a flicker of movement in her peripheral vision. Regardless of what she had found in the dining room and kitchen, she hoped it was someone who could deal with the sadistic monster who had her life in his hands. But no one shouted out to stop or grabbed the boy from behind; just a trick of the light, no doubt.

Jacob Betley lashed out again, and this time it was as she feared. His boot came down on her ankle, and something snapped. She couldn't stop herself this time and screamed in pain, which delighted her attacker.

"Funny, I came back to the village hoping I'd bump into that little shit Sillatoe, but then I saw you. Imagine that." He bent down on one knee and looked her in the eyes. "I got knocked back by a girl today, and it hurt, but a woman, especially one your age, well, you must be gagging for it."

At any other time, McCarthy would have laughed in his face and grabbed him by the balls and given them a good twist, but the pain in her leg was excruciating and her head was swimming.

"Ghost apples," she repeated, her faint whisper missed completely by her attacker, who had removed his shirt, his chest barely showing signs of puberty. He raised his fist to hit her again but stopped before he struck, his face registering first surprise then confusion as he bent his arm behind him, seeming to search for something. Twisting to see behind him also proved futile, and through her blurred double vision, Sam could just make out something sticking out of the back of his neck. Betley managed to get hold of it and tried to pull it out, but the hand pushing it in was stronger.

"Elizabeth?" Sam rasped, blinking repeatedly, unable to focus on Betley, who had stopped struggling and was fighting for breath, the stream of blood outlining every vertebra on its way down to the pool at the top of his trousers. Betley slumped and landed beside Sam as she lost consciousness, her last view of the silver letter opener jutting out of his neck.

***

When she awoke, there was no sign of the deranged boy, a small trail of blood that led into the dining room the only evidence that there had ever been a struggle.

Groggily, she felt her leg. Pain rushed up to meet her once more, and she would likely have passed out again, were it not for the deep rumble in the distance. Whether it was down to her delirious state or her desire to escape the agony by any means, her first thought was that a bomb had been dropped on Southampton, and she waited for the inevitable aftershock, the flash of light that would round off her day perfectly.

It didn't come. She leaned against the empty plinth, watching the sun slowly descend beyond the open doors and then closed her eyes, thankful she would not see the second sun in the east that day.

Chapter Thirty-Seven

ROBERT ROMSLEIGH CURSED and sat at his kitchen table, laying out the cards for a game of solitaire to distract from his feeling of disappointment. Bela hadn't shown her face all day or come home for dinner, and he swung between worrying that she had got lost—or worse—and annoyance that she was intentionally defying him. The move had been rough on her, never mind all that preceded it, but that didn't excuse being late home.

He flipped the cards without seeing their faces. The game held little joy for him in the normal scheme of things. A few rounds of crib, suddenly wiping out your opponent's twenty-point lead with a golden hand of four fives and a jack, now that was fun, but you couldn't play cribbage on your own. It was a game of psychological warfare that required someone else to stare down.

He looked at his watch again and sighed. Any later and he'd have to go out looking for her, and Samantha McCarthy was coming round. For a moment, he couldn't remember what time they'd arranged to meet, not that it mattered. Since leaving the bookshop, he'd had second thoughts about reliving the story. He wasn't even sure he knew it, not properly. He only saw the evidence on his daughter's face, and she wasn't here to refresh his memory.

***

Bela and Sarah managed to skirt the graveyard by clinging to the wall, their toes breaking further chunks off the frayed earth, each step taken with the smallest of breaths escaping as they inched towards their goal of the boundary between the church and the field. Finally within jumping distance, they looked at each other, nodded, and took a leap of faith, then ran as fast as they could while keeping low so the soldiers didn't see them. Once they had put what they hoped was enough distance between them and the church, they slowed down but kept moving.

"Where do we go now?" Bela asked, finding that she didn't want the day to end.

"Well, we could wander through the forest for a while, although it's a bit boring without a drink or any smokes, or we could get a bus out of this one-horse town. There are some decent pubs in Avoncross. The Grey Fisher used to have a really good barman, the rough and ready type, but he left to go travelling..." She shook her head ruefully. "Really, I should go home and check on my mum. I don't like to leave her too long at the moment."

"Why?" Bela asked, blushing at her brashness, but she was still curious so didn't take back the question.

"Cancer, same one as my dad. She hasn't got long. Do you want to meet her? You know, while you have the chance?" Sarah said it in such a matter-of-fact way that Bela wondered if she was joking but still nodded.

"Is there a back way, just in case my dad's out looking for me?"

"Yeah. Follow me." Sarah turned down an alley that ran behind the shops, only coming out onto the main road as they neared her house. They narrowly avoided walking straight into Belinda Bennett, who marched past, then disappeared into the forest.

"Weird," Sarah said. "She's going to see her son, but the anniversary isn't till next week."

Bela just smiled, no idea what Sarah was talking about, and followed her around to the front of the house and through the door.

"Mum?"

Receiving no reply, Sarah moved through the house, opening doors until she finally found her mother asleep at the kitchen table, her head resting on skinny arms, the radio playing some banal lullaby. Sarah gently touched her mother's hand.

"Mum? Are you awake?"

The woman stirred, still noncommittal to waking up until Sarah rubbed her hand with a little more vigour.

"I've brought a friend back. I hope that's all right."

Slowly, Mrs. Calster lifted her head, and Bela clamped her teeth together to silence any expression of shock. Pain dominated the woman's features, her skin yellow and crumpled like stretched rubber sheeting, her lips only slightly darker and caked in dried saliva. She attempted to wet them with her tongue and reached up to smooth a palm over her daughter's cheek.

"I was dreaming about your dad."

"Were you?" Sarah smiled. There was no regret from either woman, only acceptance. "This is my friend, Bela. She and her dad have just moved in down the road, the old professor's house." She turned to address Bela. "I was the one who found him, you know. He'd been dead for ages, but they said I murdered him and kept quiet about it, then had a sudden attack of remorse and broke in, acted like I'd just found him there. There was no evidence, but when my dad died, the rumours resurfaced— I'll give you one guess who started them."

Bela didn't need to guess. It was clear when she'd met the man the day before and he'd looked at her the same way her mum's male friends had that he was capable of doing her real harm.

225

"I can tell by your face you see it too. You've been abused, haven't you? Do you want to talk about it?"

"Yeah, I do," Bela said, though she wasn't sure why. She didn't know this woman and doubted her father would approve of them talking, but who else was there? Who else would understand what it felt like to be an outsider?

Sarah helped her mum through to the back room that had been converted into a small bedroom for her, unable as she was to climb the stairs anymore. "I'll make you some supper later, Mum, okay?"

A sleepy mumble came in response, and Sarah said something else to her mum, too quietly for Bela to make out the words. A moment later, Sarah returned to the kitchen and filled the kettle, keeping her back to Bela as she spoke. "I half expect to find her dead every night when I take in her supper." She turned around and smiled sadly. "Tea or coffee?"

"Tea, please. I'm sorry about your mum."

"Me too." Sarah shrugged as if to say *there's nothing I can do* and set about preparing two mugs. "She said something as she was closing her eyes. I'm guessing she's been chatting with your aunt Stella. She talks a lot, does your aunt."

"Tell me about it."

"Mum mentioned your brother."

Bela nodded. "Stuart."

"What's he like?"

"A little brother."

"A pain in the backside then?" Sarah said with a grin. "I wish I had a brother or sister."

Bela laughed, or tried to, but she'd almost said the thought she'd had so many times—that she wished she'd never had a brother—and it kicked down the final wall of resistance, letting years' worth of guilt and rage pour out. Yet there were no tears, perhaps because she had no more left to spill. She explained everything that had happened—her parents' marriage breaking down, her mother's lunacy, the fire—with a sense of great calm and maturity, as if this were her coming of age.

Sarah kept eye contact at all times, never once straying to the ripples of scar tissue covering half of Bela's face or interrupting her. After an hour, when Bela found she'd said all that there was to be said, Sarah observed, "You haven't told your dad this, have you?"

Bela shook her head and shifted in the chair, her lower spine finally feeling the hardness of the wooden seat. As she did, one of the journals dislodged from inside her clothes and fell to the floor. Embarrassed, she picked it up and shoved it in her lap.

"Did you take that from the church? Actually, you don't have to answer. I don't care either way. Nothing wrong with a bit of purposeful pilfering." Sarah smiled broadly, no recriminations, no judgement. From what she'd said, Bela had the impression she'd done far worse. "So are you going to come to church tomorrow morning? I promise it'll be fun!" Sarah's smile became a mischievous grin, and Bela returned it with a genuine grin of her own.

"Why not?" she said, standing and sliding the journal back inside her jumper. "I'd best get going. Thanks for today."

"Anytime." Sarah walked Bela to the front door. As she opened it, there was an explosion that almost knocked Bela into Sarah's arms.

"What was that?"

"I don't know, but it came from down the hill."

The two of them looked in the direction of the noise.

"Oh my God. That's the new estate!" Sarah's voice was lost to the loud rumble of tiles sliding from roofs and chimneys crashing to the ground. In the distance, a dog howled and a man shouted his wife's name over and over. The crossroads sign rose a foot into the air and cracked into two separate pieces, which toppled in opposite directions, sending up a plume of dust as they embedded themselves into the ground.

"My dad!" Bela yelled. Now the tears came as, in a blind panic, she tore down the hill towards home.

***

Robert was pacing. He had let too much time go by, not wanting to stand in the way of his daughter's development, but he also wanted to protect her. Surely she'd forgive him for that. He went into his study to retrieve his keys but forgot all about them when the table was thrown halfway across the room by what felt and sounded like an explosion in a mine, except it seemed to have come from directly underneath the house.

Then he fell.

Before (1975)

He felt humiliated, ridiculed, disgraced in front of his peers and students alike, and as he slammed the door of his office for the last time, he left the college in no doubt of what he really thought of them.

"Damn you all, ingrates, heathens, idiots!" His bitter words echoed through the faculty building. "You don't deserve science. You don't seek enlightenment or education, reasoned thought and debate. You are a gathering of fools without purpose— puerile, attention-seeking cretins."

Not another sound could be heard. Those walking through the normally welcoming halls either stopped dead as if they were under Medusa's scrutiny or hurried away with heads down as the voice of one of the university's most respected figures descended into base insults, accusing every doctor and professor as he passed their firmly closed door of producing work that was short on originality, style and substance. He was tempted to fling open those doors and remind them strongly of their responsibilities to the impressionable young adults who had chosen to study biology or zoology at this so-called esteemed institution. Instead, he cast his opinions onto the rapidly emptying corridors lest he scare the poor souls no doubt already cowering behind their books and being urged to stay quiet by lecturers convinced a beast was in their midst.

Naturally, the long corridor that led to his study was devoid of life. Nobody dared venture that far beyond their sanctuary.

They'd all heard what had taken place in the grandest of the three lecture halls, which had been named after the professor only a year before. The lavish ceremony had thrilled him, his ego swelling with every handshake, every utterance of flattery and the pièce de resistance, his confirmation as chancellor of the university. After a career dedicated to enriching the field of myrmecology and being at the forefront of the anti-apartheid movement, he knew with certainty for the first time in his life that he deserved such respect.

Alas, dreams and ego rarely make good bedfellows, and even in his ire, he acknowledged that his sense of self-worth had become bloated in recent years, dining out on the sycophancy that he had not noticed was sown with barbs until it was too late. At first, it was no more than a gentle ribbing that evolved into undisguised annoyance at his arrogance, even though the bubbles of knowledge escaping him were becoming fewer, less significant. He had reached his depth and become a caricature, a figure to be mocked behind closed doors, but for the longest time, he attended only to what he needed to. Not that he was completely blind; he saw how society was breaking down around him, but he believed the damage was inflicted by governments and leaders elected by hateful, sneering crowds who saw history as bunkum and for whom learning was anathema.

The final straw—the moment he realised that the whispers in the library, the indiscreet laughter when someone brought up the subject of African Queens, the references to comic books and pop culture were about him—had come that morning as he orated his latest lecture on the mating habits and the structure of the colony. He had made a habit of not referring to the slides behind him; it was several years since he'd needed to. The whole lecture theatre, his domain with his name in gold leaf above the door, was deathly quiet. All eyes, he had supposed, were on him, yet not a single note was taken in the first thirty minutes. He tried to not let his annoyance show, resolving to issue a spot paper and make it worth a few points towards the students' final yearly totals, but as he continued, he began to notice a few people covering their mouths to hide grins and stifle giggles, and he understood that the mirth was directed at the screen. He glanced behind him, endeavouring to keep talking, but his learnèd words lost all meaning.

There were no slides depicting his discovery of a new offshoot of the marabunta ant, no photographs of the bivouac way their colony came together, the lack of nests, no drawings skilfully sketched by his friend who had been tortured to death for loving a white woman. Instead, he was confronted by a disgraceful performance, carefully spliced together scenes from 1950s so-called horror movies featuring grotesque, giant ants that had been bombarded with radiation and on each actor's head the professor's own face, horribly bloated.

A few of the students in the hall could no longer contain themselves, and as they let rip their mockery, so too did others join in as if they were caught in a wave that pushed the professor deeper and deeper underwater until he was drowning in ridicule.

From the projection room, he heard several students laugh cruelly and one of them call, "Do you like our presentation, Professor Quatermain?" Then a door crashed open and a booming voice revealed the tricksters' identities.

"Denbigh, Fowler, Michaels and Protezni, you will report immediately to my office whence you will be expelled from this institution and your learning record struck off."

"Professor Chalk, that's not fair! I only have two papers left to submit, and I'm virtually assured a first."

He didn't hear Chalk's reply and no longer cared what any of them had to say. The damage was done; he would not be able to continue his career, not in this or any other university. Indeed, it would not have surprised him to find the entire event being satirised in the papers, an endless stream of illustrated jokes at his expense. Perhaps, had he developed a sense of humour and not abandoned humility in favour of fame, he could have ridden out the furore, waited for some other scandal to overwrite it. As it was, his bubble of pomposity was not just leaking air; it had exploded all over his life.

He continued to stare at the now blank screen and supposed Professor Chalk had switched off the projector. Behind him, students shuffled away uneasily, likely expecting they would also be held to account for the morning's uncomfortable end. When he thought they had all deserted him, he turned around, tears of shame running freely down his cheeks, and was greeted by the sight of several students who had remained in their seats, their faces still etched with horror at what he had been subjected to.

With as much dignity as he could muster and ignoring the crack in his voice that betrayed him, he asked them what they wanted, whether there was a question on today's lecture they wished to ask.

One by one, they stood up, approached the man who had steered them through three years of university life and hugged him, each telling him how much they loved his work. It was the first meaningful human contact he'd had since he'd left South Africa, when Rachael had kissed him tenderly on the cheek, her way of saying goodbye.

Aware that it would be the last time he saw them, let alone talked to them, he permitted their gestures of kindness, and as the students filed out of the lecture theatre, Professor Chalk appeared, his hands clasped together in readiness to deliver an apology on behalf of the whole university. The man stopped him before he could make it.

"How long have you known I was no more than a figure of fun, demeaned behind my back, used as a joke?"

"I assure you, Professor, this behaviour will not be tolerated at all. The four young men responsible will have left the campus before the end of the day. You are not a joke, my friend, you are a valuable asset to this university."

Fury welled up from the pit of the man's stomach; he recognised it as the same emotion he experienced when he was banished from South Africa.

"You're a liar, Chalk. I can see it in those beady eyes of yours. You gave the speech at the opening ceremony for this very lecture theatre and all but saluted me, grovelled at my feet, as you poured your fine words regarding my achievements. All deception, all lies. You might not have supplied the knives that have pierced my soul and my heart today, but you knew they were planning to treat me like Caesar, and you did nothing. You may as well have armed them yourself with a note attached saying for the use of destroying Quartermain."

Professor Chalk was visibly shocked and protested his innocence, begging to be heard. The man looked at him with contempt and, saying nothing more, picked up his notes and stormed out of the lecture theatre, the heavy wooden door flying open with ease as he pushed it with ungainly force.

Having made it clear that he was resigning with immediate effect, he stamped with ever-growing fury down the many levels of stairs and out into the square, where he shouted one last time to all those gathered for the spectacle of his downfall.

"Each one of you came here to learn, to enhance science. Through your behaviour today, you have turned it into a mockery. I damn you all."

What remained of his dignity had given him the wherewithal to leave a forwarding address for all his papers and equipment to be sent to and carried him off campus with his head held high. It was only in the near-empty carriage, as the train journeyed through the English countryside, that he began to weep, silently, uncontrollably, for his glittering career, ended by nothing more than a B-movie.

He never cried again, not even when he read in his morning paper that the lecture theatre was to be renamed in honour of Queen Elizabeth II on the occasion of her silver jubilee. A few of his former students had protested the change and demanded a formal apology, but it meant nothing anymore; he would forcibly remove himself from it all.

Chapter Thirty-Eight

DARKNESS HAD FALLEN by the time Alan Tarky crouched in the bushes that separated the farmer's land from that upon which the church regally stood, though how much longer it would remain that way, he cared not to consider. The past forty-eight hours had seen the pit surrounding it expand by a multitude of feet, thrusting even more of its once-resting flock into what one local lad had aptly referred to as purgatory.

The word sent a chill up Tarky's spine, for in his mind it had always seemed so much worse a destination than hell. It was the place for those who hadn't grasped the enormity of their sins and therefore had not asked for forgiveness—those not quite evil enough for the devil to take their souls outright, but on whom he could count to march to his tune if he tortured them enough and gave them some hope of peace—an eternal offering of Stockholm Syndrome that would see them turning their backs on salvation.

For two hours, Tarky had waited for the farmhands and their dogs to go home to their own beds so he could get the job done. In his coat pockets were several heavy-duty plastic bags that he intended to fill with prayer books and hymnals as well as the one thing he wanted more than anything: his letters, the proof of his love for Reynard. If the church was going to be sealed off, if he could not remove the evidence and an accident befell him, then his shame might be revealed. The way he had conducted himself, doing nothing to stop Reynard from committing suicide, was neither the action of a benevolent priest nor a compassionate lover, and if it came out, he knew it would be the end of him.

He could hear the two soldiers who had been on patrol since eight that evening chatting idly, cracking jokes, laughing. On guard they might have been, but their attitude towards defence left a lot to be desired. In another time, Tarky would have entertained the notion of threatening them with a sternly worded letter to their commanding officer, but his mission was difficult enough. The arc lights seemed even to penetrate the black soul of the pit, and he couldn't resist looking down into it, aware it might look back and damn him or, like Narcissus, he would be captivated by his own darkness and gaze into it forever. He forced his eyes away from the sight and concentrated on the soldiers' conversation.

So still was the night air, their voices carried the full distance of the obliterated graveyard. They had moved on to politics—the classic story of left versus right, the energetic Blair or the staid Major—and each was so determined to make his point that it gave Tarky the opportunity he'd been waiting for.

Climbing over the small wall and keeping as close as he could to the edge, he unwittingly followed the same route Sarah Calster and Bela Romsleigh had taken earlier, ending up at the back of the greenhouse he had put there many years ago, when he'd discovered the secret entrance that had been hidden from view by creeping ivy since the time of Cromwell.

The greenhouse door was open, which may or may not have been important. He never locked it, for if he did, he reasoned, it would tempt the few teenagers that lived in the village to break in, either believing there was something of value inside or simply seizing the opportunity for mischief and mayhem. That wasn't to say the door should be open, but perhaps a bored soldier had found his curiosity piqued and taken a look at the various plants growing in there.

A single thread of wool caught Tarky's attention. Not khaki but red, it dangled inelegantly from the catch on the hidden door he imagined had once been an escape route for his persecuted predecessors or for the local wench they had invited in to administer their own brand of the sacrament. Such a thought would usually have enraged Tarky and inspired a sermon on the subject of purity and lewd behaviour. Nor would he have had any problem delivering such a sermon. It was, after all, his duty to save his sheep from spiritual damnation or deliver them into God's wrathful hands. Did that make him a hypocrite? He didn't think so. He was but a vessel through which the Word of the Lord flowed.

On this occasion, he didn't dwell on the actions of his predecessors. He didn't have space for it in his blinkered, holier-than-thou mind. He had seen only one person in the village wearing red in the last couple of days, and the possibility that she had been inside his church, that she had violated this sacred place of worship, didn't fill him with rage. It made him extraordinarily scared.

He had felt fear before, but as he stood at the doorway, the loose thread resting in his hand, he was almost overtaken by the urge to vomit. In the days of Reverend Thomas Clatford, it would have been a sign of demon possession; indeed, the good reverend had burned alive several local women on suspicion of being witches before mysteriously disappearing himself. It was said that he burned to ash when lightning struck an oak that had once stood grandly opposite the church, a spot now taken up by an ornamental well, erected on the event of the village's 600th anniversary, that provided cover for teenagers' smoking and other illicit activities.

Tarky pushed open the secret door and stepped into the gloom. Taking his flashlight from his coat pocket and making sure not to lose any of the plastic bags, he inched his way to his private room, hesitating at the portal. If someone had been in there and had not yet left, they would be just as surprised to see him as he was to see them.

A distant rumble, louder and more percussive than thunder, reverberated through the old stone building, but Tarky was unfazed, intently watching the door in front of him as the sound bounced around the walls and echoed up into the rafters. For the moment, he was satisfied that no one was in there and reasoned that the red yarn could have been there for a while, unnoticed until now, when it had taken on a different significance.

Removing the chain he wore around his neck, he unclasped it and slid the key free, taking care to leave the cross in place. Keeping the chain in his hand for the time being, he unlocked the door and shone his torch over the room. The view that confronted him would have upset anyone, that sense of violation from knowing someone has searched through one's possessions, but it turned Tarky statuesque. He didn't have to move to see the drawer that had contained his letters had been emptied, and he knew then that whoever had broken in had done so with the specific intent to steal the intimate portrayals of a man who had loved another more than he should.

He looked up to the heavens, the space between him and God empty of response and meaning, no comforting words beckoning him forth for absolution. Walking towards the nave, he turned his thoughts of hatred on himself. He should have burned the letters, let the ashes float into the sky to be read by God alone, for only He could judge him. Unworthy, he knelt before the altar, and for a moment, a flight of fancy overtook him as a second rumble sounded, as if the Saviour were making himself comfortable in preparation for his loyal servant's confession.

The detonation also made him change the direction of blame. He *knew* it was Sarah Calster; she had promised she was going to make him and the village suffer. Tarky placed his hands together and prayed. He prayed that the devil in their midst would suffer the most horrific death and burn in hell till the end of time.

He had sought divine intervention from the light, but it was the shadow of darkness that consumed him. With his eyes closed, Tarky prayed harder than he had ever done. He wanted justice, retribution; he wanted Sarah Calster to suffer.

A small, quick-moving shadow crawled down the cross and onto the communion table, soon joined by others that dropped from the high rafters. As the vicar summoned God's wrath, they moved as one. So far in thought was he that he paid no heed to the scuttling sound that rushed towards him.

Bring down your vengeance, My Lord, on the person who has brought this shame upon me...

Tarky felt a bite on the back of his hand and opened his eyes, directing the torch's beam to see what creature had dared to feed on a man of God's blood in his church. A solitary ant, slightly bigger than usual, stood fearless in its spotlight. Tarky swore and flicked the creature off his hand.

Feeling a further bite on his calf and another on his knee, he quickly rose, and as he did, his eyes fell upon the moving floor of the church, a black mass congregating around him, climbing him, crawling over and inside his clothes. He swatted at them, tried to brush them off, but he was one man and they were legion, a congregation of tens of thousands devouring the body of Christ's representation on Earth.

***

Hearing the blood-curdling scream from inside the church, the soldiers stopped talking about England's chances in the European Championships and swiftly made their way to the door. It was locked, as they had expected, but with the vibrations from a third explosion that seemed to come from directly underneath their feet, they were able to prise it open enough to see what was going on inside.

Debris falling from the church roof forced them back; the sight of a human flailing in agony forced them back further. Neither of the soldiers was religious, but both made a silent pact that day, should they survive it, to attend church parade with a little more enthusiasm in future, not just for the biscuits and a couple of hours off from kitchen duties. Both soldiers later admitted that they had been scared out of their wits, that what they'd seen was a demon coming at them, a fiend covered in moving sores, its black, bloody arms clawing the air.

Tarky never made it beyond the doorframe of the building. What remained of his body fell to the ground in a crumpled, disjointed heap, and then, before the soldiers' eyes, the swathe of writhing, shiny black scurried back into the darkness.

The plague of ants, having had their fill, left the two men alone.

Chapter Thirty-Nine

DOCTOR KAHN WAS a young GP whose colleagues complimented him on his patience while also joking that it wouldn't last, and in the space of a couple of days, he'd started to think they were right. He now knew why, as 'the new kid', he'd ended up with Downmere's residents on his list. Even with Kahn's open-mindedness—some called him eccentric—the people in that village could have tried the patience of a saint, none more so than one Mrs. Belinda Bennett.

Belinda claimed she was 'a woman of the world', yet anyone who talked to her for any length of time quickly realised she was intolerant of anything that didn't fit with her very narrow worldview. She openly despised busybodies and the way some people insisted on interfering in others' lives. That extended to those whose business it was to interfere in others' lives, including doctors, but it was understandable in a woman of her years, who had lived through the war and was a paid-up member of the shrug-and-get-on-with-it brigade. However, she also had a nasty streak of racism—a double whammy for Doctor Kahn.

It was no wonder Doctor Goldman had hidden his face when the practice manager suggested Khan was the ideal candidate for taking on Downmere. They had earmarked him for the job, they said, a young, energetic GP who could endear himself to the community. It had taken a good deal of effort and compromise, but he was making progress in most quarters—Alice Calster had told him he was the only doctor who listened to her, and for as much as palliative care was emotionally challenging for even the most experienced doctor, he was glad to be able to offer her some relief as she neared the end of her life.

Belinda Bennett was an entirely different kettle of fish, as he discovered when he tried one last time to gently persuade the recently widowed woman to go to the hospital where she could be treated by specialist practitioners using modern equipment. That was when she told him to take his foreign backside out of her bedroom and not disturb her again.

Khan had let it go. He didn't want to add to the woman's suffering by arguing with her but allowed himself the pleasure of a knowing smile—*Foreign? I was born in Southampton, as were my parents, you stuck-up, bigoted buffoon*—as he snapped his bag shut and told her to get some rest.

***

Belinda Bennet looked up at the sturdy tree branch where her son had been found and whispered a prayer for him. The tablets the doctor had prescribed had not settled her at all. Having ordered her to rest, he'd left her in the hands of a neighbour and with a list of numbers to call should she take a turn for the worse. As soon as she heard his rather ostentatious car start, she'd put her clothes back on, and here she was.

She wasn't yet supposed to undertake her annual pilgrimage to the site of her son's last stand against that dreadful, consuming disease, but something inside her had gnawed away since the spirit—the shade of Lionel—had confronted her and said things she could never imagine having sprung forth from his lips in life. She'd soon realised it was her own overwrought mind that conjured those images of a demon in her husband's form, which was why she'd come to the forest to talk to her son about more fondly remembered times.

She'd taken the back way, of course. It added a further mile to her journey, but it was safer—less likelihood of a well-meaning neighbour seeing her and telling Doctor Kahn she had gone against his advice. After sweet Reynard passed, Doctor Goldman had ordered her to bed and threatened to send her to Manor Hospital, and she feared if they sent her this time, if they found out about her late husband's 'visitation', she might never return. She knew how those types of places worked, what they did to you once they had you in their grasp.

Her father had been taken away just before the war. They told her it was because he was a person of interest, that he had written letters to Prime Minister Neville Chamberlin threatening that if he didn't sue for peace with the German Chancellor, he would shoot him in the back. When Belinda was finally allowed to visit her father, she discovered he wasn't in jail but was under the care of a psychotherapist. He'd had an embolism on the brain, which they said had made him act out of character. She had been a young girl then, but she knew her father well enough to understand that he had meant what he'd written. Did that make him mad? Did that give them the right to keep him under lock and key all through the war? Belinda didn't believe so and had defended him, even when they told her she was wrong, when others pointed the finger at her and called her names. She was never wrong, and she wasn't going to be told to stay in bed by a doctor who was on their side. She wanted to talk to her son, and besides, the walk, once she had skirted the village, had invigorated her, enlivened her spirit.

The shade that the trees afforded was pleasant on her face and gave her an inner glow she hadn't felt in years. How Reynard would have enjoyed the feeling of nature surrounding him. For the first time since he had died, she saw the forest not as a holding place for his spirit, but a calm oasis, a home for the breeze to gently touch each vibrant and differently coloured green leaf. Even Lionel would have enjoyed the moment.

Bending in preparation to sit on the ground beneath the tree, Belinda groaned in pain but refused to be thwarted. For a lady of her years, it was no mean feat getting into that position, and it played havoc with her knees and right hip, but it was of little importance when this could be the last time she came to see her boy.

She closed her eyes and felt a slight wind take hold. Somewhere high above, a branch creaked and crackled. After decades of reaching out to the sun for nourishment, its spine had become hollow, insects, small mammals, birds and fungi all leaving their mark, contributing to the inevitable day when its bark split open revealing the diseases rife inside and the branch snapped and tumbled to the forest floor.

Belinda concentrated. She had come to know what to listen for, the telltale signs of the animals that foraged, hunted and found peace in the forest.

"My boy, my lovely boy. I know I'm early—I hope you don't mind. You don't have to say anything, just listen. Your father... your father has died, and he will need your help."

She returned to her silent prayer, her eyes remaining closed.

A figure shuffled soundlessly through the smallest of gaps in the thicket, its dead eyes never leaving the woman's face, discerning her intent.

Suddenly, Belinda let out a heart-rending, terrifying wail. Even in her grief, it could have stricken a man down in fear.

"Why did you have to leave? Oh, I know you say you could not take the pain anymore, that the idea of living another six months with that horrible disease left you beyond despair, but did you ever think what it would do to me? All those gossipmongers in the village telling me how sorry they were, how they understood my pain, that no mother should lose their child, and then hurrying away, they who were too afraid even to clutch your hand, and they had the nerve to point their fingers at me. 'Look! That's her! The mother whose son had AIDS and hanged himself.' It destroyed me—"

Her eyes sprang open. She felt a presence, her mother's intuition telling her that her son had come back to her. The branch gave another onerous creak, much louder this time, but Belinda no longer cared for the wind or the trees. Ahead, she thought—no, she *knew*—she could see her boy, his elf-like face sullen, his shoulders slumped in boredom as they had been so many times when his father had waxed lyrical on rural post-office life. There was no mistaking the poise and gait of the boy—the man who had been cruelly taken from her.

"Reynard, I can see you. Oh, my sweet boy. It was a sign from God, after all. You did not die. You were just buried under all my expectations."

She struggled to her feet, her knees stiff from so many years of praying night after night and whenever the mood took her. The atmosphere in the forest seemed to change, become thicker somehow, and it left her breathless. A faint mist drew over her eyes, obscuring her vision, and she reached out, not to feel her way but to be guided by God so she might touch her son's face again. A voice beckoned her, urging her to complete her mission, but was lost within the loud creaking of wood splintering and giving way.

The figure in the thicket watched on in horror, dumbstruck as the tree from which Reynard Bennett hanged himself swayed, loosening its roots from the earth, and toppled forwards.

Even the old must eventually die, the most noble must lose their crown, and so it was for one of the oldest trees in the New Forest. It had seen kings come and go; it had borne the happiness of children who had once upon a time danced around its trunk and later swung from its boughs; it bore the scars of teenagers who had engraved their initials into its bark; and it had carried a mother's grief as her son took his life to save his family more pain, more embarrassment.

As the tree lost its will to stand majestically against all that surrounded it, Belinda walked directly into its shadow where her boy awaited her. She kissed him on both cheeks and told him how beautiful he was. He smiled, took her hands, and told her to be brave.

Belinda Bennet never felt a thing. She died happy, unafraid and no longer alone.

***

The unseen observer waited for the ground to stop shaking before he crossed to where the woman's body lay. Kneeling beside her, he blessed her in a language that had not been heard in the forest for centuries. Then he rose slowly, weary from his own time underground, and went in search of help.

Chapter Forty

WESS BREATHED HEAVILY, his hands on his knees, the box of grenades at his feet. In the enclosed space, the air was hot and heavy with the same sickly aroma he had smelled in the bunker, only here it was more pungent. It got into his mouth, dangled disgustingly on his taste buds, danced on the tip of his tongue. Neither of the two men alongside him seemed to notice.

Wess wracked his brains, trying to work out what it was, if he had ever come across such an odour before. The closest he could think of was during the platoon's regulation drill for chemical and biological gas-mask training. He hadn't been paying attention and had counted wrongly. The tear gas had lingered in his nose and mouth for days.

Here in this tunnel, though, it was something else. It made his eyes water and the hairs in his nostrils shrivel in protest; this, he recognised, was natural gas, possessing the space where oxygen was supposed to be.

"Sir, we have to keep going. There's gas in the—" He was cut off before he could finish his sentence. From somewhere back along the tunnel that they had run through to escape the black swarm came a noise like the chattering teeth of a hundred young children left out in the cold. It was rapid, constant, and growing louder.

Captain Trelaryn shone the diminishing light from his torch at his map of the tunnels; he pointed silently at the area marked

Bunker 4, then at the overlay of the village of Downmere. Bunker 4 was directly below the church—by some three hundred feet.

"You reckon this tunnel leads to the collapsed graveyard, Sir?" Wess asked.

"I'd say so."

"And if it doesn't?" Dixon's question was devoid of the usual aggressive sarcasm.

"Better to try than be eaten by whatever's coming our way, Sergeant."

The tunnel that had been carved out of the earth had become narrower the further they traversed, but it was still accessible. They moved on, carefully but quickly, trying to keep as much distance as possible between them and the chattering, bone-on-bone sound, until they came to a brick wall. It also had a crack in it, not as wide as the one in Bunker 3 but still wide enough for a person to wriggle through. To the side of the wall, the unhuman tunnel continued, stretching out before them.

"The gas is coming from down there, Sir," Wess said. "Maybe a pipe's given way."

Trelaryn nodded in agreement and urged him to go through the crack in the wall first, reminding him to remain watchful without saying what all three soldiers were thinking: there might be creatures ahead of them as well as behind.

Wess removed his rifle and his pack and started to climb through, turning sideways at one point where the wall jutted in sharply. When he was out the other side, Trelaryn passed through his rifle and pack.

"Your turn, Dixon."

Dixon shook his head. "I won't fit through that gap, Sir. I'm a lot larger than you and Wess, and he had enough trouble squeezing through. If it comes to it, I'll go down that tunnel. Leave me a couple of the grenades and I'll keep guard, Sir."

Trelaryn hated heroics. It was a soldier's job to defend, not sacrifice himself, but as he sized up the crack in the wall, he realised that with the best will in the world, Dixon wasn't getting through that opening.

"All right, Sergeant." Trelaryn took off his gun and pack and left them on the ground before turning sideways and edging into the crack, only to find that he, also, was too large to fit through. He eased out again and discarded his jacket, holding out little hope that it would give him the extra manoeuvrability needed to force himself through. To his surprise, it worked; exhausted, cut in several places from old bricks and tiles and with some additional pulling from Wess, he emerged and waited for Dixon to push his equipment through from the other side.

"As soon as you get to the door, Sir, holler, then close it and run for your life."

Through the gap, they saw Dixon arm himself with a grenade in each hand.

"Don't be a fool, man!" Trelaryn implored, but Dixon was resolute, and for the first time since Wess had known the man, he seemed at peace.

Clipping the four remaining grenades to his belt, Wess once again grabbed his captain by the arm and made for the door of Bunker 4.

The room was clear of any signs of infestation, but there was no way of knowing what waited for them at the top of the stairs. No time to conduct a recce either, Wess pushed Trelaryn up the first few steps, shouted, "Clear!" and slammed the door. A few seconds later, the first explosion rocked the walls, followed half a minute later by the second, which was louder and shifted the air. Wess figured Dixon had thrown one grenade down the tunnel they had come from, aimed it at the fearsome, chilling noise. The other, he had taken with him as he ran towards the smell of gas, amplifying the impact of the explosion.

The climb up the stairs was arduous, each step feeling as if it could be their last. The shock of the two explosions had compromised the integrity of the concrete walls, the fissures spreading from below and overtaking them.

Ten steps from the end of their climb, they heard the chattering once more and both looked behind them. They could see nothing but blackness, but it was a blackness that moved.

"The door, Wess. It'll be locked. We're trapped."

Where Dixon's mind had snapped under the pressure, Wess had grown in confidence since entering the tunnels. Without waiting for an order or even running his idea past the captain, he undid his belt and tied it around one of the grenades.

"Stay there, Sir," he advised as he climbed the remaining stairs to the door, where he wedged the grenade alongside the lock, pulled the pin and virtually threw himself back down the stairs.

The resulting explosion rocked the entire stairwell, fissures now sprouting from both ends and connecting in the middle, but it had also blown the door open; the panel on the other side sparked as the electrics shorted out.

Dust and concrete clattered down the stairs, covering both men, who coughed and spluttered. This time, Trelaryn recovered quickest and helped Wess to his feet, staying behind him until they were both safely through the door, at which point he took one of the grenades, pulled the pin and threw it as far down the stairwell as he could.

That was the third explosion the villagers had felt. While each had been necessary for the soldiers' escape, they had set off a chain of events on the surface, and it was only through quick thinking that Trelaryn and Wess survived the downpour of earth, broken coffins and bones.

Above them, what was left of Reverend Tarky fell to the floor outside the door of his church.

In the hotel foyer, Sam McCarthy was startled out of her semi-catatonic state when the grand chandelier broke free of its chains and crashed to the floor, sending shards of glass flying towards her.

When they finally came to, Trelaryn and Wess looked down the tunnel to where the outside world had beckoned only moments before. Now all they saw were thousands of tons of soil and broken chunks of concrete.

Trelaryn looked up at the dark sky; the stars called to them. "Come on, Wess. Not far now."

"Yes, Sir."

They began their ascent, taking care not to tread on the bones of the dead, using broken bits of wood to steady themselves and scrape out the stubborn earth. The sound of emergency vehicles and the fizz of the one remaining arc light kept them moving upwards until, at last, they clambered out of the pit and collapsed, filthy and heaving for breath, but alive.

Chapter Forty-One

THE ECHOES OF the explosion hammered in Robert's head. As the floor of the study had collapsed beneath him, he'd raised his arms to shield himself from the rain of wood and tiles, leaving his legs vulnerable; a splinter the size of a pencil had impaled his thigh and left him screaming in agony.

Robert blinked, trying to clear the dust caked to his wet lashes, and wondered for a brief moment if he'd temporarily lost his sight from hitting his head. Experimentally, he lifted his arm, feeling above him, but the movement shifted whatever was beneath him, so he quickly lowered it again.

Robert was not a religious man. Like many within the humanities, he'd read too much to see religion as anything other than a means of controlling the unruly masses, yet he found himself willing some greater power to help him out of the hole. He was too cynical to hold out much hope, but then he began to see colour, shape…a hand held out towards him by a god saving a lost soul.

As his vision returned to normal, he saw it was no god, just his boy, his small pal. All that time he'd been concerned with Bela's whereabouts, he hadn't given his son a second thought. The fierceness of his remorse stuck the knife in and gave it a good twist.

"Stuart, where's Bela? Have you seen your sister?"

Stuart's face remained impassive, not a flicker of recognition.

"Stuart, are you all right, son? Are you hurt?"

Once again, the boy said nothing, then he began to shimmer, to flicker and fade, and Robert had the presence of mind to understand he was passing out from the pain.

***

"Wake up, Daddy."

Robert didn't know how long it had been since he had tried to communicate with his young son, but when he opened his eyes, he was dazzled by the bright light reflecting off the shattered glass around him. He felt another rumble below him, a smaller explosion this time but still enough to feel the shockwave ripple against him. The ground shifted, and half a roof tile speared down into the hole. Robert shot back instinctively, the confined space giving him mere inches to play with, but it was enough. The piece of tile jammed between the wall and his chest and put a hole in his shirt.

If I hadn't been awake, that tile would have killed me.

Then he remembered Stuart telling him to wake up. His son had brought him round just in time.

"Where are you?" He didn't dare move to look. As it was, his legs were dangling in empty space.

Then came the second explosion. It rocked the house, and a crack appeared in the ceiling above him. Robert watched it spread and widen, convinced the entire thing was going to come down on him. Plaster dust sprinkled, snowflake-like, settling on his upturned face, and Robert concluded his reason had finally deserted him. Black dots started to pour through the crack in the ceiling, like the absence of stars. Within seconds, they had covered half the ceiling, fanning out in waves, a shoreline in negative. It was only when they reached the top of the bookshelves that he comprehended what they were.

"Daddy, it's coming." Stuart's voice was distant, afraid.

"Run, son! I know I've always told you to not leave my side unless you're going to sleep or you're with Bela, but please, go now. Find help. *Run*."

Robert panted, his energy drained, but he had to make Stuart understand the danger. He listened out for his son fleeing the house, any confirmation that the boy had taken heed; all he heard was the skittering sea of black creatures moving ever closer.

"I'm scared, Daddy." His son's voice sounded close to his ear. "I don't want to leave you. Please, Daddy, don't make me leave."

"You *must*, Stuart. You must go *now*."

The blackness was enveloping him, tearing at the fabric of his reality. His son's small hand gripped his own, the touch sparking a memory of love, of anguish, of the night of the fire.

"Get ready, Daddy. It's coming."

"For goodness' sake, Stuart, do as you're told and get out of here!" He shouted at the child in desperation, fearing it was already too late as the final explosion shifted the house's foundations, tipping it sideways. The deep rumble seemed to come from all around, as if an earthquake were ripping through the English countryside, followed by the ear-splitting screech of metal being shorn in two. A pipe came crashing through the wall, and brown, foul-smelling effluence spurted from the fractured end, a disgusting wave of human waste that poured unceasingly around him and eventually over him.

Robert had no intention of dying. He still had Bela and Stuart to care for, so much to live for, so he held his breath, caught between the millions of ants racing towards him and the shower of excrement and feculence pooling around him, rising up, touching his chin and then his bottom lip in a matter of seconds.

The last things Robert saw before the floor finally gave way were the ants halting their progress, refusing to come any closer, and his son smiling, a beam of light and love shining down on him.

Robert dropped through the floor. It seemed an age before he landed, and when he did, he felt something in his spine give way, and then all he felt was numb. Above him, beyond the dust and fallen floor, the ceiling of his study was returning to its bright, white finish. He tried to move his arms, to protect his mouth and nose from the flow of waste that had finally begun to slow down, but the pain was too great, too intense, and he was so tired.

"Stay awake, Daddy. Help is coming."

Robert was instantly alert again. How had his son not been crushed or drowned?

"Stuart, where are you? I can't see you."

The flames licked up the walls; the stench of petrol burned the inside of his nose and made him gag. So much heat, yet it was cold at the same time, and Bela running down the stairs, screaming, pleading, her words inaudible in the roar of the inferno. *Save Stuart. He's locked in his bedroom.* Robert charged forward, but the policeman hauled him back. A firefighter blocked his view, shouting instructions in his face, meaningless words with his son's small fists smacking against the glass. Robert broke free of the policeman's grasp and sprinted towards the house.

Get ready to jump. Daddy will catch you. Don't be afraid.

Bela bolted from the front door and was almost in reach of the fireman when her mother lunged and caught hold of her, pulling her back.

The vision turned to slow motion, and Robert tried to escape from it, but his injuries forbade it, forcing him to live through that night once again. Yet this time, the image split in two, separated by an invisible line, a void he couldn't fill.

His ex-wife scrabbled for a match that had fallen out of the box. Grasping it between her fingers, she yelled triumphantly as she struck it and dropped it. A stream of flames raced towards Bela, and in that moment, while he was paralysed by the sight of his daughter burning alive, the policeman rugby-tackled Robert and threw him to the ground. Pinned down, unable to fight, he watched the firefighters carry first Bela and then, with somewhat less care, his ex-wife from the house.

Robert screamed and cursed, his frustration and hatred seeming to shake the tunnel in which he lay as helpless as he had been that night, when the windows shattered and the house became a ball of flame. Slowly, the image faded as his mind finally accepted that his son had not survived. Since that night, Robert had been seeing a ghost, a flicker of the boy he had loved.

He thought back to the day they had arrived in the village, when he'd asked Bela if they were both all right, and she'd replied without looking at the space where he'd thought Stuart was. There were other moments, too, when he'd caught an odd look aimed at him for talking to his son, believing the boy was at his side. He had been carrying his son with him for so long now, it was hard to let go, and he cried out in his grief, "I miss you so much, my Little Nemo."

I love you, Daddy, came the reply, a soft whisper on the wind. Robert reached out to the void, begging to be with his son once more, and felt a hand touch his, heard comforting words trying to soothe him.

He didn't want to open his eyes. If he opened them, he would have to accept that his son was gone and that, arguably through little fault of his own, he had neglected the child who had survived, had not cherished her enough. So he kept his eyes shut and wished for sleep. He'd never wanted to sleep so much in his life.

"I love you, Dad. Stay with me, *please*. The army will get you out of here, and we'll get you to hospital."

Robert didn't reply but gripped Bela's hand as tightly as he could. It was all he was capable of doing.

Underneath...

I remember falling...then blackness for a while. What brought me round, made me take a breath and regret it immediately, was the sound of an engine stopping not far from where I'd landed. I saw and heard it all—a strange voice issuing instructions, the horses being slaughtered, the fear in their eyes. It was undoubtedly scarier than what I was to go through in the next twenty-four hours, after I sank underground, into their world.

The embankment had given way beneath my feet when I fell, as it had for Kevin Sillatoe, the difference being that he landed on the ground and merely rolled into the manure, whereas I plummeted directly into it, the temperature and stench rushing past me as I plunged into a new darkness.

I can hold my hand on my heart and tell you now that I thought I was going to die and prepared myself for leaving this life immersed in crap. Like anyone who might find themselves in such a position, I imagined the headlines, the posthumous embarrassment. After all, the way we die is usually the first thing people remember when they evoke our memory in conversation.

Philip Piccolo, born of Italian parents, Scoutmaster, several O' Levels, enjoyed amateur dramatics, played

*cribbage for his local pub, not bad on a snooker
table, good son, good friend...died from suffocation
when he fell into a heap of horse manure.* It's
a natural way to think: we love our friends and
our family and endeavour to fondly remember their
greatest achievements, but dying a bizarre death
overwrites everything, becomes that person's legacy.
You only have to look at Isadora Duncan, Elvis
Presley, Henry the First of England, the Duke of
Clarence, Allan Pinkerton, Alex Mitchell. For good
or ill, we remember people by how they died. That
is the way obituaries work, and the headline stays
with us.

I witnessed the horses being slain, but I cannot
hold my head up in a court of law and point the
finger at anyone. Such was my own pain; for a time
I thought I was hallucinating.

I heard someone fall close to me. As it turns out,
it was Kevin Sillatoe, but though I shouted for
help, he must have climbed back up the embankment
as quick as a flash. Then all was quiet for a while,
until I felt the manure move, a little bit of the
ground give way. Stuck as I was, I hoped vainly
it would push me out, but instead, I was sucked
down deeper into the pile, and then I was falling
through air. I estimate I had fallen over ten feet
before I landed with a heavy thump on the hard
surface below.

I lay there for a while, dazed. Images of my
mother, sick in a facility outside of my hometown
of Perchester, came rushing over me, feeding my
guilt, pushing at my sanity. Looking up at the

structure of the earthy tomb into which I had fallen, I noticed with alarm that the ceiling, if that is the word for it, consisted of loosely packed soil that had cracked under the weight of the dung heap. That was enough to get me moving, albeit by dragging my bruised form at less than a snail's pace away from the leaking hole above my head.

It was after pulling myself along for a couple of minutes that it dawned on me just how long and wide the space was, as if it had been dug out to take utility pipes and cables, yet there was no evidence to suggest human activity. Still, I reasoned, I had to surface at some point, so I kept going, crawling through what I took to be some kind of tunnel that seemed to go on for miles. Sometime later, I reached an intersection with another tunnel, just as round and expansive, veering off at a sharp angle, which I know now took me in the direction of the church in Downmere.

I cannot say for sure how long I had been down there when I heard the deep rumble that confirmed my suspicions: the ground beneath the manure had given way. In a matter of seconds, the passage that had taken me several hours to traverse backfilled with soil, manure and debris, a steaming tsunami hurtling towards me at a frightening rate.

While I may have been born and raised a Catholic, religion as a concept leaves me cold. However, I am not too proud to say that for the first time since my mother informed me that the doctor had found the cause of her blackouts and seizures, I prayed. Then I waited for the inevitable.

It did not come. Be it by the hand of God or some other omnipotent force, the distant rumble tapered off, the tumult of dirt slowed and then stopped. My best guess: the tunnel had collapsed in more than one place, creating a temporary plug. It was a reprieve, enough time for me to keep crawling and outpace the next cave-in.

Eventually, the tunnel opened up, and it was here that I saw the first signs of human interference in the form of a bent, corroded pipe, coupled with the tang of gas in the air. I soon started to feel sick and knew I must keep moving, though I could see little in the gloomy darkness. However, I understood that the space before me was more than a tunnel; it was a cavern, perhaps as big as a house. How did I ascertain this? By its echo, of course, because it talked to me.

Be not under any illusion. I don't mean we had a conversation, but there was something in there that communicated. Something that didn't need the reason of man to justify its existence. I had no choice but to go forward. The way back was blocked; where I lay was slowly filling with gas. Whatever was ahead of me, I had to face it, but still, the noise…it got inside my head and added desperation to my faltering will.

I tested the ground ahead of me, scrabbling at the dirt lest I should fall once more into the mouth of what waited below. A foot in front of me, the ground dropped away to a gentle slope, which would have been easily navigable, but there was also a strange structure like wet papier mâché, soft to the touch, and it felt alive. I sensed the industry going on inside it and its…well, pulse. Whatever it was, it made me shrink back in revulsion.

I don't have to tell you how long it took me to crawl to the other side of that cavern. All the while, I was aware of the liquid-state object pulsing above me, talking to me inside my head, not in words but an emotion that filled every part of my being. I felt unnerved, under attack. It dug away at my reserves, making it almost impossible to continue, yet on I went.

I was perhaps halfway across the cavern when, from within that horrible, terrifying darkness, I saw a light. It was no more than the flicker of a candle flame observed in a house several miles away, but in the dead of night, your eyes are drawn to it.

Turning my head slightly, I dared myself to look upon the illumination. The pulse became rapid, and as it did so, the light increased enough for me to see that what I had conceived of as wet paper pulp was organic, a living thing, and less than two feet above me.

Looking back, I think that was the moment my mind snapped. Everything afterwards is fragmented, broken by the image that still haunts me when I close my eyes and try to sleep.

I'm told that sometime in the late afternoon on that Saturday, I was found wandering the forest calling for help. I cannot confirm or deny that this happened. All I remember is staring at the small, black dots, the creatures hurrying around, signalling one another, each directed by a higher purpose, an intelligent design based on cooperation, working as one, and it was hungry.

Why it didn't attack me, I cannot say. You have read the same accounts I have. You have heard the evidence, read the testimonies. All I can say is I suspect it was the smell—the reason I had ended up in the tunnel in the first place. I was covered from head to toe in rotting shit. I may be wrong; I could be grasping at straws, and finer minds than mine will have an explanation that suits the narrative better than anything I can come up with. Or perhaps it was just dumb luck, more than I deserve and less than some who aren't with us now.

I can't tell you how I escaped. I don't think that matters, to be honest. In the end, what matters is that the truth has been told about what I saw in that tunnel, about the lives lost to arrogant superiority, the human belief that we have the right to be where we want, when we want, to determine the fate of others by building our homes on top of theirs and then wondering why they fight back, why they wage war on us. Why they eat us. We need to remember that others were here before us, and we are the creatures destroying the planet in search of living space.

Before (1986: February)

The old man was weary of life. Bitterness had eaten through his soul, and all he had once hoped to learn, all that had excited him, had turned on him and begun to tear him apart. Exhausted, tired, alone and frightened, Professor Carlton L. Sandalwood lay down on his bed and tried to think of a time when all he was, all he could give, mattered.

His academic achievements had been for nothing, his research the same. His name no longer meant anything, not even as a footnote to others' explorations. He was forgotten, invisible. Downstairs, his private zoo was broken. He had set the ants free, returning them to nature.

The re-dedication of the lecture hall had been one thing, but to see his name discredited by a former pupil was altogether a different story. Nor did they stop at claiming his life's work had been built upon that of others. Accusations flew of falsified data and recklessness in his later research into combining the traits of one ant species with another.

The rage he felt was unlike anything he had ever experienced, and he had struck out in fury, both at the glass tanks and down the telephone at the publisher's, assuring them he would be suing for every single penny. The man on the other end laughed and told him he would never win. With blood boiling inside of him, he asked the man his name and was immediately transported back to that day when he had been made a fool of in his own lecture hall.

He looked at the name on the book in his hand, a name that had meant nothing just five minutes before but now broke his heart, shattered it into small pieces.

"Are you still there, Professor, or have you heard enough?"

"Andreas Protezni, you were a student of mine. You were expelled from the university, and Fowler, the author. I presume that's Oscar Fowler, your compatriot, your friend?" the old man asked, choking on the words, tears of regret and distress beginning to collect in the corners of his eyes.

"The same," Protezni confirmed. "He was able to transfer and collect his degree and went on to take his doctorate. His chosen specialist subject was you, Professor. He never forgave you. I could not have cared less. In fact, you did me a favour that day. My father got me the job at the publisher's, and I've made more money than I could have dreamed of. No sweating in muddy fields collecting samples, no living with tribes. I have an extremely comfortable life, thanks to you."

"So why destroy me? Why damage my reputation and deny the truth?"

"Why not? It's a game, which you thought you had won, but you ran away before our turn was over. No one has cared about you or your work in years, and I'm happy to be part of the system that buries you underneath your inflated—"

Before Protezni could finish, the old man set down the receiver and, covering his face with worn-out hands, let out a tremendous sob, then another. Not since his friend had died at the hands of white supremacists had he felt such burning injustice and absolute powerlessness to do anything about it.

Images flooded over him, threatening to sweep him away. His mother hanging from a beam in the kitchen. His father ruffling his hair as they shared a joke before he went to work that evening. The policeman bringing him a new toy to play with on Christmas day. The baseball bat smashing Gicicio's knuckles. The news of Hendrick Verwoerd's assassination and how enormously pleased he'd felt—so much so he'd framed his letter for all to see, transforming personal defeat into world victory.

He steadied himself, unable to stop the cascade of tears flowing down his face, but he had other things to do. He rang his neighbour across the road and told him he was going away for a while and asked if he would mind keeping an eye on the place, perhaps running a mower over the lawn every so often. It was all very cordial, such had been their relationship, founded on the mutual death of their parents in an air raid over Birmingham and extraordinarily little else. Next, he rang Lionel at the post office and instructed him to close his account and give the proceeds to Alice Calster.

"I know it's not much, but I still owe her for some sewing she did for me, and goodness knows, she needs it."

He listened to Lionel talk for a moment—he was a good man, stubborn like himself—and smiled at the filtered memory of them coming to blows once when Lionel had overcharged him for petrol. They had soon sorted it out; several large whiskies and a few games of cribbage always worked a treat, or was he remembering it wrong? It hardly mattered.

"Oh, by the way, Lionel. I will be leaving some books outside my front door this afternoon. Would you please deliver them to Reverend Tarky? He will be expecting them. Thank you. And please give my love to Belinda." He rang off before Lionel confirmed he would fulfil his requests. The professor wasn't being rude; he just expected them to be carried out.

As he watched ants scurry across the floor, driven mad by their freedom, he made one last phone call.

"Ah, yes good morning, Vicar. I trust the day is well... The news? No, you know I can't abide all that tittle-tattle of village life. Look, Alan, I am going away for some considerable time... Yes, back to South Africa... Well, it's the anniversary soon of Gicicio's passing, and I have received a letter from the president himself inviting me back to the country. All is forgiven, it seems... Yes, yes, good news indeed. I must say, I'm quite thrilled. I'm leaving some books for you to read—personal journals. I thought they might come in handy one day... Yes, ah, that's splendid, my dear old fellow. I won't keep you any longer. Lionel will drop them round later. Goodbye, Vicar."

The old man breathed in deeply. He hated dealing with the man, but there was no one else who would take care of his work in the way he wanted. He never doubted for a minute that the vicar would simply put the journals on a shelf and forget they were there. That was hardly his problem anymore.

An ant crawled onto his hand and stood still, as if awaiting instructions from the one who had kept them prisoner.

"Well, now, my small friend, I suppose all that is left to do is to write some letters, after which I shall go upstairs. The bed is as good a place to finish life as to start it."

He set the ant down by the telephone and stood up slowly. He suddenly felt incredibly old. So much he had seen, so much time he had wasted. He had no family, no one to admire his dedication to furthering his mind; it all counted for nothing. No, not nothing. There was still one thing he could do. He could give a person destined for trouble the advantage he had been given. The house may belong to him now, but only because the woman who had taken him in during the war had no one else to leave it to. He would follow suit; die by her example.

He had no idea if it were legally binding, but as he had never made a will before, he doubted anyone would complain. She, after all, just needed understanding. He shuffled on tired legs through to the front room, carefully withdrew his books from the top shelf and took one last look at the covers, the small sketches he had made when in deep thought. A tear sailed down his face, and he made no attempt to wipe it away. He placed the books in a plastic bag and deposited it a few feet outside the house so Lionel wouldn't miss it.

Once back inside, he went to his bureau and took out his finest pen, some paper and three envelopes. The first he addressed to his old university, the second to Sarah Calster. In his letter to the rector of the university, he spelled out in no uncertain terms that he held them responsible for the way Protezni and Fowler had ruined his name and the mockery they were about to bring down on the university, especially when all the facts became clear; of that he was certain.

The second letter contained his hopes and his apologies for not standing up for the girl in the way a gentleman should. He knew she was suffering; however hard he tried to ignore it, the gossip floating around the village about how she was a wrong'un, a daughter of the devil, still reached his ears, and he was appalled. He had, after all, seen the devil on numerous occasions, knew the faces it wore, and Sarah Calster's was not one of them.

He explained that her father had been a good man, her mother a kind woman, and how he hoped she might learn something from their examples. He finished off by saying it was only right that he leave her the house, which she could do with as she wished—bulldoze it, sell the land so her parents could move out of their sickly cottage, live in it. He signed the letter, not with any type of formality, just his first name. Carlton.

Placing the letters into their partner envelopes, he once more shuffled to the front door, opening it carefully to make sure he wasn't seen a second time, and placed them in the bag with the books. Immediately, it felt as though the weight had been lifted from his shoulders. Closing the door behind him, he went upstairs, the third envelope in his pocket, along with his pen and the remains of his notepaper.

As he lay in his bed, his neat and short will in an envelope resting on the bedside table, he began to take the tablets that had been awaiting him for a few weeks with methodical and calculated precision. Resting his head back on the pillow, he allowed Morpheus to claim him.

Days later, the first ant appeared in his room, hungry and curious about the decaying smell. Over the next few months, the ants ate their creator. There was no savagery in the way they did so; it was calm and measured, solemn and respectful, just as the man had been in life.

Epilogue

Underneath, not on the surface. That's where the truth of our existence lies, sometimes buried under years of punishment, suffocating, choking on the dirt we have carried with us so deep in our soul where no one will ever find it. Sometimes it scratches, clawing at the thin veneer of the respectable face we present to the world, hoping to pierce, to pop the bloated façade of all we refuse to acknowledge we have done.

Underneath the skin lies the dirt we have on ourselves. We hide it from the investigations of others while knowing that if we were to slice the surface and let the dirt run free, we would be liberated from this human prison in which we are securely kept...

Underneath.

***

BELA PUT DOWN her extensive notes and stopped talking, allowing the concluding paragraph of the professor's last journal to sink in. She looked around the room; the crowd assembled before her was silent, stunned by the words of a dead man who, by his own admission, had bred something terrible, something that had destroyed half the village of Downmere.

The select committee had invited several of the survivors to give their accounts of the weekend in question, to bring the series of events out into the open. Some had refused, their reasons their own, but Bela believed a number of factors were involved, and Reverend Tarky was at the centre of it all. Not everybody liked the man; indeed, many had loathed him and with good reason, especially Sarah Calster, but the way he had died made it easier to forgive him. In time, the stories would come out; the village rumour mill was always hard at work.

Sam McCarthy was one of those who had refused to attend, and she had made her reasons public, sort of, by including in her scant statement to the authorities the words 'threat to national security'. While certain officials and members of parliament were scathing in their condemnation of her, they had no choice but to accept her decision. Her husband, whose prolonged hospital stay had kept him away from the village, had also not been called.

Bela suspected both McCarthy and her husband were keeping the events of that weekend a secret, even from each other. Jacob Betley and Elizabeth Croker were among the dead, yet Elizabeth's body had never been found, and when Sam McCarthy was asked if she'd seen the girl, she didn't answer, but she also never mourned for her. There were tales that Elizabeth was still alive and in hiding, driven mad by the discovery of her mother's body, which had been slowly eaten away.

Also unfathomable was how the Croker house had stayed intact when others around it crumbled and sank into the depths of the network of tunnels uncovered by the army. Captain Trelaryn and the newly promoted Sergeant Wess were heading up the operation to make safe the tunnels and return the locale to some semblance of normality. So far, it had been six months, and the village, or what remained of it, was still uninhabitable, the old cottages and homes that had stood since before the turn of the century now lost to time.

One small miracle had happened, however, which Bela was not aware of until she heard the testimony from the two Scout leaders who had been camping in the forest that weekend. Despite losing one of their charges—and Bela didn't consider Jacob Betley that great a loss—their missing friend, Philip Piccolo, had been found wandering around the forest calling for help. He was covered in horse manure and all manner of filth, to the extent that nobody recognised him or wanted to go near him, including the ants. He had testified that he had seen the old tree fall towards Belinda Bennett and tried to warn her, but it was to no avail. On the day his friends had spoken to the committee, he sat rigid in the gallery, and afterwards, when Bela was introduced to him, she realised it was him she'd seen climb out of the sunken graveyard, the shadow against the wall.

A smattering of applause broke her out of her reverie, one person from the gallery cheering loudly in support. Bela didn't have to look up to know that it was Sarah, her friend and now official legal guardian, since her aunt had enough on her plate looking after her dad. While he had finally accepted that Stuart had died in the house fire and that what he'd been seeing was a shadow maintained by his grief, he had been through incredible trauma, which he was finally beginning to process, so in a way, it was a blessing he'd fallen through the floor of his study. Their house had not survived, though, which was not surprising, given it was the epicentre of the ants' nests and bivouac. Sturdy as they were, they could not withstand the seismic shock from the army's explosions.

The session was called to a halt for the day, and Bela endured the handshakes and congratulations for being *so brave* for offering her account and for bringing the professor's journals to light. She had the feeling the professor's name would suffer more embarrassment in some quarters, but influential people had assured her that Fowler and Protezni would face justice for the lies they had spread, fuelled by professional jealousy.

As usual, Sarah had refused to bow to convention by dressing in a more conservative manner and on her way to join Bela was intercepted by quite a few people, all eager to shake her hand. Aided by Ainsley Corbett and Christine Balker, she'd had the chance to clear her name, her in-depth interview making the front page and catching the public imagination. She'd also kept her promise to Bela to leave the vicar's memory alone, let the village heal awhile. If, when people began to return to their homes, Sarah still felt compelled to put the record straight, Bela wouldn't stop her. For now, the villagers had rallied around Tarky's memory and would likely dismiss outright the notion he had been complicit in his lover's suicide.

"Come on, let's get out of here," Sarah said, finally reaching Bela and steering her away from a person who was insisting she should turn over the professor's notes on how he had enhanced the ant's abilities. Admittedly, most of what was in those notes had gone over her head, but she understood enough to know they should not fall into anyone else's hands. The village had suffered, but perhaps it was the price that had to be paid to uncover the lies built up over time, to ensure the greater good.

Bela had read the history of the man deemed responsible for all the heartache and destruction, and she had seen how events unfold from different directions, how one tunnel inevitably feeds another. If her mother had not set fire to their home, if her dad had not moved them to the New Forest, would the journals have ever come to light? If Reverend Tarky had not been overcome by profound guilt and grief, if he had read the professor's journals instead of stowing them on a shelf to gather dust, would the village have been saved? If Germany had not gone to war with the rest of Europe, if the boy had never found those small creatures scurrying on the wing of a crashed *Luftwaffe* plane, if a policeman with an amateur interest in ants had not taken the boy in, would the professor have ever embarked on his research in the first place?

As they emerged from the dim, stuffy chamber, the sun streamed through the windows, turning motes of dust into tiny dancing fairies flapping their fragile, fanciful wings.

"Do you want to see your dad this evening?" Sarah asked with a cheeky grin. "Your aunt tells me he's been asking after you."

Bela returned the grin, and they departed the building, heading to Waterloo Station. The train to Avoncross would be waiting at the platform for them.

The End

Acknowledgements

With absolute thanks to Steffi Webster, a friend from my time at the University of Liverpool, who one afternoon answered my questions on the nature of fear for young women. It was with trepidation and a certain anxiety of my own that I broached the subject with her, as I wanted to maintain a healthy perspective on gender, or as much as I could within the confines of writing the book that you hold in your hand. Without her help, I doubt that the characters of Sarah Calster, Bela Romsleigh and Elizabeth Croker would hold the same sense of drama for me.

Underneath is fiction, but with any fiction, any tale or story, there must be truth somewhere woven into the narrative. My own aversion to insects is at the heart of the story, but *Underneath* is also not about them; it is about what flows through our veins—the fear and repulsion when confronted by something that looks so alien, so different from our own physiology—and while they are beautiful intelligent creatures, they, and in particular ants, leave me cold.

This is the truth of *Underneath*, not what we perceive as danger, but the amplification of the things that frighten us, that dig away at our resolve and leave us on edge, ready to take flight against reason.

As always, enormous thanks to my wife Judith for allowing me the freedom to hide away in the obscurity of my room, to Debbie McGowan and all at Beaten Track Publishing for believing in my thoughts, to my mother and father and my cousin, Bryan Beck, for continuing to be a sounding board.

Most of all, to you—the ones who pick up the book and take a chance, who are willing to walk awhile with me down an unlit path—thank you for that belief.

Underneath was written during the first few months of the coronavirus outbreak and lockdown of 2020: a heartfelt and personal thank-you to my friend Tony Higginson for his assistance and valuable support during what was a difficult time for all humanity.

I also need to thank many a musician who, for over an hour a day, brought me back above the surface as I revisited my vinyl collection during this period of writing. Whether it was Marillion, Pink Floyd, Eagles, Tori Amos, Joanne Shaw Taylor, The Stranglers, The Boomtown Rats or any others that were played till some sanity returned, I thank you all.

It only leaves me to say I hope to see you again—that you will be part of my nightmares, that I can take you into the forest and show you a world with webs and mist.

Underneath is dedicated to the memory of the Guv'nor, James Herbert.

Ian D. Hall 2020

About the Author

Having been found on a 'Co-op' shelf in Stirchley, Birmingham by a Cornish woman and a man of dubious footballing taste, Ian grew up in neighbouring Selly Park and Bicester in Oxfordshire. After travelling far and wide, he now considers Liverpool to be his home.

Ian was educated at Moor Green School, Bicester Senior School, and the University of Liverpool, where he gained a 2:1 (BA Hons) in English Literature.

He now reviews and publishes daily on the music, theatre and culture within Merseyside.

Please visit www.liverpoolsoundandvision.co.uk

By the Author

Poetry

Black Book

Tales from the Adanac House

Four in the Morning, Pavement Blues

Writing Out of Earshot

Novels

The Death of Poetry

Dark Chrysalis

Ghost Apples

Underneath

Sound and Vision

A Trip to a Festival (Me, Myself... Only)

Listening Out of Earshot:
A collection of words and music from the friends of Ian D. Hall

Beaten Track Publishing

For more titles from Beaten Track Publishing,
please visit our website:

https://www.beatentrackpublishing.com

Thanks for reading!